Twelve Slays
of Christmas

Also available from Jacqueline Frost

Kitty Couture Mysteries (writing as Julie Chase)

Cat Got Your Secrets

Cat Got Your Cash

Cat Got Your Diamonds

Twelve Slays of Christmas

A CHRISTMAS TREE FARM MYSTERY

Jacqueline Frost

CROOKED
LANE

NEW YORK

Published in the United States by Crooked Lane Books, an imprint of The Quick Brown Fox & Company LLC.

Crooked Lane Books and its logo are trademarks of The Quick Brown Fox & Company LLC.

Library of Congress Catalog-in-Publication data available upon request.

ISBN (hardcover): 978-1-68331-317-5
ISBN (ePub): 978-1-68331-318-2
ISBN (ePDF): 978-1-68331-320-5

Cover illustration by Richard Grote
Book design by Jennifer Canzone

Printed in the United States.

www.crookedlanebooks.com

Crooked Lane Books
34 West 27th St., 10th Floor
New York, NY 10001

First Edition: October 2017

10 9 8 7 6 5 4 3 2 1

To my parents for providing me with
a lifetime of magical holidays

Chapter One

"I have two cups of Santa's cinnamon tea, one spicy apple cider, and a peppermint twist hot cocoa," I said, setting the mugs on the table surrounded by rosy-cheeked women wearing matching holiday sweaters. They leaned forward at the sight of my mother's specialty drinks. I slipped cinnamon sticks into the tea and cider, then popped a candy cane into the cocoa.

The women smacked their lips. Soft sugary scents wafted into the air as they sipped and stirred.

I tucked the empty tray under my arm and placed a basket of warm cookies at the table's center. "Three saint snickerdoodles and one Christmas chocolate chip, all fresh from the oven."

"Ohh," they sang.

"This place really is magical," the redhead said. "Is that necklace for sale in the craft shop?"

I lifted my fingertips to the faux gumdrop on my collarbone. "Oh, no. This is something I made."

"I see." Steam crawled up her glasses as she savored her hot cider. "That's too bad. It's lovely. Whimsical." She seemed to search for a better word. "Enchanted." She smiled, satisfied. "Your brochures aren't lying. Reindeer Games Tree Farm is a holiday paradise. And you really have games! We're coming back tomorrow to play Bling That Gingerbread, and I also want to try Build a Big Frosty. I was always a whiz at snowmen."

"We love the activities," her seatmate agreed. She smoothed a wrinkled flyer on the tabletop. "Twelve Days of Reindeer Games. It's brilliant. Maybe we'll extend our stay and play all twelve games. We're retired. We can do that."

I pressed my palms to the table and smiled conspiratorially. "If you're here on Christmas Eve, don't miss the Snowball Roll. Everyone in town shows up to line the big sled run on both sides and cheer as players race to the bottom with their snowballs. The little sucker is small at the top of the hill and big enough to bowl you over at the bottom."

The lady with the cocoa fluttered her eyelids and moaned as whipped cream and sprinkles clung to her upper lip. "I can't believe we've been missing this our whole lives. This might be our first trip to Reindeer Games, but it won't be our last."

"No," one woman in the group vowed. "Certainly not," another said.

I smiled brighter. "Wonderful. I look forward to seeing you at the games this week and maybe again next Christmas." The reality of my statement brought a wave of pain that stole my breath. *How do I know where I'll be in a year? I didn't plan on being here now.*

I should've been in Portland, Maine, counting the days until my Christmas Eve wedding, but my ex-fiancé had broken it off three nights ago. He claimed he'd met someone more "Zen" at the gym. I had a feeling that was guy slang for *younger and hotter*, but I didn't ask. I rented a moving van and drove home to Mistletoe, Maine, where no one said dumb things like "Zen."

The front door swung open, smacking me with an icy burst of wind and snow. Patrons tugged their frocks a little tighter without missing a beat of conversation or a bite of their warm desserts.

A woman I recognized as Paula Beech from the maple farm next door stomped snow off her boots and scanned the room. We'd never met officially. She was older than my parents, but I'd seen her around while I was growing up. She waved at a group of locals sharing a table. "Well, she fined me. Can you believe it?" she asked them. She shook snow from her shoulders and shoved the door closed with a little effort. "She fined me fifty-seven dollars for painting the gift shop a shade of pink that wasn't listed in her goofy historical code book."

Her friends scoffed appropriately. One pushed a communal tray of reindeer gingerbread cookies in her direction and asked, "What on earth has gotten into her?"

"She's gone 'round the bend. That's what's happened." Paula loosened her scarf and shook more snow onto the floor. "Here's what I've got to say: I'm *not* paying." She fell into the empty seat between her friends.

I went to take her order. "Hello, I'm Holly. Can I get you something from the Hearth tonight?" The Hearth was the name of the tree farm's café, but I couldn't resist a good play on words. A surprising number of people didn't get it.

"Coffee," the newcomer grumped. "Black. I need to stay up all night plotting my revenge."

"Is there anything I can help with?" I smiled, hoping to diffuse the sour mood before it spread to our other customers.

"Yeah. If you see Margaret Fenwick in here, charge her double, or add fifty-seven dollars to her bill and tell her it's for wearing the wrong color hat."

"Ah." *Fenwick.* The conversation suddenly made more sense. There was an endless battle in Mistletoe between shop owners and the Historical Society. Local proprietors enjoyed leasing property in our picturesque town, but they didn't like all the rules and regulations that came with it. So they pushed the limits, and the Historical Society pushed back. A member of the Fenwick family had been president of that society for as long as I could remember.

I went to the counter for Paula's coffee.

Delores Cutter climbed onto a stool and greeted me with a smile. "Holly White! Look at you. Beautiful as always. You cut your hair."

"Hi, Cookie." I wrapped her in a big hug. Delores's late husband, Theodore Cutter, gave her the nickname because she loved to bake. I'd called her Cookie Cutter for at least ten years before I got the joke. "Thank you. It's nice to be home."

"Is that your moving truck outside the guesthouse?"

"Yep. I got in last night."

"How was the trip?"

"Good." Though it was mildly unsettling to know everything I owned fit into a truck small enough for me to drive from Portland to Mistletoe on one tank of gas. Cindy Lou Who, my rescue cat, had ridden shotgun.

"I'm so glad you're here. Did I say that?" Cookie asked. Her curly white hair formed a cloud on her head, and her big blue eyes seemed trapped in a state of enthusiasm. Cookie had seen and done things I couldn't imagine. She'd been a cigarette girl in Vegas, met Frank Sinatra, and outlived two husbands. The year after I'd left for college, she'd won the state lottery. Cookie had reasons to be excited.

"No." I smiled. "You said you liked my hair." I curled a swath of poker-straight locks behind one ear. I'd always worn it just below my shoulder blades, but by the time I hit Mistletoe, it was six inches shorter. I'd spotted a road-side beauty parlor near Westbrook and pulled in on a lark. I needed a change, so I left thirty dollars and half my hair behind.

"What's new?" I asked, enjoying the twinkle in her eyes and warm, easy smile on her lips.

"Oh, not much. I saw Margaret Fenwick out front arguing with the reindeer keeper. She says your tree farm needs a livestock permit for those guys. I tried to stick up for them, but she threatened my Theodore with the same citation."

I rocked back on my heels. "Your late husband?"

"My goat." She deposited her hat and gloves on the counter. "I named him after my husband. He's a pygmy, and he wears a nice beard just like Theodore the first did. He's not livestock, for goodness' sake. He's family."

I smiled. "Shame on her."

"Darn tootin'." Cookie hummed along to "Jingle Bell Rock" and tapped her fingers against the countertop. "How about you fix me a peppermint tea with a shot of Schnapps?"

An unexpected laugh bubbled through me. "How about just the tea?"

"Oh, that's okay," Cookie said. "You know I was only kidding." She pulled her giant quilted handbag into her lap and cracked it open. "I brought my own Schnapps."

"Ho ho ho!" My dad's booming voice from the opposite direction had me turning. "Merry Christmas!" He patted his belly and arched his back. An enormous burlap sack hung over one shoulder.

I rushed Paula's black coffee to the table by the door.

"How's my little girl?" Dad asked. He dropped the bag and wrapped me in his icy coat sleeves. Snow toppled from his hat onto my hair.

"I'm wonderful, thank you for asking."

Dad was my personal Paul Bunyan. The very definition of a woodsman. A lumberjack by trade, nature, and birthright. After fifty years of rolling logs and cutting timber, Dad was the size of a barn and just as hard to knock around. But he gave the best hugs. He released me with a kiss on the head.

I might've gotten my face and creative aptitudes from Mom, but my height and outgoing personality were all Dad. I wasn't six one like him, but at five eight, I had almost six inches on Mom. The brown eyes and hair came from both.

"Hi, Daddy. What can I get you?"

"I'd love a little renewed feeling in my fingers," he teased. "Maybe also in my toes."

"How about a coffee?"

He peeled his heavy gloves off with a groan. "I accept."

"Excellent." I went to get a mug. "What's in the bag? That thing's as big as me."

"Row markers." He wiggled the drawstring open and dragged out a piece of wood three feet long. It had been painted like a candy cane and sharpened at one end. He turned it over in his hands to reveal three letters stenciled onto the front: *FIR*. "I've got pines and spruces too. Your mom says these will make it easier for folks to find what they're looking for. She painted them up nice, and now I'm matching them with the right trees and pounding them into the ground at the ends of the rows."

"Smart. And adorable."

"I was making good time until Jack Frost insisted I come inside and warm up." He rubbed his palms together and huffed against them. "Do I smell whoopie pies?"

"Probably." Mom normally didn't stop baking from Halloween until the New Year, and those little chocolate delights were a White family tradition.

"I might call it a night if there're whoopie pies," he said. "I'll toss this sack in the barn and finish up tomorrow."

"Do it," Cookie urged. "Let me know if you want a cup of tea."

Mom manifested from the kitchen in a puff of sugar and cocoa powder. Her short brown hair was curled into loose waves and tucked behind her ears like mine. And her oven-mitted hands gripped a giant tray of fresh whoopie pies.

The room went silent at the sight of her tray. Then people began to wave.

"Coming." I went to take the cookie orders before I ate them all myself. Being home at Christmas was exactly the medicine my broken heart needed. I'd missed my family and our town. I'd missed the Hearth, with its chocolate-bar tables on black-licorice legs—every piece carved by hand. The café's interior looked like the inside of a gingerbread house, with gumdrop chandeliers hanging over candy cane–striped booths and white eyelet lace lining the windows. I'd brought all my biggest cares here as a child. Lost pets. Traitorous friends. Crushes unrequited. None of it had ever been too big for a hot chocolate cure.

The front door opened again, and another lady slid inside. The table of women who'd been complaining about Margaret Fenwick went still. Standing in a red tweed coat, the newest guest dashed the toes of her boots against the welcome mat, leaving little tufts of snow to melt at the threshold. She scanned the room with a grimace and stopped on me. "Holly White." She marched in my direction with a scowl. "It's nice to see you. It must mean the world to your folks, having you here at Christmas." Her voice was soft, creating a sharp contrast with her expression. She looked me over for a long beat before issuing a stiff nod and turning toward Dad. "I've got something here for you, Bud."

Dad smiled. "Great. Let me have a look at it, Margaret."

Margaret? I flipped my attention to Paula's table. The women pressed their mugs to their lips and watched with rapt anticipation.

This was definitely the Margaret they'd been complaining about.

"Here." She extended a piece of paper to Dad. "It's an order to bring your fencing up to code."

Dad crossed his arms, rejecting the paper. "My fencing's all brand new. It has to be up to code."

8

"No." She jabbed his hand with the paper until he took it. "You've got historically inaccurate sections around your stables and petting zoo. They're much too tall, which puts them in violation of the Historical Buildings and Operations Code. I've outlined the details in this letter and provided pictures and possible sales avenues for the purchase of replacement pieces."

Dad narrowed his eyes. "Do you know how much we paid for that amount of vinyl fencing? I can't just toss out the pieces you don't like. We paid extra for the ones at the stables and petting zoo. The added height is meant to protect the animals."

Margaret shook her head. "I'm sorry, Bud, but—"

"I'm not taking it down," Dad said.

A gasp rolled through the café. Every face pointed in our direction. All pretenses of *not* eavesdropping had been wholly abandoned.

I cringed. I hadn't heard that tone since my teenage years, and when Dad used it, he meant business.

Dad sighed. "Look. I understand your concerns, and I'm sorry you think the pieces are too tall, but I've got to do what's best for my animals. I'm happy to pay the fine."

Margaret screwed her beet-red face into a knot and hitched up her chin. "You're lucky I'm not asking you to remove the whole thing. Do you think they had vinyl fencing when this town was settled? No. And it's too close to your property lines near the road, but I'm willing to let that go as long as it meets a base level of visual expectations. I'm trying to be reasonable."

Dad wasn't moved.

Margaret pursed her lips. "You'll take down the illegal sections of fencing or I will."

He chuckled. "That'll never happen. My fencing was installed to last, and no offense, but I've got cats bigger than you."

"Oh, yeah?" Determination solidified in her milky blue eyes. "I never said I'd use my hands to take it down." She turned on her heels and blew out the door, fists clenched at her sides.

The tension was palpable in her wake, and a few guests made their way to the door. Paula followed suit, clearly done with the night's drama.

Dad deflated, dragging remorseful eyes to Mom. "I know. I have to apologize."

"You argued with a five-foot septuagenarian," she said. "It makes you look like a bully."

"Fine." He loaded his sack of tree markers onto his shoulder and went after Margaret.

Mom nudged my shoulder. "You'd better go too. He's not good with apologies, and she's likely to get him going again."

Cookie pulled fuzzy mittens over her hands and tugged a knit cap onto her puffy white hair. "I'll go with you." She put a to-go cookie in her purse.

I delivered the requested whoopie pies to several tables, then grabbed my coat.

Night had fallen outside, catching me briefly off guard. Twinkle lights illuminated the seemingly endless rows of snow-dusted evergreens.

Children huddled around the reindeer as the keeper, Mr. Fleece, told them stories about the magic needed to fly. Mr. Fleece didn't look nearly as happy as his audience. I supposed that was a result of his earlier run-in with Margaret Fenwick.

Cookie rubbed her mitten-cloaked hands against her coat sleeves. "Where are they? It's freezing?"

"I don't know." I peered into the distance, scanning every direction for signs of my dad, who normally stood head and shoulders above the crowd.

A horse pranced away in the distance, pulling a great white sleigh in its wake. "Maybe she decided to take a sleigh ride," I said.

"Yeah," Cookie agreed. "Those horses probably needed a speeding ticket."

I moved farther into the night, examining each smiling face. "Maybe Dad never caught up with her because she didn't stick around." I turned toward the long gravel drive leading off the property. "Maybe she's heading home. What does she drive?"

Cookie shrugged. "A broomstick?"

I gave her a gentle shove. "Everybody has a job to do. She's just doing hers." Though I had to admit, a little honey would've done more for her than all that vinegar.

Cookie shivered. "I might need another cup of my special tea. It's for my arthritis."

I giggled. "Are you making a gingerbread house tomorrow?"

She curved her lips into a mischievous smile. "I'm doing all the games this year. I've been practicing my icing skills and taking step aerobics for seniors at the church. I'm ready for anything."

My smile widened. "You want to be partners?"

"You know it!" She lifted a mitten for a high five.

Cookie was always my favorite. She told great stories and ran the Holiday Mouse Christmas Craft Shop. She'd let me watch her create the most amazing things while I was growing up. My parents had assumed she'd quit after her big lottery win, but I knew better. Cookie liked her life the way it was, and nothing could change that. Though I'd always wondered why she didn't start her own business. She was a creative genius. Thanks to her, I was an expert in making everything from applesauce ornaments to replica gumdrop jewelry. I still made the jewelry when I was homesick, and based on the few dozen pieces I'd packed into my jewelry box, I was homesick more than I'd realized.

"I'm going back inside before I turn into an icicle," she said.

"Okay. I think I'll take a look at the fence that's causing all the fuss." I moved slow and steady across the grounds, stretching my legs and enjoying the fresh winter air. The fence looked great to me, tall and short pieces alike.

I braced my hands against my hips and turned in place, searching the area for signs of Margaret or my dad.

A sharp scream pierced the night. I jumped, spinning and peering into the darkness for the screamer. A shadowy figure near the county road waved its arms. "Help!"

The peal of the woman's voice set my feet into motion down the drive.

I closed the distance between us at a clip, crossing under the hand-carved "Welcome to Reindeer Games" sign and landing on the road where she stood. "What's wrong?" I panted. Aside from her terror-filled expression, she appeared to be fine.

"Are you hurt? Did you see something?" I pressed. "Was it a bobcat? A coyote?"

The woman pressed one set of gloved fingers against her mouth and pointed the other toward a retired sleigh on display at our property's entrance.

I followed her gaze, hoping it wasn't a bear. "Oh, no." I darted onto the sleigh's cracked leather seat, scrambling toward a familiar red tweed jacket. "Call nine-one-one!" I yelled. "Mrs. Fenwick? Can you hear me?" Did she have a heart attack? A stroke? "Mrs. Fenwick!" I turned Margaret's face toward mine. Pale, unseeing eyes stared back. Dark sticky liquid coated the material behind her head. "No," I whispered. I shook one mitten onto the sleigh floor and searched my coat pockets with bare fingers. I swiped my cell phone to life and dialed, but I didn't need 9-1-1 to confirm what I already knew—Margaret Fenwick was dead.

Chapter Two

I sat in the sheriff's cruiser, wiping tears and working through a load of overwhelming emotions. How was it possible that a woman who'd welcomed me home tonight was being loaded into the coroner's van outside my window? It was nonsense. My mind couldn't right it, and my body was failing to process the flood of adrenaline that hit out of nowhere. I took another deep, shuddered breath, and my head grew light.

The door at my side popped open, and I screamed. Sheriff Evan Gray stuck his head inside. He'd apparently taken over for the older, wider Sheriff Dunn while I'd lived in Portland for eight years.

"Sorry. I should've knocked first."

I probably still would've screamed.

"We're about done here," he said with a faint Boston accent. "Farm's closed for the evening, and your folks said we can talk in the café. They thought you'd be more comfortable there than at the station."

I wobbled my head in what I hoped looked like agreement and not a seizure.

The door shut, and Sheriff Gray climbed behind the wheel. Dialing 9-1-1 had resulted in the whole kit and caboodle: an ambulance, a fire truck, and sheriff and deputy vehicles. The local press hadn't been far behind, but they were exiled by authorities. The coroner's van had come separately.

The cruiser crawled over our long gravel drive, jostling and tipping me with each hump and bump. The interior was warm and smelled like gingerbread and cologne, a fitting combination for the sheriff of Mistletoe. A worn paperback lay on his passenger seat.

We stopped outside the Hearth. He lifted the book above the seat's edge and caught my gaze in the rearview mirror. "It's *The Count of Monte Cristo.*"

I sat back with a flop, not realizing how far I'd craned my neck in wonder.

He climbed out and opened my door. "You doing okay?" he asked, guiding me into the building.

"No."

Dad wrapped me in his arms before I made it across the threshold. Cookie and the rest of the Reindeer Games staff were seated inside, filling the brightly colored booths with sorrowful faces. It was hard to stay sad sitting on a candy-shaped stool, but I had a feeling tonight I'd have no problem.

I sank onto a lollipop at the counter, and Dad kissed my head. "Sorry you had to see something like that, sweetie."

A low murmur of agreement echoed his words.

Mom ferried tea and peppermints to the counter. Her eyes were glossed with tears. "This'll help."

The sheriff cleared his throat and addressed my dad. "Is this your entire staff, Mr. White?"

"Yeah." Dad squeezed my shoulder, parental concern wrinkling his brow.

"Is there anyone who was on duty tonight who's unaccounted for now?" the sheriff continued.

Dad gave the room a more careful sweep. "No, sir. Gang's all here."

"All right." The sheriff walked slowly through the room, hands in his coat pockets, sharp eyes examining each staffer. "The murder weapon was recovered in a dumpster not far from the body."

Dad groaned. "Not one of our dumpsters, I hope."

"Afraid so," the sheriff said. "Want to take a guess at what it was?"

I wrapped my palms around the warm cup of tea and wrinkled my nose. "Who would want to do that?"

The sheriff turned his gaze on me. A muscle jumped and pulsed along his jaw. "I took a picture." He spun his phone to face the room. "Who knows what this is?"

Cookie put her glasses on. "I can't see it."

I could, and it was no good.

"Let me describe it to you," the sheriff said. "It's about three feet long, wooden, and painted like a candy cane. This one says, 'FIR.'"

Dad swore under his breath, then took a seat.

Cookie jerked her gaze to Dad. "Uh-oh," she said. She tucked her glasses back into her purse and brought out the Schnapps.

Mom's jaw hung open. "You can't think . . ." A gasp interrupted her thought.

I set my cup aside and gawked openly. "Are you suggesting my *dad* killed Margaret Fenwick?" Accusing a member of

16

Dad's staff was bad enough, but to accuse *him* was unthinkable. Madness. Hadn't the sheriff ever met my father? He was a two-hundred-pound teddy bear.

Sheriff Gray moved his gaze to Dad. "I'm just asking questions. Like, where were you at approximately six thirty tonight, Mr. White?"

"I was looking for Margaret," Dad said, hands extended in plea. "I wanted to apologize, but I couldn't find her."

The sheriff slid a pen from his shirt pocket and opened his notebook. "Apologize? Did the two of you have an argument?"

"Whoa." I opened my arms like an umpire at home plate. "You don't have to answer that," I told Dad. "You should get a lawyer."

Mom pressed a handkerchief to her nose. "Are you arresting my Bud?"

The room was on its feet, closing in on Mom and Dad with words of encouragement.

The sheriff watched wide eyed. "I'm not arresting anyone," he said loudly. "I'm asking questions. That's how this works. Everybody, please sit down."

The crowd slowly returned to their seats.

"What happens now?" I asked. "Will you start looking for suspects?"

Mom leaned near my ear. "Honey, I think that's what we are."

I looked around. "What? Why?"

The sheriff gave me a disbelieving look. "A woman was murdered tonight, on Reindeer Games' property *with* Reindeer Games' property, so I'm starting with the obvious."

I pressed two fingertips to one temple and attempted to control my tone. "What's obvious to me is that these people are as shocked and confused as I am. None of them would intentionally hurt anyone, and they certainly wouldn't hit an old lady over the head with a tree marker." I hoped to sound more exasperated than aggravated.

He turned to face me head on. "Everyone here had access to the murder weapon and the victim. I have witnesses who saw two of your staffers fighting with her tonight, on the property where she was killed."

I narrowed my eyes, not liking where this was going. "There were dozens of people on the grounds tonight. Everyone had access to those markers, and Margaret argued with more than just Reindeer Games' staff. The way I hear it, she's been harassing everyone."

Cookie raised her hand. "It's true. She's been picking fights all over town. Handing out those awful Historical Society citations. She even threatened my Theodore."

"Theodore?" Sheriff Gray asked.

I jumped in before Cookie could answer. "I heard Paula from the maple farm next door complaining about a fine Margaret gave her for painting her gift shop the wrong color."

The sheriff rubbed his brow. "I'm going to need written statements." He spun a legal pad on the counter and started tearing out pages. "I'd like everyone to write down anything you heard, saw, or believe might help me figure out what happened to Margaret Fenwick tonight."

Cookie raised her hand again. "What if there's someone who didn't see anything?"

"Then write that," he said.

"Well, that seems silly."

"Maybe you can write about the fine for Theodore," I suggested.

The sheriff moved to stand between us. "This isn't an open-book test, Miss White, nor is it meant to be teamwork."

I turned around, prepared to draw mean faces, but the only thing that came to mind was poor Margaret being loaded onto a gurney. I needed a lot more tea and a little of Cookie's magic ingredient to write an account of tonight's events.

The sheriff collected our papers as we finished and excused us individually with instructions to call if we thought of anything else. I slogged toward the guesthouse, exhausted. I needed my favorite pajamas, a nice warm bed, and some cuddles from Cindy Lou Who.

* * *

The next morning, tension pinched the muscles in my neck and shoulders as I dragged myself out of bed and stuffed my body into soft jeans and an ugly Christmas sweater. My boots were beside the front door, standing in a puddle.

Cindy Lou Who was in the kitchen beside her overturned bowls giving me the stink eye. Her chipped ear twitched when she saw me. "Oops. Sorry, Cindy." She hated when they were empty. I rubbed her bushy calico-colored head and righted her bowls, then added a little kibble. "I had a rough night. Forgive me?"

She turned her back to me and chowed down on her breakfast.

I selected candy cane earrings from my jewelry box, the ones with the tiny gingerbread men dangling by one hand. I'd sat up half the night beading and contemplating Mrs. Fenwick's death. I hadn't come up with any answers, but I made some lovely bracelets. "Wish I could stay and make pretty things today, Cindy, but that gingerbread's not going to bling itself."

I locked up and made a path through the snow on my way to the Hearth.

I entered with a slap of déjà vu. It was as if the entire Reindeer Games staff had slept over—everyone was in the same place he or she had been last night.

Mom met me with a large disposable cup of black coffee.

"What's going on?" I asked. "What's everyone still doing in here?"

"Sheriff Gray closed the farm. Can I get you some breakfast?"

"What?" I looked at the dozen or so expectant faces. "Why?"

"He says he needs to sweep the grounds for additional evidence. It was too dark to do it last night, though he certainly tried. Your father was up until after midnight following him around and providing access to every shed and barn stall. How did you sleep?"

I did an exaggerated blink. "How long is the farm closed? It's only twelve days until Christmas. The Reindeer Games start today."

Cookie shook her head. "Not this year."

I deflated. He'd closed the whole farm to search for clues? Margaret had been killed at the property's edge, outside the gates, along a county road. A sweep seemed like overkill. Not to mention Reindeer Games was my family's sole source of income. Closing the doors made it look like we had something to hide, and that could ruin our reputation. "Where's the sheriff now?"

Half the room pointed outside.

I snapped a lid on my cup.

"Wait," Mom said. She poured a second cup and tucked a gingersnap into a plastic sleeve. "Take him something to eat. And see if we can open for lunch," Mom said.

I pushed the door open with my hip and gave her a nod. With a little luck, the sheriff was already wrapping things up.

A line of confused tourists wandered along the outside of our closed gates beside a tour bus. A deputy was speaking with the driver.

"But we came all the way from Concord to play Bling That Gingerbread," a woman insisted.

I went in the other direction, hoping her wish would soon be granted.

The farm looked strange without people milling around. It wasn't meant to be silent or empty. In fact, after what the town had lost last night, it needed Reindeer Games to be open. Mistletoe needed to be together and do normal things. I moved a little faster through the snow, determined to make my case to the sheriff.

He rounded a building as if on cue and stopped. "Morning, Miss White. How are you feeling?"

"Not bad." I lifted the coffees and plastered a sweet smile on my face. "I thought you could use a little something to keep you warm on your wild-goose chase."

He snorted. "You say what you think. I can appreciate that. Not everyone does." Pale-green eyes searched mine as he relieved me of one coffee.

He looked different in the light of day. Less intimidating and more casual in dark pants and a bulky flannel coat. The sheriff logo on his ball cap was the only indication he hadn't come to play games or choose a tree.

"Well? How's it going?" I asked.

"The goose chase?"

A genuine smile formed on my lips. "Think you'll be here much longer?"

He tipped his head in the direction of the Hearth. "Let me ask you something, straight talker—how can you be so sure one of those people isn't a killer?"

"Because I know them. I know they love this town and all the people in it, even when they fight."

He grunted. "You have anything against Margaret Fenwick I should know about?"

"No," I balked. "Of course not."

"You don't usually live here. You came in from Portland this week, right? Are you home for the holidays?"

I squashed the tug of rejection in my chest. "Yep."

He raised thick dark brows beneath the rim of his hat. "Aren't you going to tell me about your breakup?"

I made a crazy face. "Who blabbed?"

"Pie shop." He smiled. "I think I heard your story before you crossed the county line."

I groaned. "They should close that place. People get all sugared up and spill every secret they've ever heard. It's a high school kid's worst nightmare." *Or a small-town sheriff's dream come true.*

He squinted into the sunlight, effectively dropping the lighter mood. "Everyone's got secrets. Right now it's up to me to figure out who's hiding something I need to know. For example, does this place have any nooks and crannies your dad might've forgotten about? Old storm cellars? Empty cabins? Hidey-holes?"

"Did you say 'hidey-holes'?" I tried to knock the cuckoo off that question but couldn't. "Let's make a deal—I'll give you an insider's tour, and you'll reopen the farm when we're finished."

He walked away. "Should we start in this direction?"

"Wait." I perked. "Do we have a deal?" I hustled to catch up. "Let's start at the farthest corner and work back toward the Hearth. We'll cover the most ground with the least amount of backtracking." I caught his sleeve and pulled him in a new direction. "Hope those boots were made for walking."

He gave my hand on his arm a long look but didn't protest. "No promises on the farm reopening, but I appreciate the tour. And the coffee."

"I don't like it, but I'll take what I can get. These are the trees." I swept one arm out dramatically as we passed the tidy rows. "They're planted according to species. We have eight major tree types." I missed a step as the bright candy cane markers took on a new and sinister look. My feet were heavy, and the trees looked a little melty.

The sheriff's face swam into view. "Hey. You still there?"

"Sorry," I whispered, forcing my eyes to focus.

He pursed his lips. "It's normal to struggle with what you saw last night. Don't fight it. You've got to face it to get through it."

I swallowed a painful knot of guilt. "I delivered whoopie pies."

"What?"

"My mom told me to go after Margaret when she stormed out, but I stayed to deliver whoopie pies before I went. I should've left the stupid whoopie pies . . ."

"Stop saying whoopie pies." He stood to his full height. "You didn't do anything wrong. You didn't cause her death by doing your job any more than you could've stopped it by showing up a few minutes sooner. Chances are you'd be with her now if you had gotten there before the killer disappeared. Murderers tend to frown on leaving witnesses." He fished a business card from his wallet. "If you ever want to talk to someone who's been there, you can call me anytime."

"Thanks." I chewed my lip, trying and failing to make sense of the nice man who wanted to help me but also planned to arrest someone I loved for murder. "'Anytime' is a broad offer. Don't you sleep? Have a social life?"

"Not really."

Sheriff Gray was new to Mistletoe, but I'd spent all my life getting to know the people of our town. And one of them was a murderer. My tummy lurched at the thought. "Why is this happening?"

"That's what I'm trying to find out." He scanned the horizon.

The tree farm had officially ended a few hundred yards back at the historically questionable fence. From our new position, his deputies looked like ants marching over a tiny Christmas village instead of parts of my complicated reality.

"What's over here?" The sheriff stomped into drifted snow over a slab of blue particleboard.

"No! Stop!" I jumped to catch him by the back of his coat. "It's the pit."

24

He stumbled back from the force of my pull.

I released him, then bent to grab the board under one end. "Here. Get that side."

Together, we pulled the board away, revealing a large ragged hole in the earth. I kicked a mass of snow into the air. Flakes scattered and twinkled in the bright sunlight before disappearing into the hole. "An old mine shaft collapsed when I was a kid, and this hole appeared."

Sheriff Gray inched closer and peered in. "How deep is it?"

"Not as deep as it used to be. Dad threw dead trees and cast-off limbs in there for years. Eventually, it became a survivable fall. I should know; I've been there a few times. The bruises last for a week."

"You jumped in? More than once?" He shuffled back from the opening. "Why would you do that?"

"I didn't do it on purpose. When I was young, I used to come out here and jump over it." I shrugged. "Sometimes I came up short."

"Why would you do that?" he repeated, more slowly this time.

"Why do kids do anything? Boredom, maybe. Or to see if I could. When that got too easy, I started marking how far on the other side I could land. I was pretty good by high school."

"How old are you now?" he asked. "You think you could still do it?"

I gave the hole a wayward look. "I'm twenty-six, and I don't plan to find out. What about you?"

"I'm thirty-one and not much of a long jumper, I'm afraid."

I smiled. He wasn't so much older than me, though something in his eyes said otherwise. "What did you do for fun when you were young?" I asked.

"Not that." He took a few more steps away from the hole. "Leave that open. I'll have someone check it out."

That was a short-straw job if I'd ever heard one. I dusted my palms and started the trip back at an easy pace. "How long have you been in Mistletoe?"

He fell into step at my side. "Six months. Ironic, really, seeing as how I applied for the Mistletoe position specifically because there hadn't been a murder here in forty years." He slid his eyes in my direction.

"What'd you do before you came here?"

"I worked homicide in Boston for six years, but I knew after a particularly gruesome one that I couldn't do that until retirement."

"Do you miss Boston?"

"Yeah, but I needed out."

Interesting. I felt the same way about Portland. I could've gotten a new apartment and avoided Ben without pulling up roots. Lots of people break up and don't leave town, but I'd wanted out. I'd *needed* out. "Well, lucky us. A former homicide detective is probably better equipped for solving this case than our old sheriff."

"Yeah? What was he like?"

"I didn't know him personally, but from what I could tell, he barely fit behind the wheel of his cruiser, and he rarely left the office."

Sheriff Gray laughed. "So the bar is set high."

I raised a palm overhead, and he laughed.

I squinted up at him through bright morning light. "What happened to you in Boston? Why'd you need out?"

He forced a tight smile. "It was time for a change."

Touchy subject? "Well, how do you like Mistletoe?"

He took several steps before answering. "I feel a bit like a party crasher most days. It might help if I had someone who'd put in a good word for me with the locals."

I steepled my gloved fingers and drooped my eyelids. "I see potential for a trade here."

"Blackmail," he deadpanned. "What do you want, White?"

"Can we reopen?"

"No."

"I don't think you understand how blackmail works."

He laughed, and the day seemed warmer than it had been when we left.

He frowned when the café came into view. The number of occupants seemed to have doubled. "Where are all these people coming from? You're supposed to be closed for the day."

"This is Mistletoe." I nudged him toward the door. "We're a gathering people. You might as well go inside and talk to everyone so we can get the farm open in time for lunch." I held the door and motioned him inside.

"I can't, in good conscious, allow you to reopen until I'm sure I've done my job."

"What I'm hearing is that you need a real suspect."

He made a sour face and sauntered across the threshold with me on his heels.

If the absence of a decent suspect was the only thing keeping Reindeer Games closed, I was willing to bet I could solve our problem before dinner.

I just needed to make a quick trip into town.

Chapter Three

The winding county road into town was lovely as always, even from my temporary perch behind the wheel of a rented moving truck. The forest fell away as I trundled forward, quickly exchanged for rolling hills and valleys, then the familiar smattering of homes. The little boxes popped onto the horizon, puffing smoke from their chimneys and drawing closer by the second.

I cracked the driver's side window and tilted my nose toward the crisp winter air. The truck I'd rented in Portland smelled like cheap air freshener and motor oil. A combination I'd forever associate with the tears I'd shed while loading it. Outside the cab, however, Mistletoe smelled like fresh pine and new fallen snow. It was impossible to lack clarity at those oxygen levels. Which was probably why, shocked as I was by the broken engagement, there was no doubt that things could've been worse—I could've married the guy.

My truck rumbled to a stop beneath the twisty, wrought-iron "Welcome to Mistletoe" sign, hindered by tour buses dropping riders at the square. The public benches had all been repainted a bright Santa red, and pine green wrapped the lampposts. I hadn't realized how much I'd missed it all. Even the traditional mistletoes hanging from our Main Street lanterns looked like home. Hundreds of people stood beneath them each year for selfies. I'd stolen my share of kisses on those corners.

Traffic began to move, and I took a right to circumvent the mass congestion. I drove the last few blocks to Merry Movers and parked outside.

An exiting guest held the front door for me. "Merry Christmas."

"Thanks," I said. "Merry Christmas."

A young woman met me at the counter with a smile. "Welcome to Merry Movers. Where can we move ya?"

I slid the keys and my rental paperwork onto the counter. "Actually, I just moved back."

"Oh." She perked. "Well, welcome back. I'm Annie." Her blonde ponytail bobbed behind her in a corkscrew curl.

"Holly." I did a little wave across the counter.

She processed the paper work, rubbing a thick line of freckles beneath her glasses. "You live at Reindeer Games?"

"Yep. Are you thinking of coming out?"

Her smile wilted. "Oh, um, no thanks."

My tummy tightened with the realization that she'd heard about Margaret's death and didn't want to visit a murder site. I forced a small smile. "Well, if you change your mind, I hope you'll look me up while you're there. We have a lot of fun planned this week, and I make a mean snickerdoodle."

"Okay." She didn't look convinced. "Merry Christmas." She handed me a candy cane and stepped away from the counter.

I stuffed my receipt into the pocket of my puffy white coat and saw myself out.

A parade of tourists laden with shopping bags ambled past, apparently deciding which way to go next. I stepped onto the sidewalk behind them with renewed purpose. I had to clear the farm's association with Margaret's murder before the whole town looked at Reindeer Games the way that young girl had.

Main Street was alive with holiday cheer. Banners billowed from light posts announcing the Twelve Days of Christmas, a retail celebration supported by all the local shops and enjoyed by thousands of visitors every season. A flutter of pride lifted my spirits at the sight of so many happy faces.

I bought a bag of candied pecans from a vendor's cart and surveyed my targets. There were plenty of shops in town, lots of workers and proprietors who likely saw or spoke with Margaret in the last few days. I'd never have time to visit everyone today, but I could certainly start with some coffee. I ducked inside the Busy Bean and landed in a line twelve people deep. Busy Bean was outfitted in shades of brown with punches of pink and white for pizzazz. A smiling cartoon bean with arms, legs, and a boat-shaped hat graced the windows, menus, and counter.

The line inched forward while I teetered between two of my favorite drinks. The vanilla noel reminded me of after-school laughs and coffees with my high school art club, but the cinnamon vanilla dolce reminded me of Christmas shopping with Mom.

"Welcome to Busy Bean. What can I brew for you?" An excited woman in a logoed sweat shirt perked from behind the register. "Oh, hey, Holly!"

"Hi!" I dusted sugar crumbs from my lips and rolled the half-eaten bag of nuts into my pocket. "Wendy, right?" Wendy had kept the little library on Liberty Street all through my adolescence. I'd frequented the adorable take-one, leave-one book depot regularly until I got my driver's license. After that, I traded quick trips to the little library for afternoons lost in a big-box book franchise one town over.

"What can I make you?" Wendy wrote my name on a white disposable cup and increased her smile.

"I'll have a cinnamon vanilla dolce."

"Good choice!" She went to work pumping bottles and shooting espresso into my cup. "Anything else?"

"Yeah." I leaned my elbows on the counter. "Have you heard about what happened to Margaret Fenwick?"

She stopped midpump and turned wide eyes on me. "Yes. It's awful."

"I've heard she was fighting with everyone this week, but I just got home a couple days ago so I missed what was going on." I left the implication *fill me in* hanging.

She scanned the room before leaning conspiratorially over the counter. "She was on some kind of mission to clean up this place before Christmas. Some people were less accommodating than others."

"Like who?"

She snapped a lid on my cup. "Four seventy-five."

"What?"

She opened her palm and curled her fingers a few times. "I've got to keep the line moving," she whispered. "Management gets snippy when I chitchat too long."

"Oh!" I dug in my pocket for some money. "Sorry." I handed her a wad of ones.

"Thank you." She poked the register until it opened. "I believe her nemesis's name is Paula Beech."

I believed she was right. I took my coffee and left the change. "Thank you, Wendy. Merry Christmas!"

Margaret Fenwick had been on a mission to clean up Mistletoe. Why?

A woman in pointy-toed shoes and striped leggings jammed a flyer into my line of sight as I exited the coffee shop. "Two-for-one candles." Her nose and cheeks were red from the cold. She gave my coffee a wistful look and did a little foot-to-foot shuffle. "It's warm inside," she said. "You can buy candles and sample the refreshments."

"Can I bring you something?" I asked. "You look half frozen."

"No, thank you. I'm fine."

I pointed my cup at the sign on the door. "No outside food or drinks allowed. Would you be willing to trade me your flyer for my coffee? It's cinnamon vanilla dolce. I haven't tried it yet, but I know from experience these are amazing."

Her chest expanded, and her mouth fell open. "Yes!"

I inhaled the delicious steam as the woman took it away. "Merry Christmas."

She tucked the stack of flyers under one arm and curled her hands around the cup, lifting it to her mouth with a sigh. "Bless you."

I opened the candle shop door and went to check out the refreshments. Sweet Scents Candle Company was an assault to my senses. I rubbed my watery eyes and pinched my nose to reset my system.

A row of narrow tables covered in red linens were set at the back of the store, coaxing potential buyers past all the shop had to offer before arriving at the refreshments. White doilies shaped like snowflakes dotted the tables. Upon each doily sat a tray of goodies.

"Hello." I greeted a pair of women in matching blouses and pearls. "I think I recognize you from the fudge shop."

The taller one handed me a little plastic plate. "Millie," she said, tipping her head toward her friend, "and I'm Jean. We own Oh! Fudge. We're here making a delivery."

"I'm Holly White. My mom and I were regulars at Oh! Fudge when I was younger." I filled my plate with cheese chunks, crackers, and grapes while my last name settled in.

"Of course. From the tree farm," Jean whispered. "We were just talking about what's going on up there." She scooped a sampling of their fudge from a newly delivered tray and set it on my plate. "How did you get here? Did you escape?" She stroked sleek silver hair as she awaited my response.

I tried not to make a face. "We aren't in quarantine. The sheriff's just following procedure, checking to see if whoever did this left any evidence of his identity behind."

The women exchanged a long look.

"You say 'he,' but I heard Paula was there." Jean curled a lock of hair behind one ear.

"She was," I agreed. "Does that matter?"

"Yes!" The notion seemed to spark Millie to life. She elbowed her way between Jean and the table. "Of course it matters. Paula and Margaret have been feuding for fifty years—since we were kids." Apricot-colored hair sprouted from the hem of her silver knitted beanie. "Ask her yourself," she said, sporting a grin to make the Cheshire Cat jealous. "She's selling syrup on the corner of Maple and Vine."

"Thanks, I will." I tossed a bit of salted caramel fudge between my lips and moaned. "So good."

"Give our best to your mother," they called from behind me.

At the register, I chose two roasted-marshmallow-scented candles and set them on the counter with my coupon flyer and little tray of snacks. Unfortunately, the candle clerk, a former classmate of mine, had never heard of Margaret Fenwick until her death was announced in the paper this morning, but she did offer to box up my snacks for me.

Outside, I headed for the corner of Maple and Vine in search of Paula and her maple syrup stand. I stopped at the florist, shoe shop, and bridal salon on my way. Much as I hated to think of my canceled wedding plans, the dress was ready for pickup, and there were no returns. I draped the garment bag over one arm and carried it as far as the Second Look resale shop where I hawked it on consignment. They'd call me if anyone was interested. Meanwhile, I made my way through several blocks of shops and accumulated a ton of stuff, from candles and nuts to the grapevine wreath dangling around my right arm and a number of other local treasures in two heavy shopping bags. It didn't seem right to prod businesses for details about Margaret and then leave without a purchase. Besides, who didn't need another wreath or candle this time of year?

I peered up and down the street before joining a throng of tourists in a jaywalk. I needed more time to go in every store, but with a mile of shops down each side of the street, it just wasn't going to happen on my tired feet.

"Fresh maple syrup!" a woman's voice called into the white noise of the busy street. "Samples here!"

I followed the call toward a green tent with "Mistletoe Maples" printed on the top, slowing slightly to window-shop at the art gallery on the corner. The sale on figurines and mini-statues caught my eye.

"Anything I can help you with?" a woman in black slacks and a matching pea coat asked.

"I love figurines," I admitted. "All of them. Blown glass. Marble. Ceramic. Lawn gnomes." I laughed. "Doesn't matter. I love them all, and these are beautiful." I pointed to the shelves of black-and-white kittens frozen in play. Small red bows protruded from their collars. I wiggled a finger as if I could tickle them.

The woman cocked her head and folded her arms. "I like your earrings."

"Thanks. I made them from old bottles and votive holders. It's a hobby of mine."

"They're marvelous." She extended her hand my way. "I'm Jenna Montclair. I own the gallery. What do you charge for a pair?"

I processed the strange words. "Oh, no. They aren't for sale." Though, she was the second person to ask me that question in less than twenty-four hours.

"That's too bad; they're fantastic. Do you have more?"

I glanced at a trio of women who'd stopped beside us to stare. They wore lanyards with a bus line logo and munched popcorn, apparently waiting for my answer. "Yes."

"I'd love to include some of your work in my holiday collection." She handed me a business card. "Think about it."

"Thank you." I smiled through my befuddlement. She went into the gallery. I tucked her card into my pocket and hustled toward the syrup booth.

"Fresh syrup!" Paula's hair was cut shorter than mine and barely visible thanks to the hoodie pulled over her head. Space heaters were pointed at her feet and the folding chair by her display. Tiers of syrup in three bottle sizes lined her table. Pamphlets, pens, magnets, and other giveaways were piled near a sign that encouraged passersby to stop and browse.

"Paula?" I stopped at the booth and rested my bulging bags on the table.

"Yeah?" She looked up with a curious smile. "How can I help you?" She arranged samples of syrup-soaked pancakes into a covered warming tray.

I chose a jumbo bottle of syrup and set it between us. "I'd like to buy this."

She dusted her palms and shut the warming tray lid. "All righty. Anything else?"

"Yes, actually. I wanted to talk to you about Margaret Fenwick."

She stuffed my syrup into a little bag with a grunt. "What about her?"

"I'm Holly White," I backpedaled. "My family owns the tree farm beside yours. I'm sure you know my folks, but I've been gone a few years. College and such."

My parents made a point of knowing everyone. I did what I could, but I hadn't had much reason to interact with her when I was growing up. She didn't have children, and I rarely saw her at local events. I probably would've gotten to know her as an adult, but once I'd moved to Portland, my visits home became shorter and further between.

"Anyway"—I waved a mitten between us—"last night at the Hearth, I heard you say that Margaret fined you for something."

Her chin snapped up, and her blue eyes narrowed. Wrinkles gathered in the pale skin on her brow. "Nine dollars."

I handed her a ten. "You knew her well, didn't you?"

"I knew Margie all my life." She pushed my bag across the table. "She was the same self-righteous, self-important blowhard every minute of her sixty-five years."

Heat rose in my cheeks. I checked to see who else had heard the spite-filled words, but no one seemed to be paying any attention. "If you don't mind me asking," I said, "where did you go when you left the Hearth last night?" Paula had left along with a group of other patrons right after Mrs. Fenwick, but I hadn't seen her when I walked outside with Cookie moments later.

"I got in my sleigh and went home. If I'd had to watch Margie ruin one more person's night, I would've popped her in the nose."

I'd seen a sleigh heading away in the distance. That must've been her. Hopefully it wasn't a getaway sleigh. I took the package and offered a gentle smile. "Well, for what it's worth, I'm sorry the two of you had a fight last night. That must be hard for you."

She stiffened visibly. "I'd tell her where to stick that fine all over again if I could. I'd had enough of her nonsense years ago, and she crossed the line this week." She gripped the table's edge until her fingers turned white. "It was only a matter of time until she pushed someone too far."

I gathered my packages and backed away from the booth before *I* pushed *Paula* too far. "Thank you." I wiggled the syrup bag between us. "Happy holidays."

If Sheriff Gray needed a suspect who didn't work at Reindeer Games, I had a great suggestion. Maybe it was time he visited Mistletoe Maples and had a talk with the angry tree tapper.

Chapter Four

I stopped at the corner to rearrange my bundles and bags. According to my little plastic fitness bracelet, I'd put in ten thousand steps for the day. My frozen feet and aching back would've guessed higher. Fumbling through my pockets for my cell, I hoped someone from the farm would be willing to come and get me.

I settled cross-legged on the nearest bench and plucked my gloves off.

A ragged green pickup slid against the curb before I could dial. The driver's side window rolled down. "Holly White?" a congenial male voice called. "Is that you?"

He didn't wait for an answer. The driver hopped onto the curb and headed my way with a wide, warm smile.

"You probably don't remember me," he said, combing long dark hair off his forehead. "I'm Ray Griggs. We went to high school together. I was on the yearbook staff. Student journalism staff. Photography Club."

I smiled back, having no idea who he was. "Right. Of course. How are you?"

"I'm great. You?" He took a seat on the other side of my pile of shopping bags and hooked his elbows over the bench's back. His navy-blue ski coat fell open, revealing a gray thermal shirt beneath.

"Good. Glad to be home." I reorganized my bags, filing smaller ones into larger ones and attempting to even out the weight. I sneaked peeks in Ray's direction as I worked, trying to connect his voice or face to something in my memory. Mistletoe High School wasn't very big, but nothing about him felt familiar. "You said you were on our yearbook staff?"

"Yep." His blue eyes twinkled in the midday light. "You were a senior when I was a freshman. You didn't know I existed." He laughed.

"I was a reclusive art student. When I wasn't brooding, I was dreaming of Renoir."

"Lucky guy."

A nonsensical blush crept hotly over my cheeks. "Are you out shopping?"

"Nah." He cast his attention back to me and the pile of packages between us. "I'm not sure there's anything left."

"Funny."

"Where are you headed now? Can I buy you a coffee?"

"I'm on my way home, actually." I wiggled my phone. "I was calling for a ride when you pulled up. I drove a truck back to Merry Movers and figured someone from the farm would come get me."

"You moved back?" Ray's smiled expanded, revealing a row of straight white teeth. "This isn't a holiday visit?"

"Nope."

"Well, in that case"—he stood and opened his arms like a game show host—"welcome back, Holly White." He strode to the pickup and opened the passenger door. "Let me drive you home."

I chewed the inside of my lip.

"Aw, come on. I'm not a lunatic." He came back to my side and collected my bags. "Would a lunatic carry your bags and hold the door?" He tossed my bags onto the bench seat of his bulbous old Ford.

I nodded. "If he wanted to get me into his truck so he could kill me? Yes."

Ray went around and climbed onto the driver's seat while I stared at the open passenger door. "Hey." He leaned across the seat until his face came into view through the open door. A deep crease had formed between his brows. "Weren't you getting married?"

My tummy knotted as I climbed inside. "I don't want to talk about it."

"Fair enough." He pulled the green beast into traffic with a rumble.

I buckled up and kept 9-1-1 on my phone screen just in case this really was an abduction.

"I get up to Reindeer Games at least once a week for breakfast," he said casually. "Your mom's the best cook in town next to mine. My mom's got a thing for the Hearth's snickerdoodles, so I try to get out your way and bring a dozen home with me when I can."

"You live with your mom?" I asked. Ray couldn't have been more than twenty-three if he was a freshman when I was a senior. I guessed lots of kids moved home after college or an ugly breakup.

"We lost Dad a couple years back," he said. "They had too much land for her to manage, and I didn't have time to keep up with it for her, so she moved in with me when the estate settled. Farming's a full-time job. I guess I don't have to tell you that."

I cleared my phone and stowed it in my pocket. "I'm sorry about your dad."

He flicked his gaze in my direction. "Thanks." His soft, youthful features turned hard for a long moment.

I'd scratched a wound. I needed a new subject. "So how about you? Not married?"

He gave me a goofy look. "No."

"Why not?"

He smiled at the windshield. "No comment. What happened to your engagement?"

"I was dumped for a yoga instructor."

He chuckled. "So you blame yourself?"

"No!"

"You should. You agreed to marry a moron."

I laughed. "I guess you're right."

"We all make mistakes. At least you were lucky enough to dodge yours. I'd call that a win."

I got comfortable in the warm truck, suddenly enjoying the view, the conversation, and the company. "You make it sound like I had a choice."

He cast a curious glance my way. "Would you take him back?"

"No."

"Well, then, you made a choice. A smart one, if you don't mind me saying."

"Not at all." I hummed along with the radio as the bustle of downtown slipped away outside my window. An abundance of snow-dusted trees appeared in the town's absence.

"I heard about Margaret Fenwick," Ray said. "Were you there when it happened?"

"Yeah."

"Sorry."

I gave Ray a long look. "I found her."

"You're kidding." He jerked his gaze from the road to my face and back. "Seriously?"

"I tried to resuscitate her, but the paramedics said she was probably gone when I found her. That it wasn't my fault." I pressed a mitten to my mouth. "Sorry. I can't stop thinking about it."

He watched me silently, dragging his attention back to the road only as needed to stay between the lines. "Did you kill her?"

"No!" I scoffed, twisting on the seat until my back was pressed to the door. "Why would you ask something like that?"

"Well, if you didn't kill her, how can it be your fault?"

"I don't know. I keep thinking I should've done something else. Something more." I studied the puddle forming around my boots on the floor mat. "I stayed with her until help arrived so she wouldn't be alone." Stubborn tears blurred my vision. "It wasn't enough. If I'd left the Hearth a few minutes sooner, she might be alive. My family farm wouldn't be under town-wide scrutiny. I'd be pouring hot chocolates and taking cookie orders instead of spending all my money in town trying to find out what people knew about Margaret."

"Hey . . ." Ray slowed to a crawl on the berm of our quiet county road. "This wasn't your fault."

I caught a rebellious tear with the pad of my thumb. "I know." I sniffled. "Logically, I know. It just seems like there should've been something someone could've done."

He slowly added pressure to the gas pedal, steering us back into our lane. "Yeah, the killer could've *not* murdered a harmless old lady, but you did all you could."

I fished a crumpled tissue from my purse and blotted my eyes. "Did you know this is the first murder Mistletoe's had in forty years?"

His eyebrows climbed toward his hairline. "Where'd you dig up that information?"

"Sheriff Gray."

"Ah." He bobbed his head. "Does the good sheriff have any suspects?"

"Yeah, right." I barked a humorless laugh. "You mean besides my family and every worker on the farm? Not that I'm aware of, which is why I was in town talking to everyone."

"Private investigation. I like it." Ray tapped his thumbs against the steering wheel. "Learn anything?"

"Not really." I shoved the ruined tissue into my pocket and sighed. "Do you have any tissues in here?"

"Glove box."

I leaned forward and pinched the little door open. A travel pack of tissues that'd had been jammed in haphazardly with countless receipts, pens, and notebooks fell out. A lanyard with a laminated nametag landed beside my boots. "Sorry." I scooped the fallen object into my hand and pulled it onto my lap. I liberated a tissue before replacing the items into Ray's glove box. A tiny photo of Ray smiled back at me from the nametag. "Ray Griggs, *Mistletoe Gazette*." I read aloud. "You're a *reporter*?" My tummy clenched.

"I'm trying. Mostly, I take pictures."

Nausea set my world on edge. "All your questions," I groaned. "Was this some kind of interview?"

"No. Of course not." He slowed the truck at my parents' driveway.

A few hundred feet away, the sheriff's cruiser blocked the closed entrance to Reindeer Games.

"Right." I gathered my packages. "Reporters always insist on driving women home immediately after their family has undergone a trauma, expecting nothing in return."

"I thought you'd want to talk about it."

I scoffed in his direction and released my seat belt. "Did you even go to my high school?"

He jammed the truck into park and swiveled to face me. "You seriously don't remember me at all?"

"No." I gripped my bags with unnecessary roughness. "But I won't forget you now." I popped the door open and jumped out. "Thanks for the ride."

"Holly." The sincerity in his voice stopped me short.

I turned for one last look at him.

"I take photos for the paper, and sometimes I submit articles, but I wasn't prodding you for an inside scoop. I was just being friendly. Sometimes my curiosity gets the best of me."

"If I see any part of our conversation in an article, the next time your name's printed, it'll be in your obituary." I regretted the rant immediately. "I'm sorry. That was a joke. A terrible, horribly timed, not funny joke."

"So you aren't planning to kill me?" he asked. A teasing smile played on his lips.

I leveled a palm between us and tilted it side to side to indicate the jury was still out.

Ray flipped his visor down and retrieved a business card. "Here." He pushed it in my direction. "If you just want to talk."

I snagged the little paper rectangle. "I hope you're a nice guy," I said. "I like to think the best of people—don't prove me wrong."

He did a weird salute. "It was nice talking with you, Holly White."

I wasn't sure I shared the sentiment, but I returned his salute anyway.

The rusty pickup reversed out of the drive and spun onto the road in a slow, steady fashion.

What could I do if he wrote an article about our conversation? Nothing. Absolutely nothing—once it was printed, I'd be too late. The damage would already be done.

Chapter Five

I headed toward the small guesthouse where I'd unloaded my things from the moving truck. The building had once been the tree farm's offices, but for the last fifteen years, it had housed guests. There was something sad about the fact that after a lifetime in Mistletoe, I was the visitor.

I slogged through the snow with my bags until Mr. Fleece and the reindeer came into view. He combed the animals with great care, dragging a nearly invisible brush over their fluffy manes and backs.

According to Cookie, Mr. Fleece had argued with Margaret last night. Much as I hated to think anyone in Reindeer Games' employ was capable of murder, I had to be fair. I couldn't discount anyone based on my love for the farm.

I changed direction when he looked up. "Hi, Mr. Fleece."

"Hello, Holly. Been shopping, I see." He wiggled his bushy eyebrows as I approached. Mr. Fleece and the reindeer were one of the newer additions to Reindeer Games. We'd gotten to know each other two days ago when he was kind enough to offer his assistance unloading my earthly belongings from the moving truck. Thanks to the added set of hands, plus Mom and Dad, it had only taken about an hour.

"It's good to be home." I smiled. "Thanks again for your help with the boxes. How are things going for you and the reindeer?"

He brushed the animal's back. "Not bad." Gentle as he was with the animals, it was hard to imagine him wielding a three-foot stake at an old woman. Though my recent breakup suggested I might not be the keenest judge of people.

I adjusted the shopping bags over the crook of one arm so I could get my hands on the soft reindeer before me. "Hello, you." I ran my mittens down his back and fluffed his pretty mane. "What's your name?" I asked, lifting his chin and making kissy faces at his nose.

"That's Kevin," Mr. Fleece said, "or as I like to call him, Mr. Personality. He's the team showboat." He pointed to the other two. "The one on the right is Chrissy, short for Christmas. The other is Noel. They're my babies."

Chrissy and Noel wore matching red bridles, a festive contrast to Kevin's green one.

I stroked Kevin's side. "No fun holiday name for this guy?"

"Wasn't up to me," Mr. Fleece said. "He was almost three years old when I rescued him, too old to change the name."

"He's a rescue?" My heart went out to Kevin, and I warmed immediately to Mr. Fleece. Cindy Lou Who was nearly feral when I'd taken her in.

"You betcha. They were with an abusive owner up north. Chrissy and Noel were just calves then. I took the lot of them and gave the girls their names. I didn't ask what they were called before, and they were too young to remember." He heaved a sigh. "Not that the old coot paid them a lick of attention. He probably didn't call them anything I could say in front of my mother."

"Sad."

"It was awful." He pulled a carrot from his coat pocket and offered it to Kevin, who greedily munched it down. "I never fancied myself a reindeer keeper, but it's been good for me. These guys have taught me a lot about healing." Emotion swelled in his deep-brown eyes. I'd guessed Mr. Fleece to be my dad's age, though time had worn on him in ways that Dad seemed to have escaped.

"I'm glad," I whispered, concentrating on each stroke of the reindeer's fur. "I'm sorry about what happened to Margaret. I heard you argued with her last night. That stinks, huh?"

He dipped his chin. "Yeah."

"What did you argue about?"

He turned cautious eyes on me. "Why? What have you heard?"

"Nothing more than that. I'm just trying to process what's happened. I've never known anyone who died like that before. It doesn't feel real, and everyone's carrying on today as if nothing happened."

"No," he disagreed. "We're all hurting, but life's like that. The living have to live. Some say that's the hardest part about loss."

I didn't disagree. "I've been talking to everyone who spoke with her last night. Do you know what had her so up in arms lately?"

A sense of debate hung over him. "No."

"Will you tell me what the two of you fought about?" I turned to the animals while he decided. "Cookie said something about livestock licensing."

"I lease the stable space here," he said. "Did you know that?"

"I assumed. It's the way we handled the horses until we had our own."

"I yelled at her," he said after a long silence. "I shouldn't have. I flew off the handle—it's a bad habit of mine." He clicked his tongue, coaxing Chrissy to his side. He turned the soft bristled brush on her. "I should've taken the time to explain things more clearly. Maybe she didn't understand the trouble she was causing."

"What sort of trouble?"

"Listing these guys as livestock would make me a farmer, and I can't afford to pay the agricultural taxes. I'm not farming; I'm raising pets. Besides, reindeer aren't livestock; they're wildlife, and my deer aren't wild. They've been in captivity all their lives. Fed. Bathed. Groomed. What if I registered them as livestock and managed to pay the added taxes only to have some yahoo up at the state level come down on me with orders to release them? They'd never survive in the wild, and registering the reindeer as livestock would've put a spotlight on their backs." His voice had ratcheted up with each new sentence, and he'd traded brushing his pet for pulling his own thin ponytail over one shoulder with undue force.

"Did you tell her that?"

"She didn't care!"

I started. "I'm sorry." A pool of unease circled in my stomach. I didn't like his tone or his fevered expression. I stepped away from the reindeer and freed my phone from my pocket. "I have to take this call."

He locked his heated gaze on me as I hurried away, silent phone pressed to one ear. "Hello?" I carried on a fake conversation with the quiet device until I was out of earshot, then returned it to my pocket.

I hated to see the sheriff spend any more time at the farm than necessary, and adding Mr. Fleece to the suspect pool would probably keep the farm closed longer, but it wouldn't hurt for Sheriff Gray to talk to him one more time. Mr. Fleece's temper was quick and hot, and protecting the animals he'd rescued seemed a reasonable motive for lashing out. I wasn't sure if what he'd said about taxes and wildlife was accurate, but he certainly believed it was, and it only took a second to do something rash that couldn't be taken back.

I hadn't known Margaret Fenwick, but someone had taken her life, and she deserved justice. I'd been so determined to find an off-site suspect for Sheriff Gray that I'd failed to let the weight of her loss truly register. Margaret was a local woman, exactly like Cookie or my mom, and someone had killed her.

Someone in Mistletoe was a murderer. And I might have spoken with them today.

A sudden shiver rocked down my spine, and it had nothing to do with the temperatures.

* * *

I climbed the guesthouse steps and stomped snow from my boots, then pressed the door shut behind me. Cindy Lou Who met me with a look of expectancy.

"Hello, gorgeous." I bent to pet her, but she walked away, nosing through my bags before exiting the room completely. Thus was our relationship. I fawned over her, and she was satisfied to know I was still alive. An assurance the meals she pretended to hate would continue uninterrupted.

I sloughed off my winter gear and stowed my bags in the corner. "I'm going to build a fire," I called after her, hoping she'd rejoin me. The thermostat said sixty-seven, which in Maine at Christmas was practically subtropic, but I'd been outdoors so long, the cold had settled in my bones. I needed a crackling wood fire and a hot cup of tea to truly get warm.

The logs flamed to life with little effort, and I went in search of a kettle. The guesthouse kitchen was galley style, a long, narrow addition from my early childhood after Mom decided the farm needed a guesthouse. The renovation came, coincidentally, on the heels of her father's retirement, shortly after my grandparents began making routine trips to Mistletoe.

"What do you think?" I asked Cindy when she poked her head around the counter. "Peppermint or cinnamon?" I set the boxes on the counter before her. She leapt onto the white Formica and stalked closer, crouching lower and wiping the area with her bushy calico fur as she moved.

I freed a mug from the rack and righted it on the counter. "Well?"

The boxes of tea hit the floor behind me. Cindy squinted at them.

"Gee. Thanks." I scooped them up and put the peppermint away.

I dropped a cinnamon packet into the mug and covered it in hot water. The sweet steam lifted my spirits.

Cindy was on the couch in front of the fireplace when I returned. I curled onto the cushion beside her and pulled Mom's favorite afghan over my lap. Colorful tassels danced against my legs, and nostalgia nearly overwhelmed me. The wood smoke and cinnamon in the air. Mom's blanket. The roaring fire. Snow piled on the windowsill. I rested my head back, and my eyes drifted shut.

My phone buzzed with an unheard voice mail, promptly ruining the moment. I dialed in to see what I'd missed, and Ben's voice echoed over the line. "Hey, babe, it's me."

My grip tightened on the little phone.

"So I know you probably don't want to hear from me."

"Correct," I told the recording.

"But a wedding present was delivered to the apartment today, and I wasn't sure what you wanted me to do with it. You've been taking care of all this, so I thought you'd want to call my aunt Karen and let her know about the split. She doesn't speak to my mom, so I guess she hasn't heard. If you don't feel comfortable calling my aunt, you could probably call my mom and ask her to relay the message."

My jaw dropped. "Unbelievable."

"What should I do with the gift, though?" he continued.

I had a few suggestions.

"It's that espresso machine we both wanted. Should I keep it? I mean, I hate to see it wasted." The line went silent, and I nearly hung up, assuming the message had ended. "Really," Ben's voice returned in a sullen whisper, "I wish you'd just come home and share it with me like we'd planned. Things aren't working out for me. I screwed up big time by letting you go, and I think we should talk. Maybe we can still go on that honeymoon together, work out our problems in Hawaii. Sun. Sand . . ."

I pressed the disconnect button until my fingertip was sore, then deleted the message and rubbed my temple. "Idiot," I muttered, only slightly unsure of who I meant exactly, Ben or me.

Cindy slunk across the back of the couch and batted my earring.

I caught her and pulled her onto my legs in a forced snuggle. At least one good thing came from my doomed relationship. Ben had failed to clean up after making salmon one night, and the next day I'd come home to find Cindy on the patio licking the grill. She'd looked like a mean old alley cat with her unruly fur and chipped ear, but I took her in anyway, certain that all she needed was love and security. She was so grateful for the warm bed and food that she stopped hissing when I looked at her after only a few weeks. Eighteen months later, she only hissed at bath time.

She rolled on my lap, extending her invisible claws toward my ears. I'd made a lot of jewelry lately. Maybe I subconsciously knew it was time to come home long before Ben broke the engagement. The jewelry reminded me of better days, when I knew the neighbors and didn't eat alone every night.

Cindy took an interest in chewing my feet through the blanket, and I hoisted the tackle box turned craft supply kit from the coffee table. I sorted through the small glass discs in search of the perfect lollipop tops. "People here like my jewelry," I told her.

Ben had thought my candy jewelry was juvenile. He never understood me or this town and hated visiting, which was why I'd come alone for Christmas every year at first, making excuses to my family for his absence and apologies to his family for mine. Later, I'd chosen Christmas with him over my parents. "I figured it out, Cindy. *I* was definitely the idiot."

I sipped my tea and mentally replayed the day while I wound silver wire into jingle bells and holly shapes. I didn't like the way Paula had grouched about Margaret even after her death. Was her attitude symptomatic of an awful habit? Incessant negativity nurtured over several decades or something more? I also didn't like Mr. Fleece's temper or his understandable anger. Lots of things made me mad, but I didn't scream about them, especially not to someone who was practically a stranger.

I pried myself off the couch when the tea was gone. Comfy as I was, the sheriff needed to know what I knew, and his cruiser was still at the gates. "I'll be back in time for your dinner," I told Cindy as I returned my supplies to the plastic chest for safekeeping. "Enjoy the nice warm fire."

I pulled a fresh coat and boots from the closet and stuffed my toasty arms and feet into them. An elegant navy number with a wide collar and belt, the classic wool pea coat had been in my family for three generations. My mom's mom had purchased it on her honeymoon in 1962. I always felt a little like Jackie O when I wore it. I especially loved the big black buttons, reminiscent of another time. The boots, unfortunately, were the sort of mud-soaked, calf-high rubber ordeals only found in the wilderness. I doubted the sheriff would notice or appreciate the collision of style and practicality. All he needed to know was that I'd been out on reconnaissance all morning and that I had at least two solid leads for his team.

I adjusted matching mittens over my fingers and tugged the front door open. A gust of snow swirled in, temporarily stealing my breath before vanishing into the cozy room. A line of red-and-white-striped stakes were arranged on the porch before me. My tummy dropped as the message settled in. These stakes matched the one used to kill Margaret Fenwick, and the pointed ends were aimed at my door. One word was spray-painted on each of the four tree markers:

STOP OR YOU'RE NEXT

I slammed the door shut and pressed my back against it. Someone knew I'd been asking about Margaret's death, and they didn't like it.

Chapter Six

I pulled myself together and looked out the front window. There was no one in sight. I inched the door open and scanned the stretch of snow-covered land between myself and the tree farm perimeter. No one. Whoever had left the message hadn't hung around to see that I received it. I snapped a picture of the threat with my phone, then tugged my hat over my ears and started off at a jog. I picked up the pace as the guesthouse shrank behind me and the main building of Reindeer Games drew closer. Shadows loomed behind every tree and outbuilding, daring me to wonder if the killer was watching now. If he was, would I be safe? Would my screams be heard at this distance from my family and their crew, or would the sound be swallowed by the fresh blanket of snow?

I ran toward the stables hoping to find a friendly face or two inside. The low rumble of my dad's voice pushed my feet into a sprint. "Dad!"

He came into view with a smile.

Hot tears burned in my eyes. I didn't have to be strong or calm. Dad was my refuge, and he'd make this better.

His broad strides ate up the space between us. "What's the matter?"

"I need Sheriff Gray," I said, heart pounding. "Have you seen him? Is he still here?" I blinked the tears back frantically.

"I'm here." Sheriff Gray appeared at the stable door.

A strange mix of relief and fear flooded my system. I was certain he could help, but the fact I needed a sheriff at all made the threat intensely scarier.

Dad's giant gloved hands caught mine. "What's going on? Are you hurt?" He trailed my limbs with keen parental eyes, lifting my arms at my sides like an airplane.

"No." I swallowed hard. "I'm okay, just a little shaken."

"Why? What happened?"

The sheriff stopped at our sides, creating a tiny triangle. "Tell me what happened." His cheeks were red, and his eyes glossy from the unrelenting wind.

I wiggled my hands free of Dad's grip. "I found a line of those tree markers on my porch."

"At the guesthouse?" Dad frowned.

"Yeah." I brought up the picture I'd taken on my phone. "Someone left me a message."

"With tree markers?" Dad asked, still perplexed by my story.

I handed my phone to the sheriff. "Yeah. Exactly like the one used to kill Margaret Fenwick."

"You think someone threatened you?" Dad jerked his gaze to the sheriff. "Give me that."

Sheriff Gray turned the phone over to Dad and locked cool green eyes on me. "Anything else you want to tell me?"

"I don't think so." I shifted my weight, suddenly feeling as if I'd entered the principal's office.

"We'll revisit that question in a minute." He raised the walkie-talkie from his belt and squeezed. "I need someone for evidence collection at the Whites' guesthouse. Crime scene review and photographs as well."

"Copy that," a man's voice crackled back.

The sheriff holstered his walkie-talkie and motioned for me to lead the way, but Dad turned on his boots and cut me off. We fell into step behind him like a mismatched platoon.

A few minutes later, we stood shoulder to shoulder at the base of my porch. Dad fumed. The sheriff sucked his teeth. I bit into the tender skin alongside my thumbnail.

"Well?" I asked. "It's a threat, right?"

The sheriff didn't answer. He lifted his phone and snapped several pictures before circling my house. He disappeared in one direction and returned moments later in the other.

What was he thinking? Was there something here that I couldn't see?

"Please talk to me," I begged. "You're making it worse."

Lines raced across his forehead. "Sorry. I'm thinking. Did you hear anything before you left the house?"

"No."

"See anyone? In the distance, maybe?"

I gnawed a little harder on my thumb and winced when I drew blood. "Nope." I pushed my hand back into its mitten and made a fist to ease the sting on my thumb.

He lined his boot beside one stake and snapped another picture. "Would you say these are your stakes, Mr. White?"

"They are," Dad agreed. The color in his face had bled from red to eggplant at the first sight of my porch.

I rested a hand on his arm. "Breathe."

The sheriff climbed my steps carefully, placing his feet in my prints. "The stake used on Mrs. Fenwick weighed about eight pounds. There're four stakes here. That's thirty-two pounds."

I inched closer to the objects in question. "Even if I could lift thirty-two pounds of loose wooden stakes, I couldn't carry them without looking like one-half of Laurel and Hardy."

"So whoever did this had a sack like mine," Dad said.

I mimed the size of the woodpile with outstretched arms. "If I put those in a sack, they'd drag to the ground, but I don't see any drag marks."

Sheriff Gray squinted into the sun. "She's right. Whoever carried the stakes was tall or had help." He turned in an arc, examining the area from his new perspective atop my porch. "We've got footprints, sled tracks, and hoofprints."

"Footprints could be anyone," I said, "including me."

Dad pulled a phone from his coat pocket. "I'll get someone to follow the tracks and see where they go, maybe even who they belong to."

"Paula drove a sleigh to the Hearth last night," I said. "Could she have come here today?"

Dad hovered near the marks, bent at the waist, phone pressed to his ear.

I idly wondered if Mr. Fleece used the reindeer to pull a sleigh. Maybe Santa did it.

The sheriff moseyed back down the steps to my side, phone in hand. He turned the device to face me. A close-up of the words "STOP OR YOU'RE NEXT" was centered on the screen. "Any idea what this means?"

"Me?" I asked, slightly baffled by the question. "I guess someone wants me to stop doing something."

He widened his stance and crossed his arms, effectively removing the phone from my sight. "Stop doing what, for example?"

My cheeks burned. "I don't know."

"If you had to venture a guess."

Dad turned back to us. "These tracks are too narrow for a sleigh, and there aren't any hoofprints. Looks more like a person with a large sled. Your mother's going to see if someone took one of our sleds out, then she's headed this way."

"Thanks, Dad."

Sheriff Gray's steady gaze never left mine. "Any ideas yet?"

I turned my chin left and right, lips pressed tight.

He circled me the way he had with the wood. "Why don't I believe you?"

Dad moved closer. "What's going on?"

The sheriff stopped at my back and leaned over my shoulder. "You must at least have a guess."

My eyes slid shut, ruffled further by his nearness, but my lips sprang apart. "I went into town and asked a few people about Mrs. Fenwick."

He went rigid. "Care to elaborate?"

I peeked one eye open and turned until I faced him toe to toe. "There's a possibility that one of the people I spoke to or someone who saw or heard about what I was doing wants me to stop doing it."

"Holly," Dad scolded, "what were you thinking?"

I forced an apologetic smile his way. "I'm sorry. I didn't think asking questions would cause a problem. I was trying to figure out what Mrs. Fenwick was up to before her death."

"You can't do stuff like that anymore," Dad said. "It's not safe." The ache in his voice broke my heart. "This isn't the town we thought it was. You're putting yourself in danger." He wrapped me in a mammoth hug.

I angled my head against his chest so he could hear me. "It's not like I went shop to shop asking for a show of hands if anyone had recently bludgeoned her. I just wanted Sheriff Gray to have someone to look into who didn't work at Reindeer Games. This is our busy season. We have to get those gates open. You and Mom live off this one month's income for half the year."

Dad squeezed me tighter before letting go. "That's right, *we* do. Your mom and me. You don't have to worry about us. We've made it through harder times than this, and we'll get through this too." He fiddled with the collar on my coat. "Why don't you let me worry about you instead?"

"Hey!" I smiled as a new idea formed in my head. "Sheriff Gray, my dad was with you earlier today, right?"

"That's right."

A jolt of enthusiasm pulsed through me. "If he was with you, then he wasn't putting this on my porch."

Dad looked at me like I'd sprouted another head.

"Not that you would ever do anything like this," I backpedaled. "I think whoever killed Mrs. Fenwick did this. That's the significance of the stakes. If I'm right, and Dad was with you, Sheriff, then this proves my dad isn't the killer."

Sheriff Gray seemed to mull my theory over. He rolled his shoulders. "I'm tempted to say your argument is circumstantial, but this isn't a courtroom, and I don't disagree."

I stifled the urge to clap. "So Dad's off the hook as a murder suspect?"

"Tell me this," the sheriff said, swiftly changing the subject, "who have you talked to today that's capable of this?" He tipped his head to the threat on my porch. "The police report didn't include a description of the murder weapon and neither did the morning paper. The person who did this also had access to the farm's other painted markers. Had to know where you keep them and how to get to them. Someone with a reason to think you're on to them."

I wet my frozen lips. No one had asked about the murder weapon, and I hadn't offered that detail. "I don't know."

Mom hustled toward us through the snow, a lidded basket with holiday-print liner clutched in her grip. "I can't believe this," she lamented. Puffs of white steam lifted into the air with each word. "I'm so sorry this happened to you. You must be terrified." She caught one of my hands in hers and pulled me up the steps toward my front door, careful to stay on the already trodden path. "Come inside and have a bite to eat. I'll put the kettle on."

I stopped on the porch. "You go ahead. I have to finish talking to Sheriff Gray."

"Then you should both come inside where it's safe."

"Mom," I huffed. "He's the sheriff. I'm safe with him."

"You're my daughter," she chided.

The sheriff cleared his throat, drawing Mom's attention. "Why don't you both go inside, and I'll be in as soon as my deputy arrives to cover the crime scene."

"Go on, Mom," I urged. "I'll be in soon."

She batted emotion-filled eyes. "If you two won't come with me, then I'll bring the tea to you." She swept over the threshold and shut the door.

Sheriff Gray's lips curled into a half smile. "She's not happy with me, but she's still willing to bring me tea in the cold. People aren't that nice in Boston. It's different here. Like living in a Rockwell painting."

"Not everyone's that nice," I muttered.

"Yeah? Who?"

The deputy arrived right then with a multitude of black shoulder bags crisscrossing his round belly. "Ready to get started, Sheriff." He greeted Dad with a handshake and me with a nod, then went to work photographing the area. His serious black camera made the scene feel more criminal than I liked.

I squirmed under Sheriff Gray's scrutiny.

"Who isn't that nice?" he repeated.

"Can we talk inside now?" I asked, afraid of offending Mom if we remained outside longer than necessary.

Dad moved to block the steps like a newly hired bouncer. "Go on. I'll keep watch."

I went inside and beckoned the sheriff to follow.

The fire was going strong, heating the little space with ease. Cindy lounged on the couch where I'd left her.

"Come to the kitchen," Mom called.

Hot tea and baked goods sweetened the air.

Sheriff Gray stopped at Mom's side. "Any chance you know who had a sled out this way?"

"No." She shook her head. "No one marked the log book because we're closed. It's a way to keep track when the sleds are in demand, but today . . ." She sighed. "I don't know."

She'd set the kitchen table with an array of muffins, pastries, and tea trimmings from her basket. Each type of treat had its own woven container and matching linen liner.

"What happened to the cute little baskets made from recycled paper that you love so much?" I asked. The paper baskets came in an assortment of holiday prints and made cleanup simple. Real baskets seemed impractical. Come to think of it, she'd switched to ceramic mugs in the Hearth too.

Mom waved a dismissive hand. "Throwaways seem so impersonal. These give folks the feeling of permanency, like they've just sat down to a snack at a friend's home."

I mulled that over, and it didn't mesh. Throughout my childhood, she'd touted the practicality of disposable cups and the freedom they gave guests to leave the booths and enjoy our farm at their leisure.

"Help yourself." She kissed my head. "I'm going to check on your father."

I leaned against the counter until I heard the front door close. A lot had changed while I was away.

I turned my attention to Sheriff Gray. "Paula from the maple tree farm next door was borderline hostile when I asked her about Margaret. The two women were apparently enemies for decades, but I think it's odd that Paula's just as mad at Margaret today as she was before."

"Anyone else?"

I frowned. "This isn't easy for me, you know? I'm talking about people behind their backs. I don't know who's a killer and who's just cranky. The cranky ones don't deserve to be gossiped about."

He circled a wrist between us, the universal sign to move it along.

"Don't you have any follow-up questions on Paula?" I asked.

"Nope."

I rubbed my forehead. "Fine. You might also want to talk to Mr. Fleece, the reindeer keeper."

Sheriff Gray pulled his chin back and tented his eyebrows. "Fleece works here. I thought the whole point of your little espionage mission was to steer me away."

"My mission was to make you cast a wider net. You're too focused on my family and the farm workers. You aren't even looking at the other people who hated her." I bit my lip, wishing I hadn't said "hate." "Maybe the killer didn't hate her. Maybe they were just two people having a run-of-the-mill disagreement and things escalated unexpectedly."

"Do you always do that?"

"Do what?"

He helped himself to a mug of hot tea and stirred slowly, forcing me to wait for his answer. "Always give everyone the benefit of the doubt."

"I try."

"You think it's a nice thing to do, but you're giving the killer an excuse." He blew across the steamy surface of his tea and took up a spot on the wall across from me in the narrow room.

I wrapped my arms around my middle. "You don't know what it's like to grow up in a small town. I've known most of these people all my life. I hate thinking one of them is capable of murder."

Something flitted over his expression, there and gone before it could be named. "Everyone's capable of something they never thought they could be."

I searched his eyes for the story behind those words, but whatever it was, he kept it to himself.

"Who, on this property, knew you were going into town?"

"Everyone. I was probably hard to miss in the rental truck."

"Did they all know you had an ulterior motive?"

"No. I didn't tell anyone."

He ambled back to the spread on my table. "Could someone have seen or heard you in town, become frustrated, and followed you home?" He bit into one of Mom's chocolate chip cookies and moaned. It wasn't an uncommon response.

"I don't know. Maybe."

He stopped chewing. "I didn't see the truck outside."

"I returned it."

"How'd you get home?"

"Ray Griggs."

He stuffed the remaining cookie between his lips with a chuckle. "You know him?"

"Kind of. We went to school together," I said, hoping it was true.

"Did he tell you he's a reporter now?"

"Yes." *After* I'd discovered his press badge.

The front door opened and closed with a thump. "Sheriff?" His deputy marched inside, dusting snow from his gloves. "All set out there. I've collected the stakes and photographed the scene." He tipped his hat when he noticed me staring, and a mass of salt-and-pepper hair burst free.

"Help yourself to cookies and tea," I said. "Take your time warming up. There's a fire in the living room if you'd be more comfortable there."

He grabbed a napkin and loaded the sweets into a precarious pile. "Thank you kindly. Don't mind if I do."

I refocused on the sheriff. "What's next?"

"For starters, stop asking people about Margaret Fenwick." He rubbed the back of his neck. "Don't give out any information either. If someone doesn't know something, it's because they don't need to. Got it?"

"Sure."

He turned to his deputy. "We need a list of all the people on these grounds today. I want to talk to anyone who was here and unaccounted for at the time when those stakes could've been delivered."

The deputy wrote something in a little flip notebook. "Yes, sir."

I headed for the door. "We might as well start at the Hearth. There was quite a crowd at breakfast."

Mom met us on the porch. "How's everything going? Can I get you anything else?"

"He wants a list of everyone who was here today," I said.

"Oh, dear," Mom answered. Her eyes rolled skyward as she disappeared in thought. "There have been quite a few. I can take a stab at it, if you'd like."

Sheriff Gray braced wide palms over narrow hips. Frustration colored his face. "I don't understand why this is so difficult. Who are all these people?"

"Townies," I said.

"What are they doing here? I ordered Reindeer Games to be closed today."

Mom smiled sweetly and patted his sleeve. "We are closed, dear. No one's buying anything. They're just visiting."

Sheriff Gray turned a droll expression on me.

I locked my arm in his and towed him toward the Hearth. "Welcome to Mistletoe."

He pinched the bridge of his nose as we moved. "When we get to the Hearth, I'll do the talking. You're done asking people about Margaret Fenwick."

I smiled sweetly. That's what he thought.

Chapter Seven

Sheriff Gray did the talking, but we didn't learn anything new. An hour later, he went back to searching hay bales and horse troughs for clues to the killer's identity. I went home to make lollipop lapel pins and binge-eat Mom's cookies.

The Hearth was dark when I arrived the next morning in need of breakfast. I knew Mom was inside before I opened the door. The sweet scents of her fresh-baked muffins and breads seeped into my nose and hastened my step.

"Good morning," I called, announcing my arrival.

Mom bebopped behind the counter to an acoustic version of "Jingle Bell Rock." Her dark curls bounced in time with a pair of silver bells pinned to her signature red sweater. "Good morning, angel." She stopped to address me with a notoriously bright smile. "How'd you sleep?"

"Great."

"You're a terrible liar," she said, smiling wider still. "Don't frown. It's not a bad thing. People should tell the truth more often," she mused. "It's so much easier."

"Too bad the person who hurt Mrs. Fenwick doesn't live by your code of ethics and honesty."

"Well"—she spritzed the display case with cleanser—"Sheriff Gray will find whoever did that. I'm sure of it. Are you hungry?"

"Whatever you're baking smells amazing."

"Cinnamon swirl muffins with a little brown sugar drizzle."

"Sold." I caught sight of the mouth-watering treats on a cooling tray and plucked one for myself. "Where is everyone?"

"Home, I suppose. Sheriff Gray hasn't given us the okay to open yet. Though I suspect some of the regulars will show up soon anyway. It's too bad I have to give the food away. Not that I mind being hospitable."

"He doesn't care about sales," I said. "He doesn't want people here at all. Did you see his face yesterday when it was time to make a list of visitors?"

Mom shrugged. "What am I supposed to do when they come? Turn them away?"

I laughed. "I don't know. I don't envy you right now, that's for sure." My mother hated conflict. She could no sooner send a guest home than hit them with a rock. She was raised at a boarding house for migrant workers. It was in her very fiber to bring people in, not turn them away. "Maybe we'll be open for lunch. Did he say?"

"No."

"Well, that doesn't seem fair. He has to have an idea of when he'll have things wrapped up here." I went to the window for a look at the locked gates. The deputy's cruiser was parked at the end of the drive. He paced the area outside the perimeter, apparently redirecting buses and visitors as they arrived. Meanwhile, my mom was up at dawn preparing for guests she wouldn't charge because the investigation was still open.

"Have you seen the sheriff this morning?" I asked. "I'll go and ask him directly."

Mom filled a travel mug with coffee and slid it over the counter to me. "Just the deputy's here today. And your father says I shouldn't encourage you to ask any more questions."

I pulled the cup to my chest. "No one said I couldn't talk to the sheriff." I checked my watch. "Speaking of questions, I was up half the night wondering who was closest to Margaret these days." I'd spent the other half checking my doors and windows for signs of a new threat. "She seemed pretty gung ho about her work. Maybe someone there can shed some light. Do you know what time the Historical Society opens?"

"Nine, but *do not* go there and ask about her." Mom's mouth said no, but her head nodded yes.

"Gotcha." I smiled. "Can I borrow a truck?"

"You betcha." Mom snagged a key from the rack on the wall. "Be sure to fill me in when you come back."

I tipped my drink in her direction and pocketed the key. "Love you!"

Dad kept a trio of red pickups with the Reindeer Games logo on their sides and brown reindeer antlers rising from the window frames. A big red nose was tied to each broad silver grill. I'd learned to drive in one of those trucks. It was the same one Mom and Dad had brought me home from the hospital in sixteen years before I took the driver's test. Surprisingly, when I squeezed the key in my pocket, lights flashed on a newer model. I climbed inside and tuned the radio to my favorite station, then took the back way around the property and down my parents' drive to avoid the closed gates. I wondered where the sheriff was this morning and what he was up to. I told myself the interest was purely based on my desire to get Reindeer Games back to business as usual, but I wasn't completely sure that was the whole story. I was positive, however, that I didn't want to think too long or hard about what else it could mean.

I cruised past familiar homes with the same trusty lawn decor from my childhood: inflatable Grinches on rooftops and twelve-foot snowmen near garages. This time, however, I couldn't help wondering if someone inside one of those cozy country houses had killed poor Mrs. Fenwick, then gone home as if nothing had changed. Surely someone had noticed something. Some change in their loved one, a difference that began on the night of a murder.

Strange how a town can be exactly the same and completely different at the same time. I took the next right on a whim, choosing a less-traveled route instead of the direct one. I forced the negative thoughts aside and let nostalgia warm me from the inside out.

A tenacious sun had peeled back the snow, revealing a slightly greener world. The crop of evergreens behind the old flour mill looked like something off a post card. I slowed at the crossroads to watch ghosts of my childhood skip through annual school field trips and multiple family picnics outside the building. Sadly, a "Closed" sign hung at an angle over the front window beside a banner thanking Mistletoe for one hundred years of business and support. It was easy to imagine the profound disappointment for the family who'd had to close those doors. I wished there was something I could do to revitalize the place, but first I needed to make sure Reindeer Games didn't end up in the same condition—shut down—after four proud generations of Whites had put their hearts and souls into it. A tug of emotion tightened my chest. I wouldn't let that happen.

* * *

The town was overrun with tourists, having absorbed the added busloads of shoppers who were unable to visit Reindeer Games as planned. Despite it all, Sheriff Gray was shockingly easy to locate. His cruiser had a front-and-center spot along the curb at the pie shop.

I breezed inside and smiled at the hostess dressed in a pink-and-white retro waitress ensemble, complete with ruffled apron. "Good morning! I'm with him," I said, pointing to the back of Sheriff Gray's head.

"Well, then, right this way." She gathered a menu and set of silverware from the hostess stand. "You've picked a good time to stop in. This is the second day of the Twelve Pies of Christmas."

She led me to the sheriff's booth, casting congenial glances over her shoulder along the way. "Today's pie is holiday apple. It's baked with brown sugar and locally grown apples. The flaky cinnamon sugar crust is enough to make you cry."

I slid into the sheriff's booth. "I'll just take coffee for now."

He smiled. "Well, hello. What are you doing here?"

"I came for coffee. Mind if I join you?"

The waitress slid my placemat and napkin-wrapped silverware onto the table before me.

He straightened. "Of course." He turned to the waitress. "Please get this lady whatever she wants. It's on me."

"Very generous," I said, arranging my discarded coat and purse on the red vinyl bench.

The waitress hovered another moment. "You look so familiar. Have we met?"

I rocked my head side to side. "You probably know my mother, Carol. Some people think we look alike. I'm Holly." I extended a hand her way.

Sun-spotted skin gathered across her forehead and at the corners of her eyes and mouth. "Holly White?"

"Guilty."

"Congratulations!"

Heat rose to my cheeks.

"You're getting married Christmas Eve! Everyone in town's been talking about it all month. I've overheard your mom and her ladies in here planning the details every Sunday afternoon since Easter." She patted the table. "You know what? Pie's on the house. Be right back." She spun on her white sneakers and vanished through swinging kitchen doors.

I suppressed the urge to drop my forehead onto the sparkly white tabletop.

"To what do I owe the pleasure?" the sheriff asked. "Not that I mind a surprise coffee date, but I must admit I'm curious."

"I came to see how much longer the farm has to be closed. There's only ten days until Christmas, and the Twelve Days of Reindeer Games brings in a lot of business, not to mention morale's down."

He twisted his cup on a napkin. "Believe it or not, I was headed out there next. My sweep's complete—I planned to tell your parents they could reopen anytime. I have a couple more staff interviews to do this afternoon, and I'd prefer to conduct them on the property where we can walk the grounds as we talk, but that shouldn't stop the fun."

"Thank you," I sighed in relief. The waitress reappeared with my pie and a mug of coffee. "One big ole slice of holiday apple for the bride-to-be." She placed it all on the table and sprayed a cone of whipped cream on the cinnamon crust. "Can I get you anything else?" She tucked the can back into her apron.

I puffed out my cheeks. "Actually, I can't accept this. My wedding was called off earlier this week, which is why I'm home, probably to stay."

She wrinkled her nose. "Canceled? Are you sure?"

"It's not really something you can get wrong."

"Was it your doing?"

"Nope."

She blanched. "Oh, honey. I'll be right back with some ice cream."

I cast a warning look at the sheriff and commanded my stinging eyes to give it a rest. "I don't want to talk about it."

He raised his palms.

The waitress returned a moment later with two scoops of vanilla for my pie. She left with a sad smile.

I plunged the tines of my fork into flaky, sweet, creamy heaven. "You know, you can't get away with eating dessert for breakfast in some places."

The sheriff chuckled. "This is my favorite restaurant in town. They make great coffee, excellent pies, and a mean pancake. I also like the atmosphere. It's like visiting a fifties soda shop, complete with checkered floors and vintage signs. The simple menus are a relief, and I'm partial to the uniforms."

I rolled my eyes. "Wow."

"What? They're classic."

"They're short and tight."

He feigned offense. "My mother was a waitress."

"Don't try looking innocent over there, Boston." I stuffed another bite into my mouth and savored the collision of textures.

"I am innocent," he said. "I think you're just trying to put me in the 'all men are pigs' box after that breakup."

"We aren't talking about that," I muttered around a mouthful of pie.

"Okay, then what are we talking about?" He leaned over the table, a glimmer of mischief in his eye. "You came here for more than coffee, and I was already on my way to your parents' farm, so it wasn't that either."

"I didn't know you were on your way to the farm," I said. "And if we're going to talk, you might as well help me eat my pity pie."

He lifted his fork. "Got any specific plans while you're in town today?" He took a chunk off the opposite side from where I was working.

I chewed intently, recalling Mom's recent observation about my lying prowess. "I can't stop thinking about Mrs. Fenwick. Everyone says something was going on with her lately. What do you think it was?"

He pushed a bite of pie between his lips and settled back in his seat. "I think she was a lonely old woman who'd outlived her husband and her son. Holidays are the worst time to be alone. The loneliness compounds when your home is empty and everywhere you look, there are endless lines of happy families. I can't imagine what that'd be like in a town like this. She might not have been as sugary sweet as the town wanted, but I liked her."

I set my fork aside. "How well did you know her?"

"Not well. I helped her get her cat off the roof when I first came to Mistletoe. She made me hot chocolate afterward."

"Was she upset about the colors of buildings and livestock without permits back then?"

"I don't think she was upset; I think she was extradedicated. Keeping the town's historical status up to snuff had been important to her husband, and she probably felt she was honoring him by carrying on the torch."

The waitress returned with a worried expression. "How was the pie?"

"Good," I said.

"Excellent," the sheriff agreed.

She cast a curious glance between us, then ripped a page from her little green order pad. "My nephew is about your age, if you're not seeing anyone." She slid the page my way. "He ain't the sharpest stick, but he's good looking and well meaning. He could be a great distraction." She winked.

My jaw dropped.

She mimed a phone near her ear as she walked away.

I turned the paper over to find a name and phone number. "Good grief."

Sheriff Gray smiled widely from his side of the booth. "What do you think she meant by that wink?"

"Shut up."

"See, I know you're out of practice, but that wasn't nice. Here in Mistletoe, people don't tell the sheriff to shut up."

"Would you like me to tell you something else instead?" I lifted an eyebrow.

He chuckled. "I like you. You're like the pepper on this people stew."

I laughed. "You're truly awful at metaphors."

"You don't want to be pepper?"

I laughed louder. "I don't want to be in a people stew. Jeez." I hid my goofy smile behind the rim of my coffee cup. "You're in a good mood this morning."

"I try to smile every once in a while. Believe it or not, I smile a lot more here than I ever have."

"Good."

"Old instincts die hard, though. I've gotta ask—any more problems at the guesthouse?"

"No."

"How'd you sleep?"

Not a wink. "Fine."

"Would you do me a favor? Consider staying with your parents in the big house until I get this thing figured out." He lifted a palm to stop the protest on my lips. "Humor me? I couldn't sleep last night. I nearly came over to check on you a dozen times."

"You could have." I glanced up at him sheepishly. "I was probably awake."

He rested his hands in his lap. "Well, at least I know you understand this is serious."

"I do."

The room buzzed with sounds of a dozen conversations, and I recalled two other things he'd told me about himself. First, he loved this place, and second, he had no social life. "Still looking for where you fit in?"

"Yep."

"Try making one new friend. The rest will follow."

He raised sincere green eyes to mine, a look of determination on his brow. "Can I start with you?"

"As your first friend?" I blushed senselessly and refocused on my drink. "Maybe."

"Maybe? Is this more blackmail?" he teased.

"No, but how about another coffee?"

Twenty minutes later, we finally extracted ourselves from the booth and headed into the day. When his cruiser was nothing but taillights, I drove to the Historical Society for another conversation.

* * *

The building's exterior was exquisitely crafted and meticulously maintained; it was easily the town centerpiece, architecturally speaking. The goliath Queen Anne structure had been part of a single-family estate near the turn of the last century, surrounded by elaborate gardens and hedge mazes. Unfortunately, the Great Depression stripped the family of its wealth and forced them to divide and sell their land in parcels. The home had changed hands many times since then, posing as a museum, an all-girls school, and a boarding house and eventually housing several small businesses like the Historical Society.

I approached the majestic front door with deep appreciation for its beauty and let myself inside. The interior smelled like dust and old paper, not uncommon for a home of its age, but shockingly pungent, as if it had been recently stirred. I trailed a fingertip over the directory on the wall, searching for the Historical Society's suite number.

The crash behind me nearly stopped my heart. I turned around, one palm pressed to my collarbone.

A man stood in an open doorway staring forlornly at a pile of fallen books.

"Hello," I said, moving quickly in his direction. "Can I help?"

"The bottom fell out," he answered without meeting my gaze.

"Oh." I crouched beside the books and pulled the busted box free. I'd officially located the source of the odor circulating through the building. "How old are these?"

The man dropped into a squat opposite me. Gray dress slacks clung to his thighs and lifted above his navy argyle socks. "Old. That's the job." He stacked the ancient tomes into a pile.

I followed his example.

"You don't have to do that. I can get it."

"I don't mind." I stood when the work was done, arms loaded.

He creaked upright with the lion's share of books nestled against a tan Mr. Rogers cardigan. His blue eyes widened slightly when he finally seemed to notice me. "Pardon me, I didn't introduce myself. I'm Caleb France." He stretched his fingers from beneath a stack of newly organized tomes.

"Holly White." I touched my fingertips to his and mimicked a handshake while keeping a careful hold on his books. "You work at the Historical Society?"

"Yes. The books and I are headed to the rear corner office."

I followed him down a narrow hall into a stately room with grand window furnishings and elaborate crown molding.

"You can set those anywhere," he said. "I'm still moving in. It'll take weeks to get organized."

"You're new?" I asked, unloading my achy arms.

"No. I'm on my fourth year now. I'm just changing offices. My old one was a closet in comparison."

I scanned the room, finally catching on. "This was Margaret Fenwick's office."

"Yes." He arranged the books on crowded built-ins.

Haphazard piles of dilapidated boxes lined the rear wall. A framed certificate with "Fenwick" written in calligraphy protruded from one stack. "Was this hers?" I asked, moving nosily toward the castoffs.

"I think that was her husband's."

"But all these boxes were hers?"

"Yeah. I tried to schedule a dumpster, but local companies are booked until after Christmas."

"Did you contact her family? Maybe someone wants these things." I tucked the frame under one arm and helped myself to one that had her name. Both awards were from national programs in acknowledgement of the Fenwicks' efforts in maintaining history.

"I assumed her family would've called if they wanted any of it." Caleb marched in my direction, looking significantly less friendly than before I'd asked about Mrs. Fenwick. "I'm not sure you've explained why you're here. Can I help you with something?"

"Maybe. Can you tell me what had Margaret so upset in her last days? Did something at work set her off?"

"How should I know?"

"Because you worked together. I assumed you'd have some idea as to why the town thinks she was on a sudden rampage."

After several long moments, Caleb finally answered: "I think Mrs. Fenwick's efforts were simply misunderstood. It's our job here at the Historical Society to help the town put its best foot forward during our busiest season. I suppose she was doing just that."

I waited for a laugh track or delayed punchline that didn't come.

Instead, he ushered me to the door. "If there's anything I can do to help you keep your property in accordance with the guidelines and bylaws of Mistletoe, don't hesitate to reach out." He pressed a business card into my hand, then promptly shut the door to his new office.

I stood in the hallway wondering what had just happened. Caleb France had undergone a personality switch before my eyes, and I'd never heard a more canned statement outside of Friday-night sitcoms. I examined the pair of framed certificates I still held onto. At least I got something out of the bizarre exchange. Mr. and Mrs. Fenwick wouldn't be spending Christmas with their family this year, but maybe I could at least get these mementos into the right hands.

I didn't like the idea that Mr. France stood to gain a nice promotion and a better office in Mrs. Fenwick's absence. Hopefully he didn't want either badly enough to kill for it.

For good measure, I added his name to my mental list of suspects, right behind the hotheads, Paula and Mr. Fleece.

Chapter Eight

B ack on the sidewalk, I headed for the last stop on my list, one I'd tried hard not to think about. I'd made as many wedding-related cancellations as possible via e-mail or late-night calls, but Sweet Treats Bakery didn't have voice mail. How that was possible was beyond my comprehension, but it was still true.

I rolled my shoulders back and forced my feet in the right direction. With any luck, I could avoid talking to the owner. She'd trained in Paris and made the best cakes in our time zone, but she had little patience for anything else. A cancellation one week before the wedding was likely to upset her as much as it had upset me.

I stepped into Sweet Treats with my chin held high, fully prepared to state my name, cancel the cake, and run. Soft Parisian music circulated through a white-and-pink color scheme punctuated with black accent panels. Framed photos of the Eiffel Tower and embracing couples lined the walls, expertly sandwiched between colorful shots of the bakery's work.

Behind the counter, Caroline West smiled brightly. Her fair skin and blue eyes were the perfect backdrop for her vintage red lips and reaching black lashes. "Hey, you! I wondered when you'd get here." Caroline and I had grown up together, though we'd never had much in common. She'd been interested in popular things like fashion and boy bands, while I'd preferred to climb trees and draw. Based on my shapeless cable-knit top and her fitted black minidress, not much had changed.

"Hello." I set the frames I'd pilfered from Mrs. Fenwick's old office facedown on the counter. "It's nice to see you. You look wonderful, like always."

"Aww. Thanks. You too." She tipped her head adorably over one shoulder.

I released an ugly breath. "I'm here about an order I placed several months ago. It was to be delivered next week. I need to cancel."

"It's okay," she said. "I heard yesterday. My cousin works at the consignment shop where you took your gown."

I let my eyelids drift shut before pulling them back open. "Great."

"It's fine," she continued. "These things happen. Imagine how much worse things would've been if you'd gone through with it." She pulled a three-ring binder from beneath the counter and flipped through order sheets. "I need your signature right here to cancel the order. I'd planned to forge it if you didn't show."

I laughed. "Thanks, I think." I borrowed a logoed pen from the mug on the counter and scratched my name across the paper with more roughness than necessary. "Is that it?"

Caroline made a sad face. "You should also know I'm really sorry. About the breakup, and about the fact we're keeping your deposit. You're canceling less than thirty days before the event, and she's already got your order in the queue."

"But she hasn't started," I said, knowing it didn't matter but feeling agitated enough to point out the obvious. "No amount of time or supplies has been wasted."

"That's just how it works. We've already ordered all the ingredients and fondants. And you signed the agreement, so you're liable." She opened a circular display on top of the counter and selected a petal-pink cupcake drenched in iridescent white sugar crystals with a small white candy flower in the center. "For what it's worth, when I open my cupcake shop one day, I'll never punish a bride in your situation." She placed it in a small box with a little window. "Take this. It'll make you feel better."

I slid the box onto my frames. "It's beautiful."

"Thanks," she said. "You know, I don't live far from your parents now. Maybe you and I can get together sometime for drinks or coffee. There aren't a lot of single women our age around here. Men either, for that matter. We've got to stick together. Hang out. Shop. Whatever. It'd be fun."

Why not? I wrote my cell phone number on a napkin and passed it to her. "That sounds perfect. Call me or stop by the farm anytime. We can put something on the calendar, but I have a feeling I won't be getting too far from Reindeer Games for another ten days or so."

She folded the napkin and tucked it into her apron pocket. "I'll stop and see you then."

I collected my things and waved good-bye. It might be fun to have a girlfriend in town. The handful of friends I'd had in high school were either married with kids by now or had left for college and not come back. I felt a little traitorous for having been one of the latter.

I crossed the street, making my way back to my truck. The crowd around the pie shop had steadily thickened in my absence. I pardoned my way to the driver's side and deposited my things inside. The question now was whether or not to go home or see who else might know something useful about Margaret Fenwick. A twinge of guilt pinched my gut for lying to the sheriff about my intentions today. Given the pile of tree markers left on my porch yesterday, he was probably right for saying I should stay out of it, but I couldn't help thinking I'd be safer if whoever threatened me was in handcuffs instead of on the loose. Since that person was likely to be Margaret's killer, I decided to move forward with my questions.

I locked the frames and my cupcake inside the cab and turned back to the row of busy storefronts. *Where should I go next?*

A low wolf whistle pierced the noisy crowd, and Ray Griggs appeared. He moseyed in my direction, slowly parting the masses like a hometown rock star. His black leather jacket and high-top tennis shoes made an interesting contrast to the untucked flannel shirt and jeans he'd paired with them. "Well, good morning, Miss White." He sidled up to me and smiled. "Lucky me, running into you like this."

"You just happened to run into me again? In this crowd?" I gave him my most disbelieving look.

"What? Do you think I followed you?"

"I think you're a reporter, and I'm investigating a possible story." I pondered my word choice. What else could I call it now? Having lots of friendly conversations that happened to have the same agenda?

"How's it going?" he asked.

"Depends. How long have you been following me?"

He looked away. "Just since you got to the pie shop."

"That was first thing this morning!" My eyes stretched wide enough to sting from the cold. "What'd you do? Set up camp outside my house last night?"

He laughed. "I wish." The humor dropped from his face in a cloud of shock and embarrassment. "I didn't mean it like that. I'm not a stalker, I swear. I meant that I heard about what happened yesterday, and I wish I'd have been there to stop the culprit or at least see who did it."

"How'd you hear?"

Sheriff Gray had been adamant about keeping the incident a secret. He thought making a public statement would put people on edge, cause panic, or fertilize a crop of unpredictable gossip that would be hard to undo.

"Police scanner. Tool of the trade," he said. "Any idea who did it?"

"Yeah, Margaret's killer. Before you ask, no, I don't have any idea who that could be. Yet."

"Yet?" He smiled. "I like your style, White. Always have. I bet if we put our heads together, we can name the killer before Sheriff Gray."

"It's not a contest."

"But it is a race," he pointed out.

I pressed my lips together. I'd learned a few small things yesterday, but maybe a partner would speed things up. Ray knew the town, and as a reporter, he probably had inside access to things I didn't. "Maybe."

He rubbed his palms together. "Atta girl." He slung an arm across my shoulders. "Now that we're partners, what's our next move?"

"I don't know."

"What did the sheriff want?" He leveled me with clear-blue eyes. "He wouldn't have called you away from the farm unless he had something significant to tell you."

"Oh." I smiled. "He didn't ask me to meet him. I tracked him down so I could find out how much longer Reindeer Games had to stay closed."

"Nice. What'd he say?"

"He was on his way to give my parents the green light to open, which means I should probably get back there and make myself useful."

"Excellent. I'll stop over later."

I gave him a long look, recalling he was the one who'd dropped me off before the threat was left on my porch. "Where did you go after you took me home yesterday?"

"Why?"

"Curious."

He narrowed his eyes. "You think I might've seen something."

"Did you?"

"No. I went to talk to the deputy at the gates, then headed back to town."

I made a mental note to check with the deputy for good measure. "Who do you think could have done it?"

"I honestly have no idea. This week is . . ." He mimed his head exploding.

I knew what he meant.

Throngs of shoppers swarmed around us, whacking my legs with heavy bags and occasionally ramming the backs of my feet with stroller wheels. I couldn't help overhearing bits of conversations as they passed. The farm was a popular topic, but not in a good way. Many had traveled to Mistletoe specifically to participate in the Twelve Days of Reindeer Games only to be denied entrance. Their day trips were ruined, and they'd not soon forget it. With any luck, they'd drive by one more time before heading home. Assuming the sheriff had kept his word, my folks and the staff were already working double time to make things right for our patrons.

Ray yanked a cell phone from his coat pocket and stared expectantly at the screen. "This is my editor. Give me a minute?"

"Sure." I leaned against the fender of Dad's pickup and thought about the day I'd had and the fact that it was barely noon. The strangest part was that this day was no more bizarre than the other days since I'd gotten home. *Had I brought a malady with me? Maybe I'm the malady.*

Across the street, Mr. Nettle, my dad's longtime friend and current accountant, walked out of the shoe shop.

Ray had wandered several feet away to take his call.

I tried and failed to get his attention over the crush of people between us.

Mr. Nettle beetled toward a white sedan, flipping through a ring of keys.

"I'll be back," I called in Ray's direction, but he didn't look up.

I jogged toward Mr. Nettle, threading myself around families and couples chatting animatedly about the charm of our town.

"Mr. Nettle!" I waved a hand overhead as he dropped behind the wheel of his car.

He startled, then slowly levered himself back onto his feet with a frown. "Sorry. I didn't see you there, Holly. How are you?"

"Not bad," I said, stepping carefully out of the street. "I won't keep you. I just wanted to say hello."

"Well, at least tell me how you liked Portland."

"It was a nice place, but nothing like home. I didn't realize how much I missed Mistletoe until I got here."

"Good." He pushed thick-lensed glasses up the ridge of his nose. He was broad across the chest and at least six feet tall, but the years had given him a layer or two of natural padding. "Does that mean you'll be staying?"

"I don't know. Maybe." I hadn't really thought about moving home permanently, but I couldn't imagine moving to another town on my own either. I didn't have a job. Or much savings. What I had plenty of were student loans and wedding debt. My tummy knotted. What was I doing with my life, and who got the honeymoon Ben and I paid for? I certainly wasn't making the trip with him no matter how sorry he was or how poorly his life was going.

"How are your parents doing?" Mr. Nettle lowered his voice. "I heard about what happened at the farm. It's a shame, isn't it?"

"Awful," I agreed, setting my own problems aside. At least I was alive and well. Given the circumstances, I certainly wouldn't want to trade places with Margaret Fenwick. "I don't suppose you have any guesses as to who would do something like that?"

"None. Thank goodness."

"Did you know Mrs. Fenwick?"

"As well as anyone could, I suppose. She kept to herself when she wasn't terrorizing the town. Of course, I don't keep a house in Mistletoe, so I can't be sure what she did in her free time. Our offices are in the same building; otherwise, we might not have met at all."

"Did she give you any citations?"

He chuckled. "Heavens no. It's hard to break the rules with her in the next room. She kept everything in order. I only had to show up and pay the lease."

"You had an office beside hers?"

"Across the way, but yes. Do you know the one? It's a grand old estate on Holiday Lane." He dragged a dimpled hand over his shiny domed head, mashing several strands of dark hair to an expanse of pink scalp.

"I was there today." I pulled my attention back to his face. "I met Caleb France."

Mr. Nettle furrowed his brow.

"What do you think of him?" I asked.

Mr. Nettle looked over my shoulder, avoiding my gaze. "France is an odd fellow. Not someone I'd intentionally spend much time with, but maybe that's just me."

"Yeah?"

He harrumphed. "The man's pretentious, high strung, argumentative, and rude."

"Ah." A rude representative at the Mistletoe Historical Society. Maybe that was a requirement of the job.

Chapter Nine

I waved good-bye to Ray, who was still on the phone, and climbed into my truck. He knew where to find me if he wanted to talk, and I was looking forward to seeing if the sheriff had kept his promise to reopen Reindeer Games.

The drive passed quickly as I mulled over the things I'd learned today. How the sheriff had liked Margaret, for example, but her colleague didn't have enough respect to call her family before the dumpster company, and how Mr. Nettle didn't like Caleb France either.

Traffic on the county road slowed as Reindeer Games came into view, then crawled to a halt outside the open gates where one of the seasonal helpers directed vehicles into a large grassy parking area. People in every shape and size of brightly colored winter wear traded green cash for a red handstamp. A banner announcing the Twelve Days of Reindeer Games billowed above them, and my heart swelled with thankfulness. The sheriff had kept his word.

I took the back way into the farm and left the truck where I'd found it.

The Holiday Mouse Christmas Craft Shop was surrounded with shoppers on benches, admiring their new purchases and sipping concessions carried away from the Hearth. I ducked inside to check on Cookie.

The former one-room log cabin was small but inviting, overstuffed with the typical waist-high aisles and cluttered shelves of a country craft store. There were plenty of spinning racks, and all four walls were covered in cutesy signs and paintings. Everything was winter themed, and the whole place smelled of Christmas. As a kid, I'd imagined the shop was made from giant cinnamon sticks instead of logs.

Cookie stood at the register in a red velvet dress with black buttons and a matching cape tied at her neck. Her black leggings and boots were equally adorable, but the thing that pulled it together was her natural crown of silver hair.

I wrapped her in a hug between sales. "You look like Mrs. Claus."

"Thank you." She welcomed the next guest and tapped the buttons on her machine with a shiver. "Every time that door opens, I get a blast of ice right up my skirt."

The customer giggled and slid her items onto the counter.

Cookie pulled her cape over her shoulders with another exaggerated wiggle. She rang up two boxes of hand-painted mistletoe bulbs and scooted them in my direction. "I always wanted to be a Rockette. They wear capes like mine sometimes. Lucky for me, I was too short to audition. I'd have frozen to death in New York City wearing a bodysuit and a cape."

I opened a handled shopping bag and slid the merchandise inside, then tucked a few plumes of colored tissue paper on top. "What do you mean you were too short?"

She cocked a hip and planted one palm on it. "I'm five foot two on my tiptoes. Those ladies kick higher than me. Of course, it would've been nice to know that before I drove across the country from Vegas only to be turned away. The sign on the door said you had to be five foot six! Can you believe that?"

"You've had such an interesting life," I said, passing the package to our customer when Cookie gave her the receipt.

"That's true," she said. "My mama taught me life was for living, so I had at it."

I scanned the happy crowd. "Looks like we won't have any trouble making up for lost sales yesterday."

"Darn tootin'." Cookie greeted the next guest with a hearty smile.

I kissed her cheek and slipped out from behind the counter. "I'll see you soon. I just stopped in to see how you were doing."

"That's all the help I get? One bag?"

"Sorry." I sidestepped a pair of men toting giant purses as they trailed a pair of women holding piles of holiday-print aprons, clearly lost in the clutches of indecision. "I'm going to see if Mom needs anything. If she's covered, I'll be back."

I held the door for an ambitious woman pushing a double stroller and towing a toddler. "Merry Christmas," I told them as they passed.

Inside the Hearth, Mom was spinning in circles, filling cups and plates, then lining them up on the counter.

I stripped off my coat and grabbed a tray. "Which way?" I asked.

Mom's eyes widened. "Oh, thank goodness! Table eight."

I shuttled the tray to table eight, careful not to slip in puddles of melted snow or trip over the hastily scattered "Caution: Wet Floor" signs.

A few more trips and we were caught up. I mopped up the snow and cleared tables for incoming patrons as I had a thousand times before. The process felt marvelous and freeing. It helped that the tourists were patient and kind. There was plenty to look at inside a life-sized gingerbread house.

"How are you doing?" I asked Mom at my first opportunity.

She dragged the back of her hand across her brow. "It's wonderful that the people came. I was worried." She fished a pile of cookies from a jar with red tongs.

"I know. Me too."

*   *   *

At three o'clock, the farm had gone still. Everyone seemed to have crammed into the Hearth to watch the first Reindeer Game of the year, Bling That Gingerbread. We'd filled every seat and added a dozen folding chairs in the aisles. Those who couldn't fit inside stood in the doorway or watched through the windows. With any luck, the fire marshal wouldn't stop by before the game ended.

Mom fluffed her hair and turned on the microphone. Every contestant had the same supplies and a total of three minutes to decorate their gingerbread house. When time was up, the homes would be put on display, and voting would be open for thirty minutes afterward.

Cookie and I sat at the chocolate bar table with a pair of women from Poughkeepsie.

"This is going to be wonderful," the brunette said. "I can't believe we're cutting loose like this, Donna."

Donna munched a gumdrop and nodded. "I haven't eaten this much sugar since the Reagan administration. I'm getting fat this week, Birdie, and I don't even care. You know it. It's true." She sampled a pinch of mini–chocolate chips from Birdie's tray.

Birdie gave her friend a stern face that didn't last. "If we don't start soon, we might not have any more decorations." She stole a string of licorice off Donna's tray and broke into crazy laughter.

"Stop it." Donna slapped Birdie's fingers away.

"We're gonna win," Cookie whispered.

The women stopped laughing. Birdie stuck her finger into Cookie's cup of icing.

I burst into laughter.

Mom gave our table a warning look. "Ribbons and cocoas will be awarded to the person who uses the most supplies and to the top three most appealing results. Also, I'd like to add that we at Reindeer Games are extremely sorry for the unexpected closure yesterday. We hope we didn't cause anyone too much trouble, and in the spirit of the Reindeer Games, we're having today's scheduled game immediately following this one. Build a Big Frosty will begin in the field outside this building as soon as the winners are announced here. The Build a Big Frosty competition is exactly what it sounds like—create your own snowman. You can begin anytime following this game, and you'll have until dusk to complete your work. We'll give a ten-minute warning at ten till five and begin measuring the snowmen promptly at five. Tallest frosty wins a warm pecan pie, your picture in the paper, and bragging rights for a year."

A round of applause went up with a few whistles and random hoots.

"I've never had my picture in the paper," Donna said.

"Everyone ready?" Mom's voice quieted the excited crowd. "Please put on your blindfolds." She lifted a stopwatch into the air. "Your three minutes start now!" She switched off her mic, and holiday music danced through the room.

I did my best to concentrate while the women across from me cackled, and Cookie said a few unladylike things to her uncooperative gumdrops, which apparently didn't want to stick to the blessed shanty roof. Distractions aside, I didn't like the blindfold this year. What had previously added a welcomed level of complexity and challenge only made me anxious this time around.

I pulled the cloth away from my eyes and used it to blot the sheen of sweat on my neck and forehead.

"Time's up!" Mom called. "Blindfolds off. Please bring your houses to the front. We'll line them up for judging. Don't forget to grab a pen and cast your vote."

My gingerbread house was smeared in white icing and little more. I stuck a gumdrop into my mouth and settled my breathing before carrying my masterpiece to the front. The other houses were hilarious, clever, and magnificent, but there wasn't enough oxygen in the room to laugh. My chest felt constricted, and my mouth was dry.

When the room cleared, Mom walked the line of gingerbread homes, judging the entries. She scratched a pencil against her head. "This one used all the trimmings, but I don't see any on the house."

I tried to laugh but choked on the effort.

Sheriff Gray arrived with a warm smile. He pulled out Donna's vacated chair and had a seat. "I like your style," he said, indicating my undressed house. "Simple. Realistic."

My trembling lips quirked at the dumb joke. "Shut up. I didn't finish."

"I'm serious," he said. "I've never seen anyone put enormous candies on their roof. Yours should win for most authentic."

"That's not a category." I stood on unsteady feet. "Can we talk outside? I'm not feeling well."

He extended his hand, indicating I should lead the way. "Panic attack?" he asked when we were free of the crowd.

"Something like that." I panted, still unable to manage a full breath.

Cold winter air snapped my heated skin into gooseflesh. I inhaled as deeply as possible, which wasn't very, and exhaled to a mental count of ten. Soon, I was dizzy. I leaned forward and braced my palms against my knees.

"Holly?" Sheriff Gray's face appeared next to mine. He'd dropped into a squat at my side. "Do you want to sit down?"

I nodded, slowly bringing myself upright. "Would you mind walking me home first? I don't want to start any rumors by collapsing the same day our gates reopen."

He looped his arm with mine and let me lean against him. "Of course."

I flattened a cold palm to my hot cheek. "Sorry. I'm usually more together than this."

"How was your time in town?"

"Okay." My muddled thoughts grew clearer with each fresh breath. "Did you go to the Hearth to judge the gingerbread blinging? I shouldn't have pulled you away without asking." I let my head drop forward. "I'm making a terrible impression."

He eased his hand over mine on his arm. "Actually, I was looking for you. I thought I'd see how you're doing and offer to make another sweep through your home and check the perimeter." He led me to the nearest bench and motioned for me to sit.

He didn't have to ask twice. I fell onto the icy seat, wondering what was wrong with me. Was he right? Was this a panic attack? My chest clenched at his interest in making another sweep through my home. "Has something else happened?"

"No," he assured. "It's like I told you this morning, I worry. It's my job."

I liked that he worried about me. I wasn't sure why his "It's my job" line seemed to ruin it. I concentrated on the slow spill of shoppers from Holiday Mouse and the collection of contestants at the Hearth. "I don't know what got into me back there. I think the blindfold freaked me out. Which makes no sense. I used to love that part. It made the outcomes sillier."

He took a seat beside me. "Have you considered that the trauma is getting to you? You've been through a lot in a very short amount of time."

"I haven't," I argued. "Not really. Nothing's happened to me. Mrs. Fenwick, yes, but not me. I only found her because I heard someone calling for help. Same thing with the stakes on my porch. I was on my way out, and there they were."

Sheriff Gray's eyes softened. "Finding trouble is just as upsetting as having experienced it. Don't discount that. And I hate to bring it up, but calling off a wedding this close to the date has to be slightly earth shattering too."

I shrugged. "I don't want to talk about it."

"Well, when you do, you could talk to me, if you wanted."

We sat in companionable silence for a long while, watching families come and go.

When I felt more like myself, I twisted on the bench for a look at him. "You've known me two days. You've only lived here six months. It's been nonstop drama this week, and I swear it wasn't always like this here. I wasn't always like this." I waved a hand in front of my face. "I used to be fun." I plucked gloves from my pockets and covered my hands.

"Weren't we all?"

"Have you spoken with Paula yet? Or Mr. Fleece?" Their residual anger weighed on me. Weren't those feelings supposed to subside when the object of your wrath is brutally murdered?

"I have."

I stretched my eyes wide for effect. "And?"

He shook his head. "I've got this covered. You need to let me handle it. Maybe get some sleep. It might help take the edge off."

If only I could sleep. I slouched against the seatback. "Have you ever been in love?" I asked. "Engaged?" He wasn't married, so if he'd been in love before, maybe he knew what I was going through.

He gave me a sidelong glance. "Love, yes. Engaged, no."

"Oh, sorry. I think." I cringed. "Don't listen to me. I don't know what I'm saying."

He broke into an easy smile but kept his eyes on the scene before us. "Back in Boston, I was married to the job. Everything else came second."

"Your girlfriend didn't like that, I suppose."

"No one likes coming second to morgue visits and murderers."

"Go figure," I joked. "Is that why you came to Mistletoe? Settle down. Marry a human."

His smile grew, and the color in his cheeks deepened. "I was hoping to have a chance at normal. Maybe experience what it's like to live a few consecutive days without a catastrophe. And I wouldn't mind raising a family."

"Yeah? How big?"

"At least four or five strapping young boys like me."

"Oh." I laughed. "Well, good luck with that."

He nodded along. "I'm kidding. I haven't thought beyond settling down somewhere calm and safe. Mistletoe seemed like a great place to do all that, so I applied, and here I am." He stopped moving and extended an arm toward the field. "Look at that."

The flawless carpet of snow was polka-dotted in every color of ski coat and knit hat, worn by people of every age, tossing snowballs and rolling snow boulders to support their Big Frosty. The gingerbread winners must've been announced.

Donna and Birdie waved from beside a mound of snow. "Yoo-hoo!" Donna called. "Yoo-hoo!" She dusted her gloves together and made a beeline in our direction. "I'm Donna. Remember me?"

"Of course." I pointed to Sheriff Gray. "This is our town sheriff."

She leaned back as if in awe. "Nice catch, honey. Every woman wants a man in uniform."

"We're not—" I began, only to be cut off by Donna reaching for my ear.

"I wanted to ask you about your earrings while we were talking, but then I got the giggles. Where did you find them? They're fabulous."

My hands jumped to the faux lollipops on instinct. "I made them. They aren't for sale anywhere."

She jutted her bottom lip out. "That's a crying shame." She turned to Birdie, still hard at work on their Frosty. "She made the earrings. She says they aren't for sale."

Birdie stopped working. "Crying shame."

"That's what I said." Donna turned back to me, deflated. "Well, I won't keep you lovebirds. That snowman won't build itself."

Sheriff Gray and I turned for the guesthouse in silence. When he began to murmur the lyrics to "Frosty the Snowman," I joined in. Sadly, neither of us knew all the words, and soon I couldn't sing through the laughter.

I leaned against his arm and caught my breath. "Now you're just repeating thumpity-thump-thump."

"That's how it goes."

I wiped tears off my cheeks and got myself together. "You might not know the words, but your voice is fantastic."

He turned his face away.

I released him, sensing a bigger story. "Please tell me you had a band in college."

He pushed his hands deep into his pockets. "I just like to sing."

I climbed my steps, trying not to dwell on how much I didn't know about the sheriff or how our weird, impromptu friendship would work after we'd solved the case. I unlocked the front door and stepped aside to let him in.

He made the sweep as promised but didn't stick around afterward.

After about twenty minutes, I followed his example and went to help my parents measure two dozen snowmen now that I'd calmed down.

I returned home hours later covered in snow. I kicked my boots off at the door and dropped my wet coat onto a coatrack by the fire.

Cindy Lou Who gave me a death glare from behind her toppled bowls.

"I know, I know," I said, rubbing her soft head. "I'm late delivering your dinner. I forgot how much fun it is here." I righted and refilled the bowls. "There you go."

She walked away.

I shook water droplets from my bangs and took my earrings off for the night. I'd left for college with the dream of being a painter. I'd learned freshman year that the best painting I did was on my nails, and it wasn't even that great. Until a few days ago, I'd worked in an art gallery in Portland selling other artists' creations. I'd never considered selling my own things.

I cracked open the box with Caroline's cupcake and inhaled the heavenly scent.

Maybe it wasn't too late for me. So what if I was a terrible painter? Art came in all sorts of forms. I peeled back the liner and sank my teeth into the moistest, fluffiest cake and icing ever made. "Oh, my sweet Christmas." I licked my lips and moaned. *Like this cupcake. This is a masterpiece.* I took another bite. And another. "It's like eating happiness," I told Cindy, who'd come to see what all the fuss was about.

I dropped the empty paper in the trash and sprang to my feet with renewed zeal and a fresh sugar buzz. "If Caroline West can open a cupcake shop one day, why can't I sell my jewelry? I don't even have to open a shop, Cindy. I can ask Cookie to put a few pieces on her counter and see what happens."

Cindy flopped onto her side and swung her tail lazily over the floor.

I grabbed a dry coat and boots. "I have plenty of sample inventory. All I need is a sign and a display." I grabbed my keys and stuffed them in my pocket. "I'll be right back, Cindy. We'll make popcorn and watch *Miracle on 34th Street* while we make plans for a new adventure. What do you say? It's me and you, kitty."

I counted to ten before daring a look out the window. No new threat deliveries. No footprints other than my own. Just another beautiful winter night like the dozens before it. I slid into the cold and locked the door behind me.

In some ways, I was probably safer outside than in. Inside was where I'd been when a killer had walked right up to my door and left a giant message. Inside was where bad people could do whatever they wanted to me in perfect privacy. The entire world was outside. There was nowhere to hide out here.

I zigzagged through untouched snow for fun, leaving patterns and spirals behind me. Sounds of distant laughter rose with the glow of a bonfire near the stables. Mr. Fleece and some workers must not have been ready to call it a night. Normally, I'd have gone to say hello, but I was on a mission to re-create myself as Holly the Artist.

The lock at Holiday Mouse tumbled easily. I let myself in to gather everything I needed for a proper Christmas jewelry display. Enthusiasm ripped through me. If none of the pieces sold, so what? I had nothing to lose and a box full of jewelry to keep for myself. *But what if they sell?*

I filled a shopping bag with the things on my mental list and slid back into the night. A cloud had covered the moon and obscured the stars, but the tiny orange glow of the fire in the distance remained. Happy voices rumbled and chuckled from the stables to my ears.

I started back toward the guesthouse at a brisk enough pace to keep me warm and a slow enough pace to enjoy the night.

An owl circled overhead, catching my attention. It swooped toward the land and rose again moments later with something in its claws.

My heart rate climbed, and a brick lodged in my throat. That poor mouse was out living its life, and bam! I checked over my shoulder. The bonfire was no longer in sight, and the voices had gone silent. My parents' home stood at the crest of a small hill in the opposite direction. Maybe Sheriff Gray was right. Maybe it wouldn't hurt to stay there for a night or two.

The crack of a twig stopped me cold in my tracks.

Shadows stretched through the rows of trees at my side. I suddenly identified with the mouse, alone in a field at night, making plans that would never come true because an unseen predator circled nearby.

I squinted into the darkness. "Hello?"

Another crack sounded. This time closer, just inside the tree line and less than ten feet away.

It's nothing. It's nothing. It's nothing. I clutched the sack of borrowed items against my chest and ran away from the woods. Away from the guesthouse. Away from whatever was out there. My panicked mind raced with horrible images of an angry killer on my heels.

"Help!" I shrieked, closing in on my parents' old farmhouse on the next rolling hill.

The cracking and snapping of fallen twigs and branches broke free of the forest, coming in heavy, thunderous footfalls behind me. Adrenaline burned through my veins, hammering my heart and bringing tears to my eyes.

A scream built in my throat and lurched free.

A blinding light exploded in my world, and I batted my eyes to see.

"Holly?" Dad's voice boomed from the porch of their home.

"Dad!" I ran faster than I ever had, crying loudly and praying that whoever was after me wouldn't hurt my parents too. I crashed into his strong chest and pushed him back. "Inside. We have to go inside. Someone's out here."

Dad kissed my head and directed me toward the front steps. "Go see your mother."

"No!" I clung to him. "Please come inside."

He twirled the baseball bat he kept at the door in one mammoth hand. "I've been patrolling for longer than you've been alive. If there's anyone out here, I'll find him. Go inside and lock the door."

"If?" *Hadn't the killer caught up with me yet?* I squinted against the motion light that I'd triggered over the yard. "I heard him."

"Who?"

I scanned the silent, motionless landscape. "I don't know. There was a mouse."

"A mouse?"

The front door opened, and Mom shuffled down the steps. "Come on, sweetie. Let's get you out of the cold."

I stumbled behind her, poorly navigating the steps and nearly colliding with the door she held open. "Dad," I called, "be careful."

Careful of what, I wasn't sure. From my new position inside the living room, peering out the front window, there was no one in the world except my dad.

Chapter Ten

I spent the next morning adorning reindeer bridles with fake mistletoe and wondering if I was losing my mind. I'd stayed at my parents' house until dawn, but I didn't sleep. Dad hadn't found any evidence that I'd been followed. The news should've relieved me, but it only managed to unsettle me further. Had I imagined the snapping twigs and pounding feet? Had the emotional distress of my week unhinged me somehow?

I'd passed the wee hours heating old glass bottles in dad's basement workshop, clipping and molding the material into tiny rock candy earrings. The results were adorable, but I was exhausted.

I stroked Kevin's soft reindeer fur and mumbled my concerns into his ear. We'd just met the other night, but I could tell Kevin understood me. He'd been through a lot too.

Cindy Lou Who sat on a hay bale judging me. I'd dressed her in her holiday best, a pointy green velvet hat with faux elf ears on the sides. She pretended to hate it, but we both knew she'd have chucked it off immediately if that were true.

Mr. Fleece adjusted Chrissy and Noel's bridles beside me. "Have you heard anything new about Mrs. Fenwick's death?"

"No. Why?" I angled to put a little space between us. The last time we'd had a similar conversation, he'd yelled at me. "Have you?" Was he being friendly, or did he have a reason for staying on top of the case? Like not wanting to be arrested for murder.

He dropped his gaze to Kevin. "You're a natural with him," he said, quickly changing the subject.

"Thanks. I love animals. Something about being with them calms me." Unlike the strange expression on Mr. Fleece's face, which I couldn't quite place. Was he sorry for losing his temper the last time we spoke? Was he mad I'd told the sheriff to have another go at him? "Everything okay?" I asked.

He answered with a stiff nod. "Hope you're good with kids too, or this idea of yours is going to go sideways in a hurry."

I hadn't been around children in a while, but how bad could they be?

Caroline and a pair of twin girls approached with timid smiles.

"Caroline!" A bolt of enthusiasm shot through me. It was wonderful to see a familiar face. "I'm so glad you're here. Who are these lovely ladies?"

"These are my nieces," she said. "My sister's Christmas shopping today." She did a stage wink over the girls' heads.

"Ah. Well, welcome." I performed a dramatic arm swing and nearly knocked over the camera I'd mounted on a tripod.

"Are the reindeer ready?" Caroline asked. "The girls are dying for a photograph."

"Absolutely." I patted Kevin's side and palmed a treat for him to gobble.

The girls stared wide eyed at me.

I bent to meet them on their level. "What are your names?"

They looked curiously at me, then at Mr. Fleece. He and I made quite a pair, I imagined. Me in my red wool swing coat with rosettes at the collar and tall black boots, him with his scruffy beard, stained barn coat, and knit cap covered in loose reindeer hairs.

"I could call you Pinky and Rainbow," I offered, based on the colors of their puffy down ski coats.

The taller girl took her sister's hand. "I'm Ginger, and this is Rose."

"Well, it's nice to meet you," I said. "I'm Holly, and this is Mr. Fleece, our reindeer keeper. This handsome guy is Kevin." I pecked a kiss on Kevin's muzzle. "The reindeer with Mr. Fleece are Kevin's sisters, Chrissy and Noel. They saw you coming this way, and they told me they wanted to have their pictures taken with you."

"Really?" Rose asked, a look of wonder in her eyes.

"Absolutely."

Families began to trickle toward us. Grown-ups formed a line behind Caroline while the children climbed onto wooden fence rungs and watched with uninhibited curiosity.

I helped the girls onto a stack of hay bales set before the reindeer pen. "Okay, have a seat. You'll be just as tall as the reindeer now, and they'll bring their pretty faces up beside yours."

Mr. Fleece arranged the reindeer on either side of the adorable sisters.

"Can we hold the kitty?" Rose asked.

"Cindy?" I asked in surprise.

Her chin lifted slightly at the sound of her name. Her wide green eyes caught mine and narrowed.

"Okay," I agreed, "but if she runs or complains, it's not your fault. She's kind of a stinker." I scooped Cindy up and delivered her to the girls before taking position behind the camera.

Mr. Fleece gave me a thumbs-up, then ducked out of the shot.

"Say Santa Claus," I said.

"Santa Claus!" they cheered.

I printed the picture on cardstock and stamped it three times with a green hoof stamp. "There you go, ladies. Signed by all three reindeer."

The twins crowded around their souvenir and giggled.

Caroline raised one cream-colored mitten to stifle a yawn. "Excuse me." She blinked puffy eyes. "I was up all night polishing my business plan. It's time to approach banks for financing and get Caroline's Cupcakes on its feet. Student loan payments are eating my soul, and this MBA won't pay for itself."

I was surprised. "You got a master's degree in business administration?"

"Yep. I've wanted to open a bake shop since middle school, and you'd be shocked at how many new businesses fail. I think marriage has a better success rate, actually." She cringed. "Oh, sorry."

"It's fine." I waved her off. "Your company is going to be great."

She sighed. "Tell that to my parents, Dr. and Mayor West."

A dozen memories of a younger Caroline came rushing back at the sound of those names. "You were the valedictorian."

"Yep."

I'd completely forgotten. "Weren't you also captain of the debate team and voted most likely to take over the world or something like that?"

"That's me." Her head bobbed slowly. "Unfortunately, I also earned the Destined to Break Her Overachieving Parents' Hearts by Baking for a Living Award."

"Aw." I wrapped my arms around her, immensely thankful for my unassuming parents. "Well, you can mark me down for a standing order of whatever was in the freebie cupcake you gave me. You aren't just baking cupcakes. You're making dreams come true."

Caroline laughed. "It made you happy?"

"It made me ecstatic."

She smiled wider. "Well, who can argue with wanting to deliver happiness? Thanks, Holly. I needed that."

"Anytime."

She gathered her nieces and pointed them toward the Holiday Mouse. "Now we need to pick out a cute frame." The trio of West women sashayed away, and I went back to the camera.

The line moved along steadily. Cindy greeted each new child with the same lackluster enthusiasm but never left the spotlight.

Cookie swung by on her way to lunch. "Look at that line. You always have the best ideas."

"Thanks." I snapped the next picture and smiled. "It's fun."

"Fun for me too," she said. "I'm selling Reindeer Games frames like hotcakes."

I laughed. "Well, that's an unexpected bonus." I lifted one hand for a high five.

She tapped her little mitten-covered fingers to mine. "I can't believe the printer hasn't frozen. This rig looks like a joke." She kicked snow off my industrial power cord. "Do you want me to get a tent over here to shelter it? Or a space heater or something?"

I'd fed the line through a rear window at Holiday Mouse and dragged it thirty feet to my printer, which I'd sat on a card table. The cord was lined in plastic traffic cones to keep people from tripping on it. So far, so good. It helped that temperatures were up by ten degrees from yesterday and the bright morning sunshine had melted some of the snow. If the afternoon flurries held off until my last picture, I'd call the day a ripping success.

"No, it's fine. How's it going with the jewelry?" I asked. I'd returned the borrowed display with a few of my favorite pieces first thing this morning after Dad walked me home to collect Cindy and some of my things.

"Why? Do you have anything else you want me to put on the counter?"

I chewed my lip. "I don't know. If the ones I left with you this morning aren't doing well, I don't think I have anything else." I tried not to let the rejection sting. Wearing replica Christmas goodies as accessories wasn't for everyone.

"What? Your stuff did great! They're all gone."

"Gone? Really?"

"Yep. Display's been empty since ten minutes after we opened. I'd have come to see you sooner, but we're swamped."

I struggled to imagine people choosing my products over the hundreds of other things Holiday Mouse had to offer. "That's amazing. Can I bring more tomorrow?"

"Sure, but sooner's better."

I smiled as a wave of joy rolled up from my toes to my nose. "I'll see what I can do." I passed the photo to the family who was waiting patiently beside me. "Merry Christmas from Kevin, Chrissy, Noel, and all of Reindeer Games."

Cookie pointed in the direction of her shop. "Holiday Mouse has a lovely selection of frames to commemorate the day." She struck a sudden pose, cocking one hip and pointing the opposite toe. "Follow me. I'll take you to them."

The Rockettes had missed out when they'd turned her away.

I lined up my next shot, and Ray Griggs climbed onto the hay. He arched his back in a terrible mock pinup pose.

"What are you doing?" I asked.

He kicked out one pointed toe and puckered his lips.

"Get down from there." A bubble of laughter built in my chest. "Goof."

He feigned disappointment as he dragged his long limbs away from the reindeer. "I waited in line fair and square."

"You did not," I said. "You cut in front of that little boy."

He bumped me out from behind the camera. "Hey, I paid that kid a dollar." He pointed to the child now seated on the hay with a crisp green bill stretched between two red mittens. "How about I take over for a while? I don't mean to throw my credentials around, but I'm an experienced photographer."

"Oh, boy." I made a show of rolling my eyes but kept out of his way. My clicker finger was frozen and eager to hide inside a toasty mitten. "Why are you really here?"

He shot me an impish grin. "I'm trying to pull together a piece on Reindeer Games for the paper, and before you get testy, it's not what you think." He poised the camera against his cheek, and the boy smiled. "I'm trying to shed a more positive light on the farm after what happened. Fenwick's death was a tragedy, but it had nothing to do with this place."

The printer rocked to life as my hackles went down.

"I appreciate that." I pressed the stamps onto the bottom of the paper and delivered the photo to the little boy. "Merry Christmas from Kevin, Chrissy, Noel, and all of Reindeer Games."

"Thanks!" He hustled away.

Ray leaned his eye back to the camera. "No promises that the paper will run it. I make pitches all the time. They usually tell me to stick with photography." He snapped another photo, then waved at Cindy and some kids. "Your cat is loving all this attention."

I admired her tolerance. "She's a sweetie under all that cattitude."

He laughed. "I think everyone should have a cat. If I was president, I'd make it a law."

"You'd have the little old lady vote all tied up." My chest pinched. A broad and heavy ache landed on my heart. "Mrs. Fenwick had a cat."

Ray snapped another photo and the printer hummed. "Should I ask why that seems to horrify you? You're whiter than the snow."

"She's been gone three days," I whispered, as much to myself as to him. "Who's feeding her cat?" I turned in a panic. "Can you cover me here? And keep an eye on Cindy?"

"Huh?" He looked bewildered. His gaze trailed the long line of kids awaiting their turn on the hay. "I don't actually work here."

"You do now!" I clapped his shoulder and made a run for the reindeer trucks.

* * *

I pulled into Mrs. Fenwick's drive thirty-five minutes later with a bag of kibble and a prayer. Her kitty must've been starving. No one had been home to feed or water it in three days. Luckily, the woman at the pet shop was loose lipped enough to give me the Fenwicks' address when I pretended to be the cat sitter called in to care for the feline until Mrs. Fenwick's extended family arrived. The cashier had been overtly relieved to know I was on the way. She told me that the cat had crossed her mind many times since news of Mrs. Fenwick's death turned up in the paper.

I climbed the front steps and peered through the parted curtains. "Kitty," I called. "Sweet kitty?"

A fat tuxedo cat leapt onto the window and meowed.

I launched forward, wiggling the locked window. "Don't worry. I'm going to help you," I promised, speaking into the glass. I'd seen people in movies get into homes with a credit card. I'd never tried it, but a cat's life was at stake. I checked the street in both directions for signs of lookie-loos, then fished a Portland coffeehouse rewards card from my wallet. I laid a hand on the doorknob and wiggled the card against the doorjamb. It didn't fit. Too thick.

I leaned against the door in frustration and it swung open. "Whoa!"

"What are you doing?" a man's voice asked.

I fell against the doorjamb and thrust the kibble between me and my attacker like a shield. My eyes pinched shut on instinct. I didn't want to see death coming.

"Have you lost your mind?" Sheriff Gray's voice pried my eyes open. He moved into my personal space and pulled me away from the door. "It's just me. I'm not going to hurt you, but I thought I'd save you from a breaking and entering charge." He closed her front door behind us. "I don't know whether to comfort you or arrest you. I specifically asked you to stay out of this investigation."

I hugged the cat food to my chest and panted. "Thank you for letting me in. This isn't about the investigation. I promise."

"Yeah? Then what are you doing trying to sneak into the victim's house?"

"The cat." I dropped the Kitty Yum Yums at my feet. "You said Mrs. Fenwick had a cat, and it hit me today that no one has been caring for it."

He cocked a hip. "So you thought you'd take it upon yourself to do the job?"

"Someone had to." I scanned the old home. Antiques and knickknacks burdened every flat surface. Gilded mirrors and wallpaper weighted the walls. "Hey, how'd you get here? I didn't see your car."

"I parked in the back so I wouldn't make a spectacle."

"Why are you here?"

His cheek ticked. "To feed the cat."

"When will Mrs. Fenwick's family come claim her? I have a couple of things I'd like them to have, and if they beat the dumpster to her old office, they'll find plenty of other treasures from her life."

"I'm not sure Margaret had any family. Her son's gone. He was divorced. It's hard to say what will happen to the estate in situations like these. I suppose it depends on the will and if her son had children."

The chubby cat pranced over thick emerald carpet and wound between Sheriff Gray's feet.

"She likes you."

He hefted her into his arms and stroked her head. "Yep. I saved her life once. She was thinner then. I doubt she could climb a tree anymore."

"Hey." I covered her ears with my hands. "Never mention a lady's figure. Give her here." I pulled her into my arms and buried my face in her puffy fur.

She nuzzled my cheek and purred.

"I could take her back to the farm with me," I said. "She shouldn't have to stay here alone. If Margaret's family turns up to collect her, I'll hand her right over."

The sheriff considered my offer for a long beat. "You sure?"

"Yeah."

"What will your cat think?"

I snorted. "Cindy will pretend to hate her while secretly enjoying the company."

He bobbed his chin. "What do you think, Whiskers?" He scratched the cat under her chin.

I moved her paw onto his hand. "I accept," I said in my best cat voice. I turned her collar around to check the tag. Yep. Her name was Whiskers.

"I'll get her things." He turned on his heels and walked through the archway between rooms. "Don't move," he commanded over his shoulder.

I made myself at home, examining the photo-covered walls and tables. A frame in the hallway showcased multiple shots of the same covered bridge where I'd had senior pictures done. Mrs. Fenwick and her husband slowly aged in each photo as the boy between them grew taller and broader. "You had a lovely family," I told Whiskers, still snuggled in my arms. My voice cracked with the weight of her loss.

I followed the plush green carpet into a cluttered office. This room was in direct contrast to the rest of the house. The desk was piled high with loose papers and file folders stuffed to the gills. I pushed the pile on the corner to keep it from splashing onto the floor.

Sheriff Gray reappeared in a huff. "I told you not to move."

"Look at this mess," I said. "The whole house is neat as a pin, and this looks like six filing cabinets exploded. What do you think she was working on?"

He rubbed his forehead. "Holly."

"I swear I'm not meddling, but did you find anything?" I tipped my head toward the mess. "Surely you've taken a look. What did you think?"

"I think none of this is your business." He handed me a cat carrier and a shopping bag filled with squeaky toys and a small crocheted blanket.

I took another look at the mountain of paperwork.

"Is there anything else?" he asked.

"I guess not." One curlicue header appeared on several papers. The initials HPS were surrounded by an intricately detailed oval. It was all I could do to keep from pointing it out to him, but he was the cop and I was, apparently, the hapless woman only permitted to care for the cat.

I set the carrier on an armchair and dropped the loot bag on the floor. Whiskers leaned her head on my shoulder. "I think someone was chasing me last night," I blurted.

"What?" the sheriff growled, then went rigid.

"Well, don't get mad. You asked if there was anything else!"

"You said there wasn't. Now you tell me you were followed and expect me not to get mad? It's not like a person forgets something like that!"

"Stop yelling."

He pressed his lips together. "I'm not yelling." This time, he wasn't. "Why didn't you report this last night? How am I supposed to keep you safe if I don't know you're in danger?"

"I didn't actually see anyone." Fear and embarrassment rushed through me, burning my cheeks and stinging my eyes. "I'm not sleeping well, and I saw a mouse get eaten, so maybe I was confused. Dad looked, but he didn't find anyone." I tucked Whiskers into the carrier and hung the bag of her possessions over my arm.

Sheriff Gray furrowed his brow. "You still should've called me. I would've come."

"There was nothing to report." I stepped away, tired of him seeing me so shaken—tired of being shaken. "I've got to go."

He took a long stride in my direction. "I didn't mean to upset you."

"Wasn't you," I said, turning back toward the door. "I'm late for Gingerbread Goes to Hollywood." I waved good-bye and sprang onto the porch.

"Holly, wait."

"I'm fine. Thanks for the cat."

Chapter Eleven

I dropped Whiskers off at the guesthouse when I got back to the farm. I wasn't sure I'd ever sleep there again, but my parents' house was a little farther away, and Whiskers needed time to acclimate before I brought Cindy into her life. Cindy was a lot to take in.

The reindeer photo op was shut down as I passed on my way to the Hearth.

I rounded the snack shop's edge with a flutter of parental anticipation. Where had Cindy gone? Was she safe? Happy?

Mom waved when I pulled the door open.

Cookie smiled, a poor gingerbread fellow pinched between her teeth. "Holly! Come on over." She patted the empty lollipop seat beside her at the counter. "We've been waiting for you."

"Where's Cindy?" I asked. "I left her with Ray and Mr. Fleece earlier."

"Barn," Cookie said. "Your dad took her with him to see the horses."

I exhaled a sigh of relief. "Wow. This place looks fantastic." Mom had dressed her giant gingerbread-themed snack shop to look like the inside of an old theater. Running lights lined the bottoms of booths and the base of the front counter. Silver film reels hung from the walls between photographs. An oversized line of black film twisted and coiled along the ceiling, and spotlights positioned in each corner of the room cast a cone of light into the air. "This is amazing."

"Thanks." She beamed. "I covered these old lunch tables in silver and black for a display area. What do you think?"

"I love it." I could almost see gingerbread people in tuxes and Marilyn Monroe gowns spinning through the room.

For Gingerbread Goes to Hollywood, each player receives a pile of gingerbread men, a stack of graham crackers, and a tray of gingerbread house trimmings. Contestants had all day to re-create a movie scene with the materials. People could come and go, vote on their favorites or make one of their own. Mom counted the votes and announced winners late in the evening. We'd learned early on that artistry wasn't nearly as important as choosing a movie everyone recognized. Some of the most terrible renditions had won, we assumed because the movies were dear to voters' hearts.

I took the empty stool beside Cookie and deflated. "Thanks for watching Cindy for me."

"Psh." Mom poured a coffee and pushed it my way. "She was no trouble. Now why don't you tell us where you went and why you came home with a cat?"

I balked. "How do you know that?"

"A mother knows."

Cookie cracked another gingerbread man in half and dunked him headfirst into her mug. She pointed his dripping body toward the window across the room.

"Ah." I sipped the coffee. "Spies."

Mom smiled.

"That was Mrs. Fenwick's cat," I said slowly. "I offered to care for Whiskers until someone came to claim her, but Sheriff Gray isn't sure anyone will come. You don't mind, do you?"

Mom looked worried. "What will Cindy think?"

"She'll get over it," I said. "Whiskers lost her whole family."

Cookie finished her drink and dusted crumbs from her fingertips. "I'd take her home if Theodore would allow it, but he's never been a fan of pets."

"Theodore, your goat?" I asked.

"Mm-hmm. He's not a big animal guy."

Mom swiveled at the waist and turned back to us with trays of supplies. "You two ladies might as well get started on your gingerbread scene before the place is shoulder to shoulder again. I've got tables to clear."

Cookie wiggled her fingers over the materials. "Which movie should we re-create this year? *Home Alone*? *Throw Momma From the Train*?"

I chewed my lip. "I was thinking more along the lines of *Titanic*."

She frowned. "That piece of wood was big enough for both of those young lovers. Shame she hogged it to herself like that."

I lifted the little cutout figures and placed them on my tray in different orders, hoping for inspiration. "How about before they hit the ice?"

Cookie bobbed her head. "Okay. I'll build the boat."

She and I could have each made our own, but the games were more fun together, and we'd been partners off and on for most of my life. I arranged blue gumdrops as waves along the tray's edge.

"Can I get you some food for thought?" Mom asked. "Maybe a lemon bar or an apple crisp?"

"No, thank you." I wasn't sure either of those counted as food for anything, and I was certain the lack of those kinds of suggestions had been why I'd lost twelve pounds instead of gaining the "freshman fifteen" when I'd started college. While everyone else was eating whatever they wanted, I was turning my nose up at food from drive-through windows and vending machines. After a lifetime with my mother, food had to work hard to impress me.

"Oh!" I dropped my last gumdrop into place and smiled. "Do you remember Caroline West from high school? She works at the bakery now."

"Of course," Mom answered. "She's the sweetest thing. Drops by every few weeks to see how we're doing."

"Have you tried her cupcakes?" I asked. The sweet memory nearly made my mouth water.

"Yep," Cookie answered. "I love Caroline's cupcakes!"

"Me too," I said. "She wants to open her own bakery. I thought we could help her get the word out by selling some of her products here."

Mom cast her gaze around the countertop, heavy laden with all her hard work. "I don't know."

I spread a line of frosting down the edge of another graham cracker and passed it to Cookie. "You don't make cupcakes, so

127

it wouldn't interfere with the Hearth sales, and it'd be a great way to support a neighbor. She's trying to get a small-business loan, but that could take a while."

Cookie sucked icing off her thumb. "Her parents aren't helping? You'd think a doctor and the mayor would have plenty of dough for a bakery." She stopped short, then beamed. "See what I did there?"

I dipped the tip of my knife back into the frosting. "I don't think her parents approve of the venture."

"Shame." Cookie put the finishing touches on the ship. "What do you think? Is the bow too pointy?"

"Nope."

"Maybe I'll ask to see her business plan."

"Really?" I smiled brightly.

"Sure, I've got plenty of money, and I'm told I can't take it with me."

"That's true," I said. "You'll have to let me know what you think."

I moved the pile of icing we'd been using as glue in front of the ship. "Here's the iceberg. Now all we need is a hero and heroine."

Mom wiped a rag over the counter in big wet circles. "Tell Caroline to bring a dozen cupcakes over in the morning, and we'll see how it goes. She should also have a sign with her name and company logo so people are clear that I didn't bake them. And ask her for some business cards so shoppers know where they can get more."

"Thanks, Mom." I iced our tragedy-bound gingerbread couple and stuck them atop the ship. "I'm king of the world," I said in my best Leonardo DiCaprio imitation.

Mom squinted at the stiff-legged couple. "Oh, that's clever. I loved *Overboard* with Kurt Russel and that Goldie Hawn."

Cookie snickered.

I hung my head and scribbled "Titanic" on the front of our board. "I'm going to go check on my cats."

* * *

I collected Cindy from the barn and carried her to the guest-house to meet Whiskers. I had no intentions of staying the night, but I needed to pick up a few things before heading back to my parents' home.

Cindy glared as I stroked Whiskers's head. "Cindy," I said sweetly, "this is your new friend Whiskers. Whiskers needs a nice place to spend the night. She might need to stay forever. We don't really know." I lowered the chubby tuxedo cat to the floor. "Why don't you show her around while I get some things together?"

The cats circled one another in a slow sharklike dance. Cindy growled. Whiskers meowed.

"How about a little kibble?"

I went to the kitchen and righted Cindy's overturned bowls. "Kitty kitty kitty," I called, shaking food into both bowls. I grabbed a third container for water and settled it between the kibble dishes. "Sometimes it's easier to get to know someone over dinner."

My tummy groaned. I checked the fridge and instantly regretted turning down Mom's offer of apple crisp. The guest-house fridge had the makings of a hearty salad with fruit and yogurt sides.

I closed the door. "Maybe a little hot chocolate instead."

I set a kettle on the stove and poured a packet of instant cocoa into the cup. Hot water over chocolate powder seemed incredibly unimpressive after ladling creamy chocolate heaven into mugs at the Hearth all week, but I definitely didn't want a salad.

I settled on the couch to wait for the water to boil. I patted my knees and tapped my feet. Sitting still had never been my best event. I grabbed my laptop and typed "HPS" into a search engine to pass the time. The logo had appeared so many times on letters in Mrs. Fenwick's home office, it must've been important. Hundreds of pages of possible matches came back. I did a long whistle. I needed to narrow things down. "HPS Mistletoe, Maine," I said as I typed the adjusted query. My new batch of results began with the Historical Preservation Society in California.

I clicked the top link and scanned the About Us section of the organization's website looking for a link to Mistletoe. HPS was a national organization that evaluated needs and allocated federal grant monies to historical towns like ours. Next, I took a visual stroll through their digital photo gallery. Surprisingly, a snapshot of our old flour mill was among the images. "Huh." I clicked to enlarge the picture. It looked exactly as it had when I'd driven past it earlier. I could only assume our mill was in the gallery because the preservation society had donated money to its restoration. I liked that idea. The mill was a wonderful place to learn about history. Renovations probably wouldn't begin until the spring, given Maine's unpredictable ice and snow patterns from December through March.

The kettle whistled, and I set my laptop aside. I checked the front door before leaving the living room. No new porch threats. The snow twinkled with the last spears of light from a setting sun. Streaks of gold and apricot painted the bellies of narrow clouds as heavenly shades of twilight spread across the sky. I needed to get my things packed up as soon as I finished my drink.

I dashed into the kitchen for a steaming mug of subpar cocoa and stirred the thin liquid all the way back to my seat before the fire. I pulled my feet onto the couch and tucked them beneath me. The sun was setting in Maine, but in California, it was much earlier. I traded my cocoa for a cell phone and dialed the number on the HPS website.

"Thank you for calling the Historical Preservation Society," a perky female voice answered. "How can I direct your call?"

I tapped a finger against my chin. "Hello," I stalled. "How are you today?"

"Quite well, thank you. How can I help you?"

I made a face at my laptop. *How can she help me?* I needed to start making plans before I did things. "Um, yes, I'm with the Mistletoe Historical Society," I lied horribly. My traitorous voice hitched and wobbled on every word.

"Of course." The clear click-clack of fingers on a keyboard ticked through the line.

She was five seconds away from calling my bluff, I could feel it. The sheriff had had time to sort through Mrs. Fenwick's desk, and he'd probably already been in touch with this organization. If the woman on the other end of the line mentioned my call to him, he'd be furious.

"Ah. Here you are."

"I am?" I chewed the edge of my thumb and winced at the sting.

"Mrs. Fenwick, correct?"

"Yes?"

"It looks like we have a team prepared to visit your town before the holiday."

"A team?"

"Yes, but, off the record, I feel you should know it would be highly unlikely for the HPS to fund a second project in one year's time. I'm not really supposed to say things like that, but it's Christmas, you know? I don't want to see you too disappointed."

I nodded at the cats who'd taken a sudden interest in my discomfort. "Right. Thank you." So Mrs. Fenwick had been angling for more funds? Why? I opened my mouth to ask, but the lady cut me off.

"That said, if our team determines everything in Mistletoe to be as it's described in your letters, I'm sure a grant to save the covered bridge won't be a problem."

The covered bridge. That made sense. The Fenwick family had taken a photo there every year. The bridge had been special to them, and the sheriff pointed out how difficult holidays can be for the grieving. No wonder Mrs. Fenwick had been acting crazy lately. She was on a time clock. A team was coming to evaluate the state of our historic town before Christmas, and she was down to the wire, battling residents and shop owners who probably didn't want to be bothered with extra work until after the holiday. If the town didn't comply, she risked losing funds to save the bridge.

"Is there anything else I can help you with, Mrs. Fenwick?" the woman asked.

"No. Thank you. It's wonderful to know your team is coming. It would mean a lot to her—I mean me—to see the bridge restored." I knocked a fist against my forehead.

I also appreciated the dump of information I'd gotten by simply dialing my phone. No trekking into town and questioning everyone in sight. I toyed with the idea of saying goodbye and not pushing my luck, but I couldn't stop myself. "I also want to thank you for all the help you've provided in the restoration of our flour mill."

"You're very welcome."

So I was right again. The mill was the other reason the HPS had sent money this year. The new question was why Mrs. Fenwick had been pushing for more money so soon. Work hadn't even started at the mill. What was the hurry?

"Anything else?" the woman pressed.

"No, but thank you very much. You've been extremely helpful."

I disconnected and dropped the phone onto my lap.

Was Mrs. Fenwick's push to save the bridge the reason someone had killed her? Could someone have wanted to stop the restoration from happening? Who? Why?

More important, how was it that every time I found a new answer, ten more questions arose?

Chapter Twelve

I woke to an empty house the next morning. According to the note on their kitchen table, my parents had already left for work on the farm and breakfast awaited me at the Hearth. I showered and dressed in worn jeans and a soft cowl-neck sweater that might've been on upside down for all I knew. I needed a caffeine IV to snap me out of my fog. I hadn't had a proper night's sleep since finding Mrs. Fenwick in the sleigh, and I'd found it even harder to close my eyes since the invisible man chased me home. I'd already exhausted Mom's entire stash of old glass bottles and milk jugs, converting them into candy-themed jewelry as an alternative to staring at the ceiling. I hadn't left Dad's basement workshop the last couple nights until dawn.

I dropped the cats off at the guesthouse where I could check on them more easily during the day, then hurried to the Hearth. It was long after nine, and the breakfast crowd had thinned to loitering coffee sippers.

"Good morning, sleepy head," Mom said when she saw me. "You look miserable. Get over here and let me feed you. What'll it be? Breakfast? Brunch?"

Dad smiled behind a steaming mug.

"Coffee." I patted the counter with my eyes closed. "Must have coffee."

She poured a mug full and set it in front of me.

I sipped from my glorious cup of wake-me-up. "Ah. It's as if I can feel my brain cells awakening."

"Good. What can I feed you?"

"Apple crisp?" I couldn't help myself. It'd been on my mind since I'd turned it down the day before.

"You've got it. What's on your agenda today?" she asked. Her soft brown eyes locked on me.

I curved my palms around the broad, bowl-shaped cup. "I don't know. Maybe if I had some apple crisp . . ."

She laughed. A moment later, a pastry appeared, and the sweet scent of apples and cinnamon danced around my head. "Talk."

"I don't know what I'm going to get into today. Do you need me here?"

She waved as the last table of customers wandered out the door. "Thank you! Come back tomorrow. I'm making crepes!"

The door sucked shut behind them, leaving my little family in silence.

Mom tilted her head like a puppy. "How are you holding up?"

"Fine." I chewed more slowly, trying to figure out her question. "Why?"

"One week till Christmas Eve," she said.

Dad folded his hands on the counter. "It's not every day a person breaks an engagement; this week isn't exactly going the way you'd imagined."

"It's fine." I stuffed another hunk of baked apples into my mouth. "I don't want to talk about it."

"You have to," Mom said. "Talking is what will help you get through it."

"Being here with you will get me through it." I sipped my coffee and searched for a way to change the subject. "What do you guys know about the covered bridge in Pine Creek?"

"It's pretty," Mom said. "You had your senior pictures taken there."

Dad groaned. "Those photos cost a fortune. Do you know I found a box of them in the attic? What'd we buy them for?"

"Tradition," Mom said.

I lifted a finger in the air. "Have you been to the bridge lately? Is it in bad condition? Has it been damaged or is it in need of repair?"

"I haven't been there in years," Mom said, "and I haven't heard anything about its condition. Have you, Bud?"

Dad shook his head. "I don't get out that way much. You could talk to Paula. I believe Pine Creek runs along the far east end of her maple trees."

I swiveled to face him. "You're kidding." Well, that was interesting in a mildly disturbing way. Paula and Mrs. Fenwick fought about everything else, why not about the bridge that lined her farm? I needed to get out there and take a look at the situation. I worked on my coffee a bit longer. Another question came to mind. "How well do you know Mr. Fleece?" I asked. "He seems to be great with the reindeer, but he has a bit of a temper."

Dad blanched. "Has someone complained?"

"No." I waved a hand between us. "Nothing like that. It's just that when I asked him about his fight with Mrs. Fenwick on the night she died, he got pretty angry just retelling the story."

Dad's brow furrowed. "Did he yell at you?"

"No. Not at me. *About* her." Though it had certainly felt as if he was yelling at me.

The muscles in his shoulders relaxed by a fraction. "Holly, what are you doing?"

"Nothing." I stretched my eyes wide. "What? We're talking. I'm a naturally curious person."

"You are, and your mother and I love that about you, but with things the way they are now, it seems your natural curiosity is taking a dangerous path. There's a killer in Mistletoe," he said as if I could've forgotten. "If this is about Margaret Fenwick, Sheriff Gray told you to stop poking into that. *I've* told you to stop that. For goodness' sake, you were chased home the other night!"

"Yeah, by the wind," I muttered. "I'm only wondering if you've ever seen Mr. Fleece angry. It's a little scary."

Dad's cheeks reddened. "You're still pushing. Why?" He turned to my mom. "Did you know she was still doing this?"

Mom jerked her shoulders up and shook her head.

"You're both terrible liars." He climbed off the stool and poured his coffee into a disposable cup. "I'm supposed to be the head of this household. You're supposed to take my advice."

Mom and I gawked, then burst into laughter.

"I'm leaving." He marched toward the door. "You're both lucky to have such a tough guy to protect you."

"We are," we agreed with matching smiles.

"Don't go," Mom said.

He rolled his eyes. "If I stay and listen to your anarchy, I'll get another ulcer. Let me know if you need anything."

"Okay," I called. "We love you."

Mom turned expectant eyes on me. "What'd you find out yesterday?"

The door opened again and Dad poked his head back inside. "Do you want Holly to go do that thing we talked about earlier? I've got some time now. I can keep an eye out for peekers."

"What thing?" I asked.

Mom stripped her apron off and rounded the counter. "No, I want to do it."

"Do what?" I asked again.

Mom threaded her arms into a white ski coat and stuffed a matching knit cap over her head. "You and I will talk later. I've got one more round of pickles to hide." She grabbed a giant jar from the floor beside the door and smiled. "Since you don't have any plans, will you lock up when you leave, then come back to prepare for lunch? I've got kitchen help coming last minute, but the seating area will need to be tidied and prepped."

"Sure." I'd nearly forgotten about Hide the Pickle. It was something Mom's family had done when she was young. Of course, back then they only had one Christmas tree in the living room, not hundreds of trees on multiple acres. Mom hid big ballpark pickles in the trees, and shoppers collected them for prizes. It was a hit every year.

I checked the cuckoo clock on the wall. I had to get moving. My fibbing record had reached an all-time high this week.

I did have plans—I wanted to get a fresh look at the Pine Creek Bridge, and now I needed to be back in an hour.

*   *   *

The drive to Pine Creek was as beautiful and peaceful as ever. The curving mountain stream was nestled in a winding gorge, always on the move, racing away to somewhere new. I'd been like that stream the last time I'd visited the bridge.

I parked at the gravel lookout and walked the short path to the bridge. Cars didn't travel the structure anymore, but hikers and mountain bikers still crossed the bumpy wooden slats with enthusiasm.

I kicked stones through tire tracks as I faced the old wooden planks, immediately lost in a fog of nostalgia so thick, I could smell my prom date's Drakkar Noir.

I took my time, recalling Margaret's family photos and thinking about the fact that all the Fenwicks in those pictures were gone now. They'd spent decades making memories where I stood, but for them, there would be no more. I paused to watch a couple lean over the railing and admire the clear water below. I'd sat where they stood, many times, feet dangling over the stream, watching leaves and sticks crash into protruding rocks and then swim away. I'd watched the stars from there. Kissed boyfriends. Laughed with best friends. Cried over heartbreaks. The bridge was a piece of my history too, though I'd never given it much thought before. It was just another stop in the town I loved.

The bridge had been built as part of the main passage into town. Over the years, more direct roads were forged, leaving Pine Creek on a route used mostly as a scenic byway for tourists. From the looks of it, hikers still used the gravel off-road parking as a trailhead. A dozen "No Trespassing" signs lined the trees in a row that climbed straight up the hill beside the bridge. It took me a minute to get my bearings, but I was nearly certain that land was east, and according to Dad, it belonged to Paula and her maple tree farm.

A fresh set of footfalls pulled me back to the moment.

I hurried out of the way, stopping when my tummy met the waist-high wooden railing. "Excuse me." I smiled over my shoulder. Then I recognized the newcomer.

Sheriff Gray stared back, half-shocked and half-angry. "We have to stop meeting like this."

I turned casually against the railing. "Hello. Beautiful day today." The words lifted from my mouth in a puff of frozen fractals.

"Should I even ask what you're doing here? And do *not* tell me you're here to feed the cat." Cold winds fluttered the dark hair on his forehead and over his ears.

I stretched a smile over my lying face. "No. I'm just taking some time to enjoy the view."

His expression went cocky, and his pale-green eyes crinkled at the corners.

"I meant the view of the stream." My cheeks burned. "Not that you aren't a nice view." I pressed my lips together.

He stared past me into the woods. "You make it hard to stay mad at you."

"You were mad at me?"

"I told you to stop snooping."

"I'm not."

He ambled to my side. "You are, but I was looking for you, so I'm glad you're here."

Yesterday's phone call rushed back to mind. "She narc'd on me, didn't she?"

"Who?"

I bit my tongue. Maybe he didn't know about Margaret's arrangement with the Historical Preservation Society. Maybe I should keep my mouth shut.

He scrutinized my face. "I don't know who you mean, but I will."

I struggled to lower my eyebrows from my hairline. "You said you were looking for me?"

"Yeah. I checked out the woods near your house. You said you thought you were followed, but your dad didn't see anyone."

My spine went rigid, and ice slid into my boots. "Yeah?"

"I found partial prints, broken branches, and the leg from a frozen gingerbread man just inside the trees."

My jaw dropped. "I was right."

"Afraid so."

Well, at least I wasn't crazy. "Did you say you found part of a gingerbread man? Like the ones we sell at the Hearth?"

He nodded.

I pressed a steadying hand to my middle. Someone had bought my mom's cookies, then stalked her only child? What kind of lunatic was this? "Anything else?"

"I made a few passes along the trail. It was loud. I can see how you'd think the person was closer than they really were."

"So?" I asked. "Are you saying I overreacted or that I had reason to worry?"

He shifted his weight, studying my face. "I think someone was trying to scare you, make you think twice before pressing your investigation any further. And on that note"—he leveled me with his detective stare—"why are you really here?"

"I noticed a logo on the papers in Mrs. Fenwick's office, so I looked it up last night and found a national organization that funds repair projects for things like this." I tried to look casual, despite the erratic pounding of my heart. "I called and learned that Mrs. Fenwick was trying to secure a grant to restore the bridge, but to get the money, she had to whip the town into historically accurate shape before the review team got here. That's why she was so nutty those last few days. This was really important to her."

Sheriff Gray stepped deep into my personal space. Warmth radiated off him, confusing my addled mind. The same sweet scents of gingerbread and cologne I'd recognized in his cruiser the night we met lifted from his jacket.

I had to crane my head back to see his face.

A hot mix of anger and something else flared in his eyes. "Do I have your attention?"

I nodded like a dashboard bobblehead.

His voice was soft and smooth, as if we were sharing a secret. "What you're doing is dangerous, and I don't want you to get hurt." Sincerity swam in his eyes. "I know what I'm doing. I don't need your help, and I can't solve this case if I'm constantly worried about what you're up to. Do you understand?"

More head bobbing.

"Final warning." He lowered his mouth to my ear. "Leave my murder investigation alone. Go home. Stay safe. I've got this. Understand?" He pulled back an inch, bringing his face too close to mine. His breath washed over my lips.

A myriad of impulses curled my fingers inside the sleeves of my coat. "Mm-hmm."

"Good." He straightened with a devilish smile and stepped away.

Fire scorched my cheeks. I blinked the haze from my eyes and marched woodenly to my truck, determined not to run or look back, but as I pulled away, the sheriff was still smiling.

Chapter Thirteen

I found Mom, Cookie, and Caroline at the Hearth when I returned to open for lunch. They were lined up at the window inside sharing nudges and giggling.

"What are you doing here?" I asked. "I thought you went to hide the pickles."

"I did," Mom said. "It only took about fifteen minutes. When I came back, I saw a couple of beautiful women waiting at the door. I figured I might as well bring them inside to warm up."

I smiled. "Well, that sounds like you."

I followed Mom to the counter as Cookie and Caroline climbed atop the lollipop stools. Cookie's feet dangled beneath a crushed velvet skirt, nowhere near the ground, while Caroline easily anchored one high heel boot against the floor. Her cream-colored leggings disappeared beneath an ice-blue angora tunic.

Mom went back to hostess mode, filling mugs with hot cocoa. She added a fourth cup for me.

I sipped and sighed. It was good to be home, despite everything that had gone wrong the last few days. My warm memories were especially thick and comforting this time of year. I turned to Cookie with a knowing smile. "Are you ready for the pickle hunt?"

She slid her eyes my way.

"I hope you caught a glimpse of where she hid them," I teased. "Maybe if we cheat, we'll have a fighting chance."

Cookie made a soft raspberry noise. "I could've helped her hide the darn things and we still wouldn't stand a chance."

I laughed. She was probably right. The only person on Earth worse than me at finding the pickles was Cookie. Our joint efforts were borderline ridiculous. People had walked in front of us over the years and collected pickles we literally couldn't see while looking at them.

"I'm not doing it," she added. "My show's on tonight, and I promised Theodore a pot pie. Besides, I'm whooped. I was worried when Reindeer Games closed for the day that it might hurt business, but I think we're busier than ever. I can't keep my shelves stocked. My feet are killing me."

Mom smiled. "It's true. We've more than made up for the lost day in ticket sales, but our bottom line is still lower than last year. I can't understand it. People come for the food and games, but I guess they aren't buying as many trees. We might have to rethink our business strategies before next season."

"Is that the real reason you stopped buying disposable cups and food boats?"

Her pretty face worked into a rare frown. "I just want to see this place put a little money aside. I'm glad for the patrons, but I can't help worrying about the reason they're really here."

I did too, since sales at the Hearth and Holiday Mouse weren't enough to keep the farm afloat long term. We were a tree farm. We needed to sell trees. "What does Dad think?"

"He says everything is fine." She stared through the front window. "The local news crew has been stationed at our gate for three days, and the six o'clock broadcast gets bolder every night."

"What do they say?" I asked, suddenly feeling guilty for not following the media's take on us more closely.

"They rehash the fact poor Mrs. Fenwick was found here after fighting with your father and another staff member." Mom made a sad smile. "They say you called nine-one-one and have been seen with the sheriff several times since then."

"Are they implying we have something to hide? Do they think I'm guilty?"

She patted my hand on the counter. "You know how reporters are. They look for ways to sensationalize everything because crazy sells."

"Good to know local reporters aren't above making an old lady's death into a spectacle," I grumped.

I glanced at the window where Mom and the others had been standing. "What were you guys looking at out there?"

"Ray Griggs is back," Cookie said. "He's taking pictures for the paper."

I crept to the window and peeked out. "He says he's trying to sell a positive article about the farm."

"Well, that's awfully nice of him," Mom said. "I'm glad he's here."

"Yes," Caroline agreed. "Plus, he's fun to look at."

Outside, Ray knelt beside a little girl making snow angels. He chatted happily with her for several seconds before shaking a woman's hand at the girl's side. He dusted snow from his jeans and marched to the next family with an outstretched hand.

"He's cute," Mom said.

I twisted at the waist to make a face at her. "I went to school with him."

She hiked her eyebrows under neatly curled bangs. "I'm just saying the man's handsome. There's nothing wrong with a little polite observation."

I stepped away from the glass and retook my seat. "He's young."

"So what?" Cookie asked.

Caroline made a puke face. "Younger men are only fun until it's time to go home and you remember they live with three other guys in an apartment that smells like burnt food and dirty dishes."

"Ew," I said. "Ray has a house, and I doubt it's anything like that. He said his mother lives with him now."

Caroline turned back to the window. "That's right. His father died," she whispered. "I forgot."

Mom rested her elbows on the counter. "Ray sounds like a nice young man. Maybe you should get to know him."

Caroline's smile widened.

"Maybe," I admitted, "but seeing as how I was supposed to get married next week, I'm not really interested in Ray right now."

Their faces went slack, and the room went quiet.

"Sorry," Caroline whispered.

Cookie rubbed my arm.

"It's fine. I'm not upset, I'm just grouchy. I ran into Sheriff Gray at the covered bridge, and he peeved me off."

"Sheriff Gray," Cookie parroted. "Now he's something. Ray's a cutie, but that sheriff . . ." She trailed off with a wolf whistle.

"What do you mean?" I forced back the memory of his face too close to mine.

Caroline made a choking sound. "What do *you* mean? He's a gorgeous, mysterious man in uniform. It's too bad he doesn't date," she said, looking more than a little disappointed.

I scoffed. "He doesn't date?" Hadn't he told me that he'd like to settle down and have a family?

"Nope. Ask anyone. I think every single woman in town made a trip to his doorstep when he first moved here last summer. Some kept after him for months, but he wasn't having any of it. Eventually they all gave up."

"Really?"

"Yep. He never accepted a single invitation for dinner, lunch, coffee, anything."

"Huh." I pressed my mug against my lips and processed the strange information. Why tell me he wanted to settle down if he didn't? The hamster wheel in my mind creaked into motion. Maybe he told me what he thought I wanted to hear. He knew I'd been recently engaged, and he probably thought he could influence me by being like me and pretending to want the same things that I did. My backbone straightened. Sheriff Gray thought he could manipulate me into doing as he said.

Caroline tapped her crimson nails against the counter. "Hey, I haven't had a chance to thank you. Your mom told me you asked her about selling my cupcakes here."

I stopped throwing mental eggs at the sheriff's cruiser and focused on Caroline's bright smile.

"It means a lot that you'd do that. You have no idea how much."

I returned her smile. "Your cupcakes are delicious. You're definitely going to be rich."

She laughed. "I'd be happy just making enough to open a shop in town."

"Well, you won't have any problem with that."

"Oh!" Cookie perked. "That reminds me—would you like some money, Caroline?"

Caroline choked on her hot chocolate. "What? Why?" she sputtered.

"I thought I could help with your new business." Cookie's wide eyes twinkled. "It's a brilliant plan, really. You need money, and I'm loaded. Plus, I love your cupcakes, and you'd be doing me a favor. It's getting harder to find new adventures around here, and I've never helped open a store before."

Caroline slowly abandoned her imitation of a statue. Her head began to bob. "Okay. Um." She rifled through her large leather bag and retrieved a hot-pink file folder. "I was planning to give this to the bank. It's a business plan, my proposed budget, staff requests, inventory estimates, and a chart of projected sales over the first five years."

Cookie blinked.

"This is everything you'll need to decide whether or not I'm a solid investment. Take it home. Read it over, and I'll meet you for coffee to answer any questions you have."

Cookie dragged her gaze from Caroline to the folder. "I didn't know there'd be homework."

Mom barked a laugh.

Cookie pushed the folder back toward Caroline. "I already know it's a solid investment—I'm investing in you."

Tears sprung into Caroline's eyes. "Are you sure?"

"Yeah. I talked it over with Theodore last night. We think you're great, and so are your cupcakes. He even eats the little polka-dotted liners. Oh!" She swung her gaze to me. "I almost forgot—I need more of your jewelry for my counter. People were asking for it this morning, but I'm still out."

"You only had a few pieces yesterday," I said. "How can anyone be asking for it?"

"The people who bought me out are wearing the stuff in town. When other people ask how to get some for themselves, they direct them to Holiday Mouse. Business folks call that 'word of mouth.'" She formed air quotes around the term.

Mom tipped her head. "You always had a creative mind. Probably why you're so interested in what led up to poor Mrs. Fenwick's death. Your imagination gives you clever ideas. That's what I told Evan when I saw him earlier."

It took a minute for the name to register. "Sheriff Gray?" I whipped my face toward hers. "You saw him?"

"Yep. I was hiding pickles, and he was walking the tree line, looking into the noises you heard the other night."

"What did he say?"

"Just that you were still pushing your own agenda and that you needed to stop. I told him I'd talk to you."

"Did you mention that *you* encouraged me to keep asking questions?"

She made a droll face. "I told him I'd talk to you, and now I have."

Caroline stilled her tapping fingers. "How often do you see the sheriff?"

"Every day, I guess."

"What's he like?"

"Honestly," I said, choosing my words carefully in case she liked him more than I did, "he's a little abrupt."

"But handsome," she said.

"Maybe, but I think he's been manipulating me, and I don't like it."

"I'd let him manipulate me." Caroline wiggled her perfect eyebrows. "But he doesn't give any regular ladies the time of day."

"I'm irregular?" I laughed. "That would explain so much about my life."

Cookie wagged a finger. "You found a dead body. That put you in his path and not the other way around."

"Oh." I had no idea what that meant. "I ran into him today at the Pine Creek Bridge. I think Mrs. Fenwick was trying to raise money to restore it before she was killed. Have you guys heard anything new about it? Did someone buy it recently?"

"Not that I'm aware of," Caroline said, "but I'm an indoor cat. I don't get a lot of local information beyond retail sales and community events."

Cookie shook her head. "Theodore's not much for sight-seeing. He loves to climb, but he's a real pain to transport. Pees in the car. So we mostly stay home."

Mom choked on her cocoa. Tears brimmed in her eyes as she ran to the kitchen.

I pushed Cookie's disturbing imagery out of my mind and pressed on. "It can't be a coincidence that Mrs. Fenwick was killed while trying to clean up the town and restore the bridge. Right?"

Caroline's blue eyes sharpened. "You think she was killed over something that had to do with the bridge?"

"It's possible." A swell of hope rose in my chest. Maybe I was finally on to something and we could put this mess to rest. Get justice for Mrs. Fenwick and put the shameless, speculating news crews in their places. "I need to prove I'm right about the reason she's dead. With evidence, I should be able to figure out who had motive to do it."

"What do you need to find out first?" Caroline asked.

I rubbed my chin. "I'm not sure. I guess I need to know who wouldn't have wanted the bridge repaired and why."

Mom returned, wiping a cloth over her sweater. "Pardon me for that awful exit," she said. "I was listening though. Your father said the bridge is right beside Paula's property line. Maybe she didn't want a bunch of workers and equipment damaging her maple trees?"

I didn't know why a repair crew for the bridge would disturb Paula's trees, but anything was possible. It was worth taking another shot at Paula. "I'll stop by the maple farm and see what she thought about the restoration," I said. "Who else?"

Caroline shrugged. "Everyone was mad at Margaret this week."

"I know," I said, "but I think the bridge was really important to her, and she was in a pinch trying to secure the help she needed to save it. I almost can't blame her for being so pushy, but I wish she'd have told people what she was up to. I'd like to think the locals here understand that kind of thing." I slumped on my stool. If my theory was right, then I was wrong about at least one person. "Or maybe it had nothing to do with the bridge. Maybe someone was just tired of being pushed around and they overreacted."

Cookie hopped to her feet and shrugged a heavy cape over her shoulders. "I don't know what happened, but the whole thing's got me exhausted." She flipped the hood over her silver hair and gave me an apologetic frown. "I hate to disagree with you when you're working so hard, but I doubt her death was a crime of passion."

"Why?" I asked, hungry for any tidbit that could put me on the right path to naming the killer.

She lifted a palm between us in exasperation. "Well, for one thing, Margaret Fenwick's gotten on people's nerves for forty years, but no one's ever killed her before."

The woman had a point.

Chapter Fourteen

As luck would have it, Reindeer Games was forced to close the next morning due to weather. A late-night storm had frozen our world into a skating rink, bowing power lines with ice and leaving half the town without electricity. At least there wouldn't be a horde of people outside the gates being turned away by a deputy this time, and hopefully poor road conditions would be enough to stop the nosy news crew from seeking a scandalous story where there wasn't one.

I'd padded into my parents' living room in time to say good-bye to Dad just after dawn. He'd built a roaring fire and kissed my head before going to feed the animals. I stayed behind helping Mom mix dry ingredients for cookie dough. We sealed and labeled the bowls for quick preparation when the power returned. She'd only needed to add the butter, cream, and other liquid parts before getting them into the oven when the time came. It was nice working with her in the kitchen again, but she left me too when boredom and snickerdoodle addiction drove a few hearty locals to the Hearth for lunch.

My parents' six-bedroom farmhouse was lonely without them. It was easy to imagine my great-grandfather's family of thirteen bounding through the halls. He'd built the place with the help of his sons and began the tradition of passing the property along to each new generation. At the moment, the cavernous space was unforgivably eerie with silence.

I went in search of a good book and a warmer top. Pictures of my ancestors climbed the wall beside the staircase—all faces of the men and women who'd treaded these same steps long before me. Similar photos covered the library walls like personalized paper. In a way, the White family was just like our town: long suffering, proud, and in the habit of documenting its history.

I bundled up around three and went to the guesthouse. I liked the idea of being that much closer to the Hearth and the stables where my mom and dad were working. The snow was deep, but the storm had passed, and the sun glowed warmly overhead. I toted the cats in my giant quilted overnight bag. They weren't thrilled about sharing the space, but so far they hadn't killed each other.

I stomped excess snow from my boots and let myself inside. No sooner had I set the bag on the floor than a pair of complaining kitties zoomed out. Whiskers hid behind the couch. Cindy stared up at me in silent complaint.

"Be glad you didn't have to walk," I told them.

I made a fire and checked the sink to be sure the pipes hadn't frozen. "We have water," I told the cats. "Who wants a fresh bowl of H_2O?"

I didn't get any takers, so I put on a kettle for tea.

Half an hour later, the little house was toasty warm, and the cats rolled on the floor beside the hearth, stretching and enjoying the lazy afternoon. I'd finished half a kettle's worth of tea, and for the first time in days, I felt at ease. I had nowhere to go and nothing was expected of me. I hadn't realized how much I needed a break until I got it.

I kept my mind mostly off Mrs. Fenwick's murder by beading necklaces and reading four chapters in *The Count of Monte Cristo* before sunset. I'd been less successful, however, at keeping my mind off the sheriff. I couldn't help wondering if he'd read the book before, if this was his first time, or if it had been on his seat that night by chance. Was it even his? I tossed my copy aside. For all I knew, it was another ploy of some sort. Maybe another suspect of his was a librarian.

I gave the cats a long look. "What should we do now, girls?" I asked. "I've finished enough necklaces to open a franchise, and I'm not ready to head back to the farmhouse alone. Maybe we should wait until we're sure Mom's at home making dinner."

Cindy's chipped ear rotated at the sound of her favorite word: dinner. She pawed my castoff paperback and chewed the curled corner.

"Fine." I shoved myself upright and headed to the kitchen. "I'll feed you, but you have to promise not to dump the bowl."

Cindy followed me into the next room, observing silently as I prepared her kibble. "I mean it," I warned. "No spilling." I placed the bowl in front of her.

Whiskers arrived a moment later and wound around my feet. "Hello, sweetie." I stroked her soft fur and poured a second bowl.

The familiar crash of crunchy tuna triangles bouncing over hardwood floors turned me around.

Cindy made eye contact before walking away from her overturned bowl and scattered dinner.

"Don't be like her," I told Whiskers. "Stay just the way you are." I delivered her bowl to the floor and went to clean up Cindy's mess.

I took a pile of junk mail back to the couch and covered my legs with an afghan. An ad from a local baby store caught my eye. They had a sale on plastic bowls with suction cups on the bottoms. I gave Cindy a warm smile and pulled out the coupon.

Mistletoe Magazine was buried under a dozen letters addressed to "Owner or Current Resident." I tossed those aside in favor of our town's quarterly edition. Photographs of the town square in twinkle lights graced the magical holiday cover. I turned the page and scanned the table of contents.

Mom's ringtone poured from my cell phone speaker.

"Hello?"

"Where are you?" she asked a bit breathlessly, the distinct note of fear in her tone.

Goose bumps rose over my arms and twisted my tummy into instantaneous knots. "I'm at the guesthouse with Whiskers and Cindy. Is something wrong? Your voice is weird."

She gave an uneasy chuckle. "You weren't here, and the trucks are all parked in the lot, so I panicked."

"Sorry. I wasn't thinking. Given the week we're having, I guess I should've called or left a note."

"I'm just glad you're okay. When are you coming home?"

I smiled against the receiver. I could see her home from mine. "Whenever you want. Now?"

"Anytime. Your father and I are having coffee with Mr. Nettle at the Hearth in an hour so we can touch base about the financial impact from this week's happenings. We'll be right home after that."

"Is everything okay?" She'd mentioned tree sales were low. "Are you worried?" Were things worse than she'd let on when the subject had come up yesterday?

"No, no, nothing like that. We always make enough to keep going, but there never seems to be any extra, and it'd be nice to put a little something away for retirement. Hopefully the last seven days of Reindeer Games will pack a punch."

"Is there anything I can do?"

"No. Nothing for you to worry about. Are you hungry?"

"A little."

"I put a roast in the oven. Help yourself if you beat us home and the scent is too much to bear. We'll understand."

"Very kind, but I'll wait for you. Will you call me when you get home? Then I'll run right over."

"Sure thing. Another storm's coming, so we'll be quick. We don't want Mr. Nettle stuck in it. How does dinner at seven sound?"

I checked the time. Five fifteen. "Seven sounds great." We disconnected, and I put the phone back on the coffee table. My refrigerator chugged to life, and the microwave beeped. Power was back. Thank goodness. Sitting alone by candlelight after sunset wasn't something I'd been looking forward to. I turned a few more pages in my magazine before a two-page spread with the words "Magnificent Mistletoe" drew me in. The article showcased local families repairing historic homes, barns, and businesses.

The old flour mill and covered bridge came back to mind. What if the Historical Preservation Society was a hoax? Maybe Mrs. Fenwick never got the money they promised for the flour mill and that was why the renovation hadn't begun. I skimmed the page for some indication that the smiling owners in the photograph had gotten help from a third party, but the source of the money wasn't noted.

My usual carousel of thoughts came full circle, as it always seemed to do. Right back to Mrs. Fenwick and the covered bridge. Had she gotten those funds for the flour mill or not? If so, what was the rush to get more for another project? Why did she put herself under so much pressure to get the HPS people out here before Christmas? Even if money for the bridge was approved, work couldn't begin in weather like this. Her project would've had to wait just like the flour mill. I raked a hand in frustration through my already messy hair. If she'd gotten a grant for the mill this year, why not finish that job before planning another? Or if the bridge was more important than the mill, why didn't they pursue that grant first?

I grabbed my phone and dialed the number for the Mistletoe Historical Society printed along the bottom of the article. It was high time I presented my questions to the cranky Mr. France. We might not have hit it off as best friends forever, but he certainly shouldn't mind answering a few straightforward questions about his work and our town. If he did, then maybe Sheriff Gray should talk to him next.

Wind whistled around the door and window frames as I waited for him to pick up. I pulled both feet under me and tipped my head onto the arm of the couch, curling into a tiny ball beneath a blanket that smelled like my childhood. Mr. France's voice mail picked up, and I left a lengthy, overly friendly message with a list of my questions and a number to return my call.

I set the phone aside, and Cindy came to sit on my head. A surefire way to know I looked comfy. Whiskers climbed into my lap.

"This is nice." I stroked Whiskers's downy fur and concentrated on relaxing each of my bunched-up muscles. Soon, I'd be home eating roast with my folks and climbing into my cozy bed for a long night's sleep. Tonight, I'd rest. I was certain of it.

I closed my stinging eyes, and a cloudy dreamscape crept over my consciousness. My cheeks stung, and I blinked against icy blasts of snow and wind. I was out in the storm, barely able to keep going without losing one of my precious felines to the fast-moving snow. "We can do it," I told them. "We can't give up." I leaned into the next blustery gale and pushed on through knee-deep drifts, teeth chattering and skin burning.

A crash sent me scurrying upright on the couch, jerked immediately back to reality. My heart rate raced, and my mind scrambled to grasp reality. I wasn't outside in a storm. The storm had come inside.

I struggled to free myself from the blanket, now wrapped around my legs, and two lamenting felines. "What happened?

What time is it?" I asked them. According to my watch, I'd been out for almost an hour, but I'd only closed my eyes a moment ago—didn't I?

The front door banged loudly against the wall once more, and I shrieked. "Oh, my gosh!" I stumbled into action on half-frozen legs and pressed my back against the door until it shut. My teeth rattled against one another, determined, it seemed, to break themselves. The fire was out, and tiny snowdrifts had formed on the carpet and windowsills.

Fear tightened my chest. Someone had opened every window and door while I slept.

It only took a fraction of a second to know who would do such a thing. *The same person who warned me to stop looking into Margaret's death. The same one who killed her.* A powerful round of shivers rocked my body and gnashed my teeth. I worked my frozen fingers, bending and stretching them, breathing heavily against the bluish skin and kneading them against one another. I couldn't feel my fingertips as I tapped the sheriff's number against my screen and waited.

"Holly?" He skipped the normal hello. "Everything okay?"

"N-n-n-n-o." I grimaced, unable to stop the brutal tremors. "S-someone." I closed my eyes to steady myself and realized my eyes were as cold as the rest of me.

An engine roared to life on his end of the line. "I'm on my way. Stay on the line."

"'K-kay." I shut and locked the windows one by one. *Someone tried to kill me—I could've frozen to death!* I could've frozen to death!

"Can you tell me what happened?" the sheriff asked.

I dragged the dial on the thermostat to eighty, then wobbled to the fireplace. I lowered myself onto the hearth and searched for the box of matches I normally kept on the mantle. They were probably knocked down by the wind. "S-someone broke into my house w-while I s-slept." My teeth knocked louder each time I tried to talk.

"I'm five minutes out. Are your parents with you?"

"N-no."

He cursed under his breath, and the sound of his cruiser's engine grew louder.

"G-guesth-house." The box of matches came into view from my new perspective, fallen, as I'd suspected, and spilled across the hearth. I reached for a handful of the little sticks, and a gasp broke free from my lips. A fresh jolt of fear sent me onto my backside.

A festive new box of matches was positioned on the cooled logs in my fireplace. A little sign dangled from a satin ribbon around its middle.

No more warnings. The farm will be next.

Chapter Fifteen

I pulled piles of outdoor gear from the coat closet and layered them over my clothes. I couldn't start a new fire until the sheriff arrived, and I couldn't shake the chill in my bones. I didn't want to disturb the note or the matches. I made another pass through the little house, dressed like I was headed into the arctic. I checked the windows and door locks and peered through each icy pane of glass in search of the sheriff who'd promised to be here in five minutes seven minutes ago.

Unable to sit or relax, I dialed my mom's cell phone.

"Hello?" Her voice was pert and jovial.

"Hi. How's it going?"

"Holly? What's wrong?" A chair scraped heavily over the floor on her end of the line, and the hum of white noise grew soft. "Have you been crying? Do you need me?"

A wedge of emotion clogged my throat. The mere fact she knew I was upset made it harder to pull myself together. "I'm okay. Just checking to see if dinner is still at seven."

"Oh." She paused. "We're running a little behind, but don't wait on us if you're hungry. The roast should be ready now. Help yourself."

"Okay." I ran the sleeve of my coat under my nose and pressed a mitten to each eye.

"Why don't we talk after dinner? Just us girls. Just like old times. It's been too long since we've done that. I miss it."

I nodded despite the fact she couldn't see me. A fat tear slid over my cheek. "Me too. That sounds really good." I said good-bye before I told her the whole sordid story of my near-death experience. The coward in me hoped the sheriff would break the news to my parents while I concentrated on look-ing unscathed for their benefit. I couldn't possibly deliver any more bad news this week. I was becoming a nuisance.

I moved to the next window and peeked outside when the sound of an engine reached my ears. A big black truck barreled into view, throwing snow in its wake and carving a path from the entrance gate at Reindeer Games all the way to my house. The beast stopped out front and settled a massive metal plow blade near my steps moments before the truck went still.

Sheriff Gray exited the cab with a lethal look in his eyes. He climbed the porch steps like a panther, so wholly focused I could practically feel his intensity through the glass. He approached the door with one hand at his back, presumably on a concealed handgun. A black duffel bag hung over his shoulder.

No cruiser. No uniform. No badge. For a moment, I wor-ried that he was the killer, and I was the idiot who kept calling him to report his crimes.

I hurried back down the hall to the front door and opened it slowly, hands raised.

His eyes widened a split second before pinching into slits. "What are you doing? Put your hands down." His dark jeans and leather jacket looked anything but official. His hair was dark, probably still damp from a shower, and his cheeks were clear of stubble. Where had he been when I'd called?

I waved him inside and pointed to the fireplace. "That arrived after I fell asleep, and I don't think it's from Santa. Watch your step. Some of the snow's beginning to melt."

He cast his gaze around the room, then back on me. "Start from the beginning."

I took a deep breath and retold the story while he bagged the threatening note and matches. He took a million pictures of my house, inside and out, before building a hearty fire to warm us when the fireplace was clear. "This week just keeps getting worse for you." He tucked the collected evidence into his black duffel and contacted a deputy to bring the official crime scene equipment.

He returned to the couch with a big green thermos. "I'll need a written statement on this."

"Okay." I made room for him beside me, shooing cats and straightening pillows. "Thank you."

"For what?" he asked, making himself comfortable at my side. He poured a lid full of something sweet scented and steamy, then passed it my way.

"Coming to my rescue. Again."

"You don't have to thank me. You may recall that I'm the sheriff. Rescues are in the job description."

I accepted the offering and gave it a closer inspection. "What is this?"

"Hard cider. It's a big deal where I'm from. I thought you could use a little after the way you sounded on the phone."

He'd had me at "hard cider." I tipped the cup to my lips and drank. "It's delicious."

His sharp eyes moved slowly, gliding their attention over me and then every detail of the room before us. "I had no idea what I'd find here. You sounded terrified."

I held out my empty thermos lid. The fire and thermostat were warming my skin. The liquor was working on my insides. I liked it.

He gave me a refill. "You're tougher than you look. Most people would be packing for Portland right now."

"I'm not brave. I'm hardheaded. Besides, this is my home." The truth of the words rang in my heart and head like a gong, reverberating until I wanted nothing more than to make sure that fact never changed. "I should've never gone to Portland. There was nothing there for me."

He watched the flames dance in my fireplace. Reflections of orange and blue swam in his serious green eyes. "You're different because you were there. Experiences like that change us." His gaze met mine. "Even the ugly stuff like this."

"I know."

The downturn of his mouth worried me. He had more to say on the topic, maybe even something personal, but he wouldn't, and I had no right to ask. I barely knew him, and I'd already ruined his night.

I took another long sip from my cup. "What were you doing when I called?"

"Why?"

"You aren't dressed for work."

"It's my night off. I was going to see someone."

I crossed my arms, painfully aware of my appearance. Even beneath Dad's giant hunting coat and snow pants, my ratty sweats and old high school hoodie had seen better days. I had thick ski socks over my softie pink ones, and my hair was a wild mess. I tugged off the knitted cap I'd donned to stay warm and felt my wild waves lifting under the influence of static electricity. I'd intentionally skipped blow-drying last night because it was late and my parents wake up early. The results were horrifying, but no one was supposed to see me today. The pitiful amount of makeup I'd applied before dawn was surely long gone after all I'd been through. What time hadn't erased, a deluge of stubborn tears surely had. In other words, Sheriff Gray was dressed for a date, and I looked like a homeless woman.

He twisted on the cushion to face me. Concern lined his forehead. "Do you want to talk about this? Do you have questions or is there anything else you want me to know?"

"Maybe."

"Shoot."

I finished the cider and set the empty cup on my lap. "Why aren't you yelling at me like last time?"

His brows dove together. "I've never yelled at you."

"Wrong." A blister of sweat sprouted on my brow. I stripped off Dad's giant coat and folded it over the arm of the couch. "You yell at me all the time. It's practically our song."

His cheek twitched. "We've got a song now?"

"Sure." I eased upright and shoved Dad's pants down to my ankles, revealing ten-year-old Mistletoe High School sweat pants. I stepped out of the giant bottoms and sat back on the couch, pulling my double-socked feet up with me. "Our song goes like this: You tell me to stop everything. Stop talking to people. Stop asking questions. Stop nosing around. Stop messing up your investigation." I tried to copy his Boston accent and failed miserably. When I dropped my *R*s, I sounded like a baby. When he did it, he sounded like Matt Damon.

He leaned toward me with a smile. "It's good advice, but I wasn't yelling. I wouldn't yell at you."

"Well, then you were scolding me."

He made an unreadable face. "I was encouraging you to make better use of your time before something like this happened. Or worse."

My jaw dropped. "You're doing it again. You just turned this into an I-told-you-so situation. Plus, it sounds like you're saying this is my fault for not listening to you."

He rolled his eyes dramatically and took a swig from his thermos.

I flopped back on the couch and faced him. "Do you really think whoever did this would burn down our trees?" It would ruin us. Trees took years to mature enough for anyone to take home.

"That's the thing about killers—they don't care who gets hurt. They sure don't care about your trees."

"It doesn't make any sense. Burning the farm would ruin my parents, and they haven't done anything to anyone."

"Yes, but you care about your folks," he said. "Whoever left that note either knows it or assumes you'd want to protect the trees because you'll inherit them one day. Either way, this is about you, not your parents or their trees."

I covered my face with my hands and groaned. I didn't want to think about inheriting the farm. That'd mean my parents were no longer able to care for the property or, worse, that they were gone. I leaned against Sheriff Gray's shoulder, not caring if it made me seem weak or needy. At the moment, I was both, and I didn't have the energy to pretend otherwise. "How am I supposed to leave this alone now? Someone tried to kill me. They threatened the farm. I have to find who did this before I wind up like Mrs. Fenwick."

I braced myself for the rebuff that didn't come. Instead, he wound one strong arm over my shoulders and tucked me more tightly against his side. "I'm not going to let that happen." He patted my shoulder. "Believe it or not, I'm a good detective. I'm an asset that you keep treating like a roadblock." He squeezed my shoulder. "Maybe we can work together."

"What do you mean?"

"Well, I don't for a minute think you're really going to leave this alone. As soon as the shock wears off, you'll be right back out there poking bears, and I can't have that. What if you start thinking about us as if we're a team instead? A relay team," he explained. "You went first, and all your legwork is done. Now we can weed through what you've learned together and see what we can make of it. If anyone else needs to be interviewed, I'll do it. I've got the baton now, and it's your turn to rest."

"Okay." Much as I wanted to keep going, I had an obligation to protect the farm that had provided for my family over four generations. "I can do that."

"I also think you should stop coming here for a while. Stay with your parents exclusively. You're too easy to get at here."

I lifted my head off his shoulder and worked to put some space between us. "I agree, but what if whoever did this goes after me at their house?"

"Do you mean before or after your dad shoots him?"

"That's not funny," I said. "I mean it. What if I bring this nightmare to their doorstep? Someone walked all around this living room while I slept on the couch. Who's to say the same person won't help themselves to my parents' house just as easily?"

"You're safer with them than you are on your own. Plus, it'll make me feel better to know you aren't alone." He scooped my fallen paperback off the floor. "What's this?"

"A book." My face heated. He probably thought I was reading it because I knew he was.

He fanned through the pages. "I read this every winter."

"You do?"

He gripped the paperback in both hands and gave me a wistful look. "My dad died when I was fourteen. He was a cop. He was shot." A slow smile changed his features into something proud and strong. "Man, he loved to read. He begged me to go to college and be a professor. He wanted me to teach English and get kids from the city to love books like we did. We read this one every Christmas break."

I slid my hand over his and curled my fingers around the edge of his palm. "I'm sorry you lost him."

"Me too," he whispered. "I followed his dream for me. I got an MFA from Boston College and a fat stack of student loans to prove it, but my blood runs blue, you know?"

I smiled at his hopeful expression. "We can't change who we are, I suppose. Still, I'm sorry I came home and messed up your plans to settle down somewhere quiet. I even ruined your date tonight."

His lips quirked into a smile. "Why do you think I had a date?"

"You said you were going to see someone."

His cheeks darkened, and his head bobbed. "I was coming to check on you. I knew the snow had closed the farm. Figured you'd be home and bored. The roads were clearing up, so I thought you might want to go for a ride."

"Oh." My heart sprang ridiculously into double time. "I would've liked that. I was alone all afternoon." I shivered. "I *thought* I was alone, anyway."

"Why don't we get out of here? If you want to get your stuff together, I'll see how far out the deputy is. I'll drive you over to your parents' house when you're ready."

I checked my watch. "They should be home now."

"Have you told them about this?"

"No." I gathered a bag of books and a couple spare sets of coats and boots, plus all my jewelry-making supplies.

Sheriff Gray followed me room to room asking questions about the people I'd spoken with regarding Mrs. Fenwick. I filled him in on the HPS and my concerns that Mrs. Fenwick's death had something to do with her campaign for renovations to the covered bridge, but nothing I said seemed to surprise him.

Half an hour later, I climbed into the cab of his running truck and balanced a quilted tote of cats on my lap. My legs and feet were smothered in bags of stuff I wasn't willing to leave at the guesthouse for an indefinite amount of time. The green dashboard clock said precisely seven.

Sheriff Gray shut my front door and placed a line of crime scene tape across the jamb. He made a call from my porch before climbing behind the steering wheel. "Ready?"

Nope. "Sure."

He shifted the truck into gear and headed for my parents' farmhouse. "The deputy stopped to help a car out of a snowdrift. He'll be here after that."

A thick plume of smoke rose from the chimney of my parents' home, and footprints led the way up their sidewalk to a newly shoveled set of porch steps.

Breaking the news to my parents was guaranteed to be the worst part of my horrible day. I could imagine the fear and hurt in their eyes when they learned I'd been in danger again. They worried too much about me already.

"Hey." Sheriff Gray's low tenor pulled my attention back to him.

He parked beside Dad's four-wheel drive and snuffed the engine. "It's going to be okay. Your parents are good people. They'll be scared for you, but they won't be mad, and I won't let anything like that happen to you again. Understand?"

I nodded, though I didn't see how he could make such a promise. Hadn't I already been threatened twice? And possibly chased once?

He reached for his door but paused. "You've told me everything?"

"Yeah."

"Then we're good, and I'm gonna catch this sonofa—gun."
He gave an apologetic smile.

I swallowed a wedge of emotion, still terrified the lunatic
who tried to freeze me to death would make good on his threat
to burn down my parents' trees—or worse, their home—while
we were sleeping.

My phone buzzed in my lap. Ben's face scarred the screen.
I slid the little red line to reject the call.

Sheriff Gray clucked his tongue. "Ben is the ex-fiancé,
right?"

I gritted my teeth against a brewing tirade on the topic of
Ben. He'd betrayed and humiliated me. His selfish actions had
uprooted my life and sent me packing back to Mistletoe. In
hindsight, the last part was blessing, but he hadn't meant it to
be. And now he was sorry? Hah! I'd rather go to Hawaii with
Cookie's goat. "I don't want to talk about it."

Sheriff Gray climbed out of the warm cab. He rounded
the hood of his truck and opened my door. He offered a hand,
but I gave him a cat instead. Then I climbed out with Cindy
pressed to my chest and two bags in my free hand.

"It's okay," he said. "We can talk about it later."

I gave him my best *no way José* look and marched up the
steps to face my parents.

* * *

The sheriff left soon after breaking the news to my folks. He
assured us that everything would be fine, but his attention
was divided when he glanced at his buzzing phone. After what
seemed like fifty rapid-fire texts arrived, he cut our coddling

short and practically ran out the front door. Whatever those texts were about, I wanted to know. Unfortunately, my parents looked like they might never let me leave the house again.

We ate pot roast in near silence. Dad watched me as if I might disappear, and Mom told me she loved me after each forkful of potatoes. When I pushed them to talk to me, Dad complained that I hadn't called him, then he took his frustrations out on dinner, using excessive force to skewer each tender bite. Mom dabbed tears from the corners of her eyes with a napkin, ashamed that she'd sensed something was wrong and hadn't pushed for an explanation.

I apologized profusely and pled my case for their safety, but when I offered to get a hotel room outside of town until this was over, they threatened to lock me in my room.

Eventually, the meal ended, and I dragged myself upstairs, praying for a short-term coma.

I kicked an old pair of tennis shoes against an unpacked book bag from my last day of high school and groaned. Life used to be so predictable and peaceful in Mistletoe.

I collapsed on the bed and pulled a pillow to my chest. What if the killer came for me tonight? What if he hurt my parents or burned down the farm? What could I do to stop him?

Nothing.

The cats curled on the edge of my bed and batted the soft white curtain billowing under the power of a heat vent.

"I want to keep my promise to Sheriff Gray," I told Whiskers and Cindy, "but we need to catch the killer before he hurts anyone else, so I don't think I can leave this alone. What do you think?"

Cindy turned on me with a leap. She batted my face and bit my hair.

"Hey, stop."

Whiskers walked over my belly and attempted to climb onto my head.

"Ah!" I rolled away snickering into a pillow. They had an effective way of changing the subject, I'd give them that. "You guys are terrible at giving advice."

My phone buzzed with an incoming call, and I nearly fell off the bed trying to get to it. Maybe the sheriff had found something. Maybe all those texts had led to the killer. I swung my legs over the bed's edge and snatched the device off my nightstand. A wave of sadness pulled my shoulders down. It was Ben again. Frustration stung my eyes and blurred my vision. Ben was supposed to want to spend the rest of his life with me, but instead he'd walked away the minute something more appealing came along. I didn't want him back, but the betrayal ached deep in my gut every time I thought of him. I slid my fingertip across the screen to reject his call. "You can have the espresso machine," I told the now quiet phone. "You can have the honeymoon. You can have whatever you want, just *please* stop calling." I tipped forward, socked feet brushing old wooden floorboards. Cindy and Whiskers poked their heads beneath my elbows. Apparently sensing my mood, they curled gently at my sides.

I fell back, dragging them with me. A woman who feared being a cat lady had obviously never owned a cat.

Chapter Sixteen

I spent the morning working with Mom at the Hearth. The roads had been cleared overnight, and the skies were a cloudless blue. Tour buses lined the county road outside Reindeer Games, dropping eager shoppers off for a day of memory making. This was exactly what six days until Christmas was supposed to look like in Mistletoe. I, for one, was thankful for a return to normalcy.

Mom's favorite Andy Williams Christmas album played through the crowded room. She lined warm cutout cookies on a rack behind the counter. Rows of colored icing bags stood at the ready. I hummed cheerfully as lyrics to "Happy Holiday/The Holiday Season" carried me around the room. I refilled drinks and took cookie orders with a joyful heart and a sugar high. Hard to believe there was a killer on the loose when the world inside our little bakeshop was so perfect.

I ferried hot chocolates and fancy cookies to a table near a window. "There you are." I unloaded the tray and tucked it under one arm. "If you're around at four, I hope you'll stop back for Holiday Bingo. Winners get free snickerdoodles and apple cider. We provide the cards and the peppermints to mark your spaces." I braced one stiff hand beside my mouth to share a secret. "The markers are also delicious in cocoa."

The woman on my right straightened her little green pill-box hat. "That sounds delightful. We'd hoped you were still doing bingo. It was scheduled for yesterday, but that wretched storm closed half the town." Her slow southern drawl was sweet and strong.

"We couldn't skip bingo," I said. "It's an annual hit. We're going to play yesterday's bingo and today's trivia back to back this afternoon."

"Wonderful." She fiddled with the napkin beneath her cup, lining it perfectly with the table's edge. "We were stranded in our rooms all day. It was maddening."

The other woman at the table fluffed her thick salt-and-pepper hair. "I suggested a walk to take photographs, but that idea was dismissed." She slid a polite gaze toward the woman with the hat. "We never see snow like this in Georgia."

"You came from Georgia?" I asked, a little thrilled. I'd never been that far south. "That's incredible. How did you hear about us?"

"We're part of the Macon Historical Society. We visit other historic towns every fall. This is our first time in New England. We pushed the trip back by a month this year just to see what Mistletoe was all about."

My smile widened. "What do you think? Aside from the blizzard," I teased.

"Beautiful," she said. "Absolutely stunning, and the weather does nothing to diminish that. Your Historical Society deserves an accolade. I hope the people here recognize the efforts."

A bud of sadness bloomed in my heart for Mrs. Fenwick. It seemed as if everyone in Mistletoe had preferred to argue with her. "Thank you." I excused myself with a nod.

I paused passing the front window. Dad was helping a family tie their new Christmas tree to a car roof. Others loaded freshly chopped evergreens into the beds of pickup trucks. A farmhand flagged the trees' ends with red ribbon, lest traffic follow too closely.

Cookie blew inside a moment later. Her puffy white hair was a mess, and her boots were covered in snow. "Next year, I'm buying a snowmobile," she huffed. She unraveled the scarf from her neck, then dusted loose snowflakes from her coat sleeves. "You think I can get a sidecar for Theodore?"

I wrapped an arm around her shoulders and squeezed. "If you can't, I bet Dad can make you one."

"Good. I'd pay for that. Theodore hates being left behind."

"True, true." I walked her to the only available booth and sat across from her for a much-needed break. "Are you staying for bingo?"

Her rosy cheeks rounded with a broad smile. "I'm the caller."

"What numbers are you going to call first?" I asked with a wink.

"Hey, there's no cheating in bingo," she said. "The cheating comes later, during trivia."

I laughed. "Not this year. Mom is insisting we turn our cell phones facedown and keep our hands where she can see them. There were too many accusations last year about who should've won."

Cookie made a face and patted her purse. "Then I'd better finish my brandy now. Bring me a pot of tea with a dollop of cream and heap of sugar."

"On it." I went to put another kettle on.

I kept up a frantic pace until nearly three, taking and delivering orders until the lunch rush ended and the last customers finally cleared out. Then it was time for phase two. Holding the Reindeer Games at the Hearth was convenient, but it required an extreme hustle. I wiped the tabletops and seat cushions, then ran a dry mop over the floor to eliminate any traces of melted snow while Mom cleared the counters and put on fresh pots of everything in the kitchen. We had less than thirty minutes before the early birds would show up to secure their spot for afternoon bingo. Even with folding chairs lining the room, space would be tight.

Cookie swished a mouthful of her "special" tea and did a dramatic sigh after swallowing. "B-10," she called suddenly.

I jumped.

"B-10. B-10. B-10." She spouted the letter-number combination in different accents. "I liked that last one. Did you?"

I looked over my shoulder to find her staring. "Yep."

"It was British."

"Yes." I laughed. "Very."

"I think people will have more fun if I sound foreign. It'll make the experience exotic." She opened the holiday bingo set and dumped the chips into a little cage with a handle, then cranked them until they were mixed. "I always wanted a man with an accent."

I grabbed a stack of well-worn bingo cards and turned them all around and right-side up.

The door opened, and a trio of women made a beeline for the corner booth farthest from the entrance. Wise—that'd be the warmest seat in the house.

I took their orders and handed out bingo cards and a mitten-shaped bowl of peppermints to be used as markers. "We'll get started in about twenty-five minutes."

I checked my watch and hustled into the kitchen to pour their hot ciders.

Mom hefted a large tray of cookies from the oven and slid them onto the stove top. She wiped her brow with an oven mitt and smiled. "How's it going out there?"

"We've got our first arrivals," I said, loading mugs onto a tray. "Do you need any help back here?"

"Nope. You'd better get going. Your job's about to get a lot harder than mine."

I darted back to the table of women and dropped off the drinks before taking orders from three more booths that had become occupied in my absence.

The entire room was packed to the perimeter by four sharp, and I was beat.

Cookie shuffled to the front counter and cranked the cage of bingo chips. She poised the mic before her lips and cleared her throat daintily to start the show. "'Ello," she said in an *Oliver Twist*–worthy accent. "You may cover your center squares at this time. Right-O. Now let's see what we've got in here." She cranked the handle a few more times for dramatic effect.

I hurried to get bingo cards into the hands of a couple passing over the threshold. "There are folding chairs along the wall. Feel free to pull up to any open table, and just wave if you need anything once you get settled."

"Hey, lady," a weird voice called on my return trip toward the counter, "I got a kiss for you."

I turned a death stare in the man's direction.

Ray Griggs burst into laughter, dangling a Hershey's Kiss from its tiny paper stem. "Clever, right?" He looked like a frat boy in loose-fitting jeans and an open flannel button-down. The baby-blue shirt beneath worked well with his eyes.

I took the kiss from him. "Gimme that." I put it in my pocket and collapsed onto the limited space at his side. He had the outside spot in a booth with three older women.

He looked at the woman positioned between him and the wall. "Did you see that, Ma? This lady stole a kiss from me."

I kicked his shoe beneath the table. "Stop being goofy."

The woman leaned around him. "Lucky you. She's as pretty as you said."

I looked to Ray for an explanation.

"Holly White, this is my mom, Fay Griggs. Mom, this is Holly White." He smiled at the two women seated across from them. "These are my aunts, Kay and May."

I raised an eyebrow.

He pressed a palm to his heart. "I swear it."

His mom smiled. "Our family loves to rhyme. That's how he got his name."

I couldn't stop the smile from spreading over my face. "Do tell."

Ray swung an arm over the backrest behind me. "I have two older sisters, Shae and Renee. I was lucky. I could've been named after my uncle Gay."

A rocket of laughter burst through me. I wished I'd remembered him from high school. Was he always so silly and fun? I could've used that drop of sunshine then as much as now. His natural disposition seemed to run on happy thoughts; mine was fueled by concern. Concern for the weather, my friends and family, strangers, families on long-distance telephone commercials, and everyone holding a telethon. "Stop it. You're kidding."

"No," his mother assured. "My brother was Gay before it became all the rage."

I slapped my knee. "Now I understand where he gets his sense of humor." I offered a hand to his mother. "It's wonderful to meet you, Mrs. Griggs."

"You as well."

I shook hands with his aunts next. The women looked alike, all fair haired with blue eyes and freckles. They seemed close in age but much older than my mother, who'd had me at twenty. I puzzled at the notion. If I'd had a baby at twenty, I would've had to drop out of college, and the baby would be nearly seven by now. Good grief. I looked toward the kitchen with renewed appreciation for Mom. How had she done it? I could barely make my ten AM classes at twenty.

"I-21," Cookie called in her fake accent.

Ray's Aunt Kay put a mint on her card. "I love this bingo caller. I could listen to her all night. She sounds just like Mary Poppins."

I covered my laugh by pretending to sneeze.

Ray chuckled. "Cookie's a hoot. You should hear her do Arnold Schwarzenegger." He pushed his bingo card in my direction. "Want to help? I'm failing miserably. My markers keep disappearing."

I looked at his blank card. Not even the free space had a mint on it.

His mom snickered. "Ray says you went to school together?"

I put a mint at the center of his card, and he ate it. I leaned against him with another round of soft laughter. "Yes. Though I'm sorry to say I don't remember him."

"He remembers you," she said.

Ray caught my eye with a warm smile. He'd told me as much, but I'd assumed it was a lie or a line.

"How's your article coming?" I asked him. "Have you found enough material to use?"

His brows pulled together. "The editor's a tough nut. He says feel-good pieces are fine for Christmas Day specials, but people want dirt the rest of the year."

"Right." Sad but true. "Too bad for us our season ends on Christmas Eve."

"You still deserve the nod. This place is the heart of Mistletoe. I haven't found a single person who disagrees."

I shivered as a gust of frigid air blew down my back. Ray rubbed a warm palm over my shoulders where the chill had landed.

"Ray." Sheriff Gray's voice startled me.

I spun in the little space and gawked.

He approached our table with slow, confident strides. "Mrs. Griggs." He tipped the brim of his sheriff's hat at the women before turning an odd expression on me. "Holly."

I did a little waist-high wave. "Hey."

Ray's mom reached for his hand. "It's nice to see you again, Sheriff. Join us, won't you? Pull up a chair."

"Oh, no. I don't want to interrupt. I just wanted to see how everyone was doing." His gaze slid to me.

"You already know Holly?" Mrs. Griggs asked.

He gave Ray a strange look before answering. "I do."

"She went to high school with my Ray," she said. "I'll bet she was lovely in high school—just look at her now."

He grinned. "What was she like at sixteen, Ray?"

"I don't know." Ray worked the mint around his mouth. "She was a senior when we met, but she was smart. Elusive. Always had her nose in a book. What was it that you carried with you everywhere?"

I shrugged. "I don't remember."

"I'll think of it," Ray promised. "Give me a second."

Sheriff Gray looked more amused than I preferred. "Let me guess. Had to be a Brontë novel. No. Wait. *Pride and Prejudice*?" He smiled in my direction.

I squirmed.

Ray snapped his fingers. "*Count of Monte Cristo*."

I felt my lids fall shut. *How did he possibly remember that? And why did he have to think of it now?* I dared a look at the sheriff.

His blue eyes had zeroed in on Ray's hand on the backrest behind me. "We were just talking about that book. Funny, she didn't mention that at all." He opened a folding chair at the end of our booth and stuffed it beneath him. "You know what? I have a few minutes. Maybe I can stay for one round of bingo."

"B-4," Cookie called in perfect examples of strained British and cosmic timing.

Sheriff Gray cast a weird look in her direction.

I pushed onto my feet and hugged the remaining bingo cards to my chest. That last call was destiny. As in I should definitely go *B-4* our crowded booth became any more uncomfortable.

Chapter Seventeen

I tied a crimson ribbon around another box of Mom's famous cutout cookies and sighed. Five more days until Christmas, and I was already dragging. I hated to think of the condition I'd be in by Christmas Eve, possibly curled under the tree, covered with the skirt and resting my head on a tissue paper pillow. I stuck a sprig of evergreen in the bow's knot and tucked a Reindeer Farms card underneath. It was my third cutout cookie order in thirty minutes. The only things selling faster were Caroline's cupcakes. She'd delivered two dozen this morning on her way to work at the bakery, and I'd sold them all before lunch. With flavors like white mocha truffle, how could anyone leave them behind?

A yawn split my face, and I stopped organizing cookies long enough to refill my coffee. This was traditionally the last day of decent tree sales. From here on out, very few trees would leave the farm. I needed to pep up and get my game face on. For the next four days, my parents would rely on gift and food purchases alone to line the coffers until next season. It seemed like a lot of pressure.

The swinging door to the Hearth's kitchen swung wide, and Mom arrived in a puff of powdered sugar and enthusiasm. "I've iced another batch of cutouts. What can I do out here?"

I scanned the room in search of something I hadn't gotten to or thought of. "Nothing. Why don't you have a seat and rest?"

She collapsed onto the stool in front of me without argument. Slowly, she lowered her head to the cool marble surface. "Ah."

I laughed. "I don't know how you do it. I'm exhausted, and all I do is take the orders and box up your work."

"You do much more than that," she said, lifting her head for a better look at me. "How are you feeling? You know . . . otherwise?"

I wasn't sure how to answer. I was feeling shockingly good about the canceled engagement. A week in Mistletoe had put things into perspective. I was sad I hadn't come home more often over the last few years, but I was extremely proud of what my family accomplished every year with dedication, teamwork, and love.

I sipped my coffee and scrutinized her expression. Maybe she was thinking about Mrs. Fenwick or the person who'd threatened my life and her farm. Those things terrified me, but what could I do about either? "I'm not sure what you mean."

"You've been through a lot lately. I worry about you." A little smile rose on her lips. "It looked like you were having fun at bingo last night."

"I was." I set my coffee aside and folded another pastry box into existence. "You never told me how it went with the pickles."

She dropped her head back and made a strangling sound. "Terrible." She righted herself and frowned. "I don't think anyone found the pickles I hid before the storm. Either no one's looking at our five-year blue spruces this season, or they aren't checking for the pickles."

"Bummer." I frowned. "I can go out and take a look at the situation if you want."

"No. We're too busy for that. The pickles will keep, and I can always store the prizes for next year or reassign them to another game. Speaking of . . ." She gave me a curious look. "How do you feel about helping out tonight?"

Tonight's installment in the Twelve Days of Reindeer Games was called One-Horse Open Sleigh. Though sleigh rides weren't much of a game, we did our best to make it special, and folks who didn't live on a tree farm seemed to enjoy the experience. Plus, the rides were free with a tree purchase. "I love the sleighs. Of course I'll help. Did you think I wouldn't?"

She fidgeted with an invisible crumb on the counter. "I just want you to be comfortable. That's all. If you want to take the night off, your father and I would understand."

"Comfortable?" I glanced at the crowded tables around us where the soft buzz of conversation and clanking of silverware mixed with the sounds of Michael Bublé. "What are you talking about?" I whispered.

"The romance. Your breakup. I don't know, honey. I've never been through what you're going through, and I don't want to make it worse by asking you to help happy couples share a blanket and a romantic sleigh ride."

I leaned my elbows on the counter, bringing my eyes in line with hers. "I'm okay, I promise. I was heartbroken when I came home, but so much has happened." I stood up. "I've got a new lease on life. I want to spend mine with people who could never willingly part with me, and definitely not with someone who might drop me for the next yoga instructor." Plus, in hindsight, Ben wasn't the nicest guy. I'd attributed his occasional smart mouth and bad attitude to having a stressful job, but truthfully I was glad I didn't have to worry about what sort of mood he'd be in at every turn. I wanted a life partner. Someone who treated me the way I treated him. I hadn't done a lot of dating, but surely that wasn't too much to ask.

Mom pulled herself off the stool. "I have no doubt you'll find a man that recognizes the treasure he has in you one day. He'll even give you goose bumps after thirty-two years of marriage if you're lucky." She patted my hand. "I'd better get back to work. Let me know when Paula gets here, would you?"

"Paula's coming?"

"Yes. I used that bottle of syrup you gave me to try a new scone recipe, and I loved it. I made a little maple butter too. They're both delicious. I'd like to add them to the menu and maybe sell her syrup on consignment."

"You made scones and maple butter without telling me?"

She rubbed her tummy and disappeared through the swinging door.

I was sad to have missed the maple butter, but this could still be my lucky day. Mom was making maple scones, and I'd get to talk with Paula again. Every time I'd thought I could slip away for a visit next door, another wave of customers had appeared and stopped me. *Now she's coming to me.*

"Oh, Holly?" Mom called.

"Yeah?" I turned to see her brilliant smile.

"Have I told you today how glad I am that you're home?"

I smiled back. "Me too."

I spent the next hour or so topping off hot beverages and organizing my questions for Paula.

Caroline slunk through the door looking like a really sad cover model. Her long blonde locks had been flatironed to perfection and anchored behind her ears with bejeweled bobby pins. Her lips were pinup red, and her eyes were nearly the same. "Hello." She exhaled the word. "Dating stinks." She plopped a white bakery box on the counter and dutifully unloaded the contents.

"What happened?"

"I only attract boneheads."

"Oh." I placed her fresh delivery of cupcakes into the glass display case. "I'm sorry."

"Why don't nice guys ask me out?"

I gave her daunting beauty another long look. "Maybe you intimidate them."

She snorted. "Yeah, right. None of the men who talk to me ever seem intimidated. They seem more like they were raised on a New Jersey construction site."

I wrinkled my nose, unsure what that meant exactly. "Too confident?"

"Obnoxious," she countered. "I mean, who cares if a guy can bench press me ten times if he has trouble counting that high?" She flattened the empty box and gave it an extra few smacks.

I smiled. "Is this what you look like when you're angry?"

"Yes. Mom didn't think ladies should be angry, so I'm not very good at it."

I closed the display door and stared into her glossy blue eyes. "You weren't allowed to get mad?"

She lifted her eyebrows. "Anger isn't becoming of a young lady, and frowning gives you wrinkles."

I did a long blink. "Wow."

A bubble of laughter rocked free from her lips. She climbed onto a barstool lollipop with a moan. "I got all dressed up for a blind date who thought we should get the good-night kiss 'out of the way immediately' so he wouldn't be nervous all night about it."

I took the seat beside hers. "He met you and immediately asked to kiss you? Before the date?"

"Yep."

I rubbed my forehead, completely at a loss. "Who set you up with that guy?"

"My dad."

I cringed. My dad would've wanted to break that guy's lips, not send me somewhere alone with him.

She rolled her eyes and slid off her stool. "He's some political incumbent's son. I guess it would've helped Mom's campaign for reelection if we'd gotten along." She pulled her keys from her pocket and waved good-bye. "In other words, I'm sure to hear about this in the morning."

"Where are you going?" I asked. "Hang out awhile. I'll get you something to soothe your woes. Maybe a little of Cookie's special tea and a couple delicious cupcakes."

"No thanks. The last time I tried Cookie's tea, I needed a designated driver. I'm going to go soak in the tub and sleep in sweat pants."

That sounded like a plan I could support. "I hope you feel better," I told her retreating frame.

I drifted back to the bakery display and sampled one of her cupcakes to confirm the quality. I had a second to double-check my observations.

I was on a sugar high when Paula finally showed up, towing a wagon with wide knobby tires and a metal-grated frame filled with boxes of syrup bottles.

"Hello!" I jumped into her path. "How are you? We're so glad you're here."

"You," she groaned. "What are you doing here? Have you finished harassing the rest of the town already, or do you just have a thing for me?" Her lips twitched. I assumed that was as close to laughter as she ever got. "Where's your mother?"

"In the kitchen."

She sidestepped me.

I raced ahead to block her path. "If you'd like to have a seat, I'll bring you something to drink and let her know you're here."

She braced one hand on her hip and stared.

"Please?"

Paula rolled her eyes and dropped into an empty booth. She pulled her wagon between her feet. "Tell her I don't have all day. I have to get back to my farm."

"Absolutely." I turned to leave but spun back, one finger lifted between us. "I was wondering . . ."

"Are you serious? Didn't you hound me enough in town?"

"I didn't mean to upset you. I'm just trying to make sense of things."

"It was murder. There's no making sense of it." Emotion flickered in her deep-hazel eyes. "Talking about it all the time makes it worse, so let it go. We all need to move past Margaret's death and get on with our lives." Her tone was sharp, but her eyes were glossy.

Paula put on a good show, but I finally saw what she'd been hiding behind all that anger: *pain*.

I slid onto the seat across from her. "I'm really sorry about your loss. I should've said that when I spoke to you last time, and I should've led with it now."

She looked away. "I don't know what you're talking about."

"I think you do." There was no denying the remorse in her eyes. Remorse for what, I couldn't be certain. For a lifetime wasted arguing, I hoped, and not the alternative. I didn't want Paula to be a killer. I wanted her to be a friend. She'd been running a farm by herself for as long as I could remember, and I couldn't begin to imagine what that must've been like. Growing up, I'd assumed she was a recluse like Ebenezer, making money but not friends, but suddenly she just seemed lonely. Exactly like Mrs. Fenwick had been.

I steeled myself for another rebuff, but I had to ask. "Did you know Margaret was lobbying for a grant to restore the Pine Creek Bridge?"

A flash of shock blew across her face, but she didn't answer.

I pressed ahead. "I think it was important to her. She had photos taken with her husband and son there, but also it was kind of her job to keep Mistletoe historic."

"I was married there."

"What? When?"

She swallowed long and slow. "I lost my Herbert to Vietnam in 1965. We were just nineteen."

I tried to imagine her as a teenage bride, kissing a brave young groom in uniform. My heart broke. "I'm sorry. I didn't know."

"How would you?" she asked. "That was long before you were born. Besides, this town thinks I'm a mean old spinster. Maybe I am now, but I wasn't always."

"You never remarried. Why?"

She forced a small smile over her sagging face. "There was no replacing Herbert. Love like that doesn't come along twice."

For the sake of every other young widow and widower, I hoped she was wrong, but I didn't argue. How could I? "Can you think of a reason anyone wouldn't have wanted the bridge restored?"

"Besides the fact that it's fine the way it is?" she snapped. "So what if we don't drive cars over it anymore? It's perfectly fit for bikers and hikers. Things age. People age. Should I get a makeover too? Some surgery to look like I did forty years ago? For a town bent on honoring the past, you'd think people would stop trying to change everything."

"Did you see Mrs. Fenwick when you left in your sleigh that night?" I asked.

Paula pulled in a long breath. "No." Her chin kicked up a notch. "I stopped to see Chip and invite him over, then I went home to wait for him."

"Chip?" Was she saying she couldn't have killed Mrs. Fenwick because she'd had a date? "Is he a local?"

"I believe you call him 'Chip Fleece.'"

I worked to keep my expression neutral. Paula and Mr. Fleece?

Strangely, I could see it.

"Paula!" Mom hurried to our booth with a look of delight. She bent over to hug Paula around her shoulders. "It's always so good to see you. Thank you for coming. We've got lots to talk about. I can't wait for you to try my maple butter."

Paula gave me a long look before following Mom to the kitchen.

I sat there, alone and flabbergasted. Paula didn't like the idea of renovating the bridge, but she'd just provided an alibi for herself and Mr. Fleece at the time of Mrs. Fenwick's murder. Unless she was lying to create a cover she didn't think I'd check out. If so, was the cover for her benefit or Mr. Fleece's?

I worked the odd talk over in my mind until Cookie arrived in an elf hat shaped like a corkscrew. The little jingle bell on top bounced and tinkled as she walked.

Her green dress and tights were adorable, as if she'd arrived directly from a North Pole workshop. "How do you like my costume?" she asked. "I made it myself. It's got one of those nice swing skirts that look so pretty when ladies twirl." She turned in a small circle to show off her handiwork.

"Very nice." I circled her with a smile. "I always wished I'd learned to sew."

"You should have," she agreed. "I made all my show costumes when I lived in Vegas. I wasn't allowed to touch my casino uniforms, though. They had to be identical to the next girl's. In-house seamstresses made sure we showed off the goods, if you know what I mean, but those were the sixties."

I tried to imagine Cookie in her twenties, strutting across a Las Vegas stage or selling cigarettes in a casino.

"Wait until you see what I made to wear to the Christmas Tree Ball," she said.

"Aw, jeez." I rolled my head over one shoulder and pinched the bridge of my nose between my thumb and forefinger until it hurt. "I forgot about the Christmas Tree Ball."

Her jaw flapped open.

The Christmas Tree Ball was Reindeer Games' annual fund raiser. Sponsors bought and decorated trees. Mom and Dad displayed the finished products inside the massive renovated barn we reserved for events like baby showers, birthday parties, and my wedding reception. Mom decked the barn to the rafters in holiday cheer and used the trees as decoration until they were raffled off, fully decorated, to the lucky winners. A local children's ballet troop performed pieces from *The Nutcracker*. It was all very adorable. Mom always brought in local musicians for after dinner, and prizes were awarded for the most festive attendee costumes. The ball was a huge deal, and I'd completely forgotten about it.

Cookie worked her mouth shut, exchanging shock for confusion. "What are you going to wear?"

"I'll figure something out," I told her. "I'm sure Mom kept all my old costumes. Maybe I can wear one of those. I'm sure with a little updating and embellishments, no one will know it's a repeat from last decade."

Cookie examined her cuticles. "If only you knew someone who could sew."

I hugged her. "Thank you."

"Don't thank me yet. I haven't agreed."

"Please?"

"I'll do it."

Sheriff Gray opened the door and held it for an older couple to pass. He strode inside with his hat pressed to his chest and a peculiar expression on his face. "I forgot to buy a tree, so I came out here to choose one."

I stepped toward him. "Maybe I can help you choose. We have really pretty firs."

He rubbed a hand through his hair and screwed his hat on tight. "I already got one. It's leaning against my truck." His brows worked together. "But it's got a pickle in it. Is that normal?"

I laughed. "It means you win a prize."

He didn't look convinced.

I went around the counter to grab a Hide the Pickle flyer. I slicked it against the counter and made a sweeping motion with my hands. "Voilà."

"Congratulations," Cookie said.

Sheriff Gray puckered up and laughed out loud. "What did I win?"

Cookie looked at her watch and ran behind the counter. "You win a sleigh ride. Doesn't he, Holly?" She shot me a "don't argue" face.

"Sure," I agreed. "Why not?"

"Well then," she said, "I'll take over your post, and you go get him set up with a sleigh."

The sky outside the Hearth window had darkened to ethereal shades of periwinkle and gray. My favorite time of day.

"You know what?" Cookie went on. "Why don't you go with him? Take as long as you like. Relax."

"Um . . ."

Sheriff Gray caught me in his gaze. "Looks like we'll get that evening ride together after all."

I stripped off my apron and threaded tired arms into thick wool-coat sleeves, though I doubted I'd need help staying warm with the sheriff at my side.

Chapter Eighteen

I led the way to our barn with an unnecessary number of butterflies flapping in my tummy, obviously the result of sleep deprivation and not the man I barely knew walking beside me. I pressed a hand discretely to my middle in an effort to eradicate the strange flutter. I hadn't experienced the sensation in a decade, and I preferred to keep it that way.

Twilight had triggered the property's twinkle lights, illuminating our largest trees and outlining the Reindeer Games buildings.

Sheriff Gray moved silently beside me like an overstuffed ninja in his heavy uniform coat and boots. Despite it all, he didn't make a sound. I checked behind us to be sure he made footprints.

"Everything okay?" he asked, watching me from the corner of his eye.

"Yep." I shoved my hands deeper into my pockets. "How's your investigation going?"

He laughed quietly. "We didn't even make it to the barn."

"What?"

"I assumed you brought me out here to prod me for information, but I thought you'd at least wait until we were in the sleigh."

I bristled at the accusation. "I didn't bring you here. Cookie sprung this on me, and I agreed because it was polite."

"Sure." He stepped into the broad cone of light outside the stables and turned to me. "You two didn't plan this at all?"

"No." The hurt and frustration in his eyes set my blood to boil. "You think I'm a schemer? That I plotted to get you alone in a sleigh and prod you for information? If I had questions, why wouldn't I just ask them? Why the sleigh?"

He worked his jaw and averted his eyes.

I glanced at the dimly lit world around us, and his thoughts seemed to project to mine. I scoffed. "You think I dragged you out here to attempt to seduce the details out of you?" My cheeks burned stupidly at the word *seduce*. "I don't know what sort of women you've had in your life, but I'm not like that." I crossed my arms and marched woodenly toward the nearest sleigh.

One of the farmhands acknowledged me with a nod. He climbed into the driver's seat and waited.

I hopped into the back and fanned the blanket over my legs. Hurt and anger had extinguished the butterflies. I folded my arms and debated climbing out and heading home.

The sheriff watched me from a distance, probably thinking the same thing I was.

"Well?" I grumped. He couldn't leave. It was my idea first, and I couldn't leave if he did or it'd look like I only left because he did. "Come on."

A storm brewed in his steady eyes. Behind that blank cop stare, he was mad.

I patted the seat. I wouldn't have Sheriff Gray thinking I was the sort of person to set him up on a sleigh ride for selfish reasons. "Move it, Boston."

Finally, he reached for the sleigh.

I scooted over as far as possible, but there was no way to avoid touching him at the shoulder, hip, and knee. We were bundled for the weather, and the sleigh was meant to be cozy. I crossed my ankles and tried to remember I was mad at him. He sat back and stretched the blanket over his knees.

A moment later, the sleigh began to move, slowly at first, then faster as the horse found a comfortable stride along the path. Icy wind stung my cheeks and nose. I buried my hands beneath the blanket, only to find the sheriff's there. "Sorry."

He smiled. "You sure I was wrong about why you lured me out here?"

I jerked my hands back on top of the blanket. "I did not lure you. Cookie surprised me just as much as you with her offer."

"Then why'd you agree to come?" he asked. "Don't tell me you were being polite. I get the feeling you don't do things you don't want to do too often."

"Why'd *you* come if you thought I had such sinister motives?" I countered.

We locked gazes for a long beat before he looked away.

I couldn't shake the hurt. "Why do you assume the worst about me? You don't even know me."

"It's in the job description." He focused on the dome of darkened sky and galaxy of ancient stars.

Suddenly Sheriff Gray was the second person I'd felt sorry for tonight. "That sounds lonely."

"It can be." He turned back to me with a look of blatant curiosity. "What was it like growing up here?"

I lifted and dropped one shoulder. "Magical."

"You grew up on a Christmas tree farm."

"Yeah." I smiled at the wonder in his voice. "I loved it."

"I bet. Ever have any problems here before this week? Break-ins? Vandalism? Theft?"

"No." I admired the beautiful property. "I always felt safe here."

"What about now?" Shame ruined his handsome face. I'd become afraid for the first time on his watch, and he clearly hated it. So did I.

"Honestly? I've never felt more protected."

The blaze of emotion I'd recognized earlier returned. His gaze fell briefly to my lips before pulling back. "I shouldn't have given you a hard time earlier. I accepted your invitation because I had questions of my own."

"Ah, hypocrisy."

His mouth formed the lazy smile I loved. "Yeah."

"Well, what do you want to know?"

He hesitated, obviously weighing what he would say next. A trait I was learning to hate. "I wondered if you were still asking questions about Mrs. Fenwick's life or death." The look on his face said that wasn't what he'd planned to say, and whatever it was still lingered unspoken.

"Not intentionally," I said.

He cocked a dark eyebrow.

"I spoke with Paula before you got here, but she came to me. She says she has an alibi."

He snorted. "It's not as if the killer is going to admit what he did. Or she," he allowed. "Criminals will say anything."

"She was with Mr. Fleece."

"I know."

I fought the irrational irritation of having to share all my details with him when he clearly didn't do the same. "I saw her sleigh heading home that night, and Mr. Fleece was outside with a bunch of kids and the reindeer, but are we sure neither of them had time to hit Mrs. Fenwick?" I lowered my voice to a whisper, trying to keep our sleigh driver from overhearing too much.

Sheriff Gray leaned impossibly closer. "I'm handling this. Let it go."

I scowled.

"Look," he said, "I've got my fingers on a thread in this case that I think is going to unravel it. So no more asking questions, even if the suspects come to you. This is a small town, and you're already on the killer's radar. If he thinks you're still pushing this . . ." The sheriff stopped to rub a leather glove over his forehead. "Just stop, okay?"

I wiggled closer and tipped my face to his. "Who do you think is the killer?" Scents of cologne and aftershave wafted over me, and I shivered.

"Are you cold?" He tugged our shared blanket higher on my waist.

I shook my head and pressed my lips together. Whatever my body thought was happening, it was wrong. I couldn't be attracted to this man. I still called him Sheriff Gray, for goodness' sake.

"Tell me what you're thinking right now," he said. "You can't keep anymore secrets. It's too dangerous."

I made an idiotic sound.

"I mean it, Holly. What were you thinking just now? You should've seen your face."

"Nothing." My voice hitched, caught in another lie. "Something personal. It had nothing to do with what you were saying, I swear."

He shot me a flat expression. "I'm giving you, possibly, the most important advice of your life, and you're thinking of something unrelated. That's terrific." The sarcasm was thick. I didn't like it.

"That isn't what I said."

"What'd you say?"

"I don't know." I waved my mitten-covered hands. "I was thinking about Whiskers."

"You were thinking about a cat."

"She's doing great," I said, deftly changing the subject to what a good caregiver I was. "Cindy gives her a hard time, but Whiskers handles herself well."

He narrowed his eyes.

A proverbial lightbulb slowly flickered to life. "You were there to feed her that day." I recalled the sheriff at Mrs. Fenwick's house, and an idea popped into mind. "Would you like to keep her?"

"Me? Why? You just said she's doing great with you."

"I know, but it's good for a man to have a cat. They make great companions, and chicks love them."

He laughed.

"She'd be a lot of company for you. Cindy's a brat, but sometimes she's the only person I can talk to."

"You can always talk to me," he said.

"Okay."

"I have to ask," he said, "why do you read *The Count of Monte Cristo*? I've told you why I do, but I have no idea why it appeals to you, and I'd like to."

I released a slow breath, hoping not to sound silly as I confessed the truth. "I liked the strategy and restraint. He was smart. He planned. I admired that the first time I read it, so I read it again. I get something else out of it every time. People think it's only about revenge, but I barely think of it that way. I think it's about a man who set an outrageous goal and nailed it."

Sheriff Gray smiled. "You like smart guys."

"I do."

The barn came back into view, and I worked my coat sleeve up to check my watch. The sleigh ride was typically thirty minutes. It was hard to believe we'd been talking that long already. According to my watch, it had been closer to an hour. The driver must've kept us moving after the usual route was finished. I folded the blanket into squares as we eased to a stop.

Sheriff Gray climbed out and offered me his hand.

I thanked the driver, and he winked. I had a feeling Cookie was behind my impromptu sleigh ride somehow. She'd never offered to cover the Hearth for me before, and she practically jumped behind the counter tonight. She must've known the sheriff was here before he came in to ask about the pickle in his tree.

Sheriff Gray rocked back on his heels. "I'm up for taking Whiskers, but maybe we should ask her what she wants to do."

I smiled. "I guess you'll have to walk me home for that."

We turned up the long path to my parents' house in companionable silence, taking measured strides and dragging the trip out.

"So you knew Ray Griggs in high school?" the sheriff finally asked.

"No." I shook my head and laughed, baffled. "He remembers me, but I swear I've never seen him before this week. His family's hilarious, though. I wish I'd known him then."

"Really?" He looked confused. "He made it sound like you'd been good friends, maybe even dated. He seems to know a lot about you."

"No. Nothing like that. He had a crush, maybe? I don't know. I was a senior. He was a freshman."

"What do you think of him now?"

"As what? A suspect?" Alarm raised the hair on the back of my neck. "Is Ray the lead you're closing in on?" I'd spent too much time with Ray this week for that possibility to make me comfortable.

Sheriff Gray set his jaw. "No. Never mind."

I watched the side of his face as he concentrated on anything other than me. "Are you trying to ask me if I like him?" I guessed, half-joking, half-thankful Ray wasn't the sheriff's suspect as a murderer.

He let his gaze bounce off me. "I was just asking."

I curled my arm beneath his on a whim and tugged him against my side. "If he asks me out and we start dating, will you run a background check for me?"

"I already have," he said dryly.

I laughed because I believed him. "Always looking out for me. I like it." I also liked the feel of his arm twined with mine, so I held onto it as we walked. Another interesting idea came to mind. "Did you run a background check on *me*?"

He shot me an impish grin. "You found the town's first murder victim in forty years. What do you think?"

"I didn't find her!" I protested. "I responded to a screaming woman's plea for help."

The motion light outside my parents' home snapped on, and Dad strode into view. His attention locked immediately on our arms, and Sheriff Gray dropped mine like a hot potato.

"Holly?" Dad asked. "What are you doing?"

"We came to get Whiskers. Sheriff Gray is going to take her home."

Dad gave the sheriff a pointed look before dragging his attention back to me. "Your mother sent me to put the slow cooker on low. Help yourselves if you're hungry. I'm needed at the stables, so lock up when you leave."

"I won't be long," I said. "I promised Mom I'd help with the sleighs tonight."

"I'll let her know." He headed for his truck.

I used my key to let my guest inside.

He watched Dad's truck through the front window until its taillights vanished in the darkness. "I get the feeling he didn't enjoy your dating years."

I tugged my mittens off and turned the lock behind us. "You assume anyone in Mistletoe was brave enough to ask me out."

"No high school sweethearts?"

"I went to prom and met guys at parties, but Dad made it as complicated as possible by hating everyone."

"I can't say I blame him," he said with a smile.

I crossed my arms. "Did you date in high school?"

He barked a hearty laugh. "Oh, yeah."

"Kitty," I called, finished with that conversation. I flipped lights on as I moved through the room.

Cindy lumbered into view outside the kitchen. She looked us over, then walked away.

I grabbed a red tote bag filled with Mom's old copies of *Mistletoe Magazine* and emptied the contents onto her coffee table. "That reminds me—I was reading the holiday edition of that the other night." I pointed to the magazines. "It looks like a lot of people fund their own renovation projects. Do you know who owns the Pine Creek Bridge? We know Mrs. Fenwick wanted it repaired, but I wonder why she didn't insist the owners handle it."

"That bridge is owned by the county," he said. "It became part of the road system in 1955."

I stopped short. "You've been looking into it too." So I *was* on to something.

He tapped the sheriff emblem on his coat.

I made a face and went to gather kibble and the bowls Mom had assigned to Whiskers when she moved in.

Whiskers was in the kitchen standing sentinel before her dinner. Cindy's dishes were upside down, and she was watching Whiskers from the windowsill.

I plucked Whiskers off the floor and dropped her things into my bag. "You're moving again, pretty lady. Looks like you get to be the woman of Sheriff Gray's house." I kissed her head. "Keep an eye on him for me, would ya?"

The sheriff leaned against the doorjamb. "Worried about me?"

I handed him the cat. "Give me a minute to grab her bed. It's just an old pillow I made in high school home ec, but she seems to like it." I darted up the steps and grabbed the lop-sided corduroy oval off my bed.

Sheriff Gray was at the front door when I got back. Whiskers was tucked against his chest in one arm and the bag of cat things hung from his free hand.

I stuffed the pillow into the bag.

"Anything else?" He backed up a step and bumped his hat against the ring of mistletoe hanging from our doorframe. "What the . . ." His blank cop expression turned mischievous. "You make a habit of kissing everyone who comes through the door?"

"No. Mom hung that for Dad. It's not for you."

Sheriff Gray leaned forward until his breath warmed my ear. "I definitely shouldn't be kissing your mom." He straightened with a grin "You've got a lot of land here. If your dad caught me, I doubt anyone would find my body."

I made a completely incoherent noise, trying not to swallow my tongue.

Sheriff Gray pushed the front door open and held it for me to pass. He gave the little greenery with a pretty red bow another look. "You might want to take that down before Ray Griggs stops by again."

I turned my key in the lock. "Why would I want to do that?"

His eyes stretched briefly before falling into a squint.

"I'm joking."

"Hysterical," he deadpanned.

I led the way off the porch.

He unzipped his coat and tucked Whiskers inside until only her fluffy face peeked out at his neck. At the Hearth, he went to his truck, and I went to help at the stables and tried not to think about that blasted mistletoe any longer than absolutely necessary.

Chapter Nineteen

The Christmas Tree Ball was just three days away, and preparations to turn the renovated barn into a winter wonderland were well under way. I stared at the freshly cut blue spruce in front of me, waiting for inspiration to strike. Mom strung lights around the rafters, supported by a motorized ladder contraption not unlike the ones used by utility workers when repairing telephone and cable lines. Dad manned the base, keeping an eye on Mom and guiding the machine as she worked cheerfully overhead. Tough as Dad looked, he feared heights like I feared ducks, and neither of us liked to talk about it.

I circled my spruce, utterly perplexed. Outfitting a few trees for the raffle had always been fun—I'd never lacked ideas in the past. Mom had a brilliant plan to dress her tree with products sold at the Holiday Mouse in an effort to boost sales. I, on the other hand, only had terrible ideas that were guaranteed to lose the unspoken competition. Yes, the raffle was luck of the draw, but there was always one tree everyone wanted most. Ball guests would linger at its side, whispering about how it surpassed the others in creativity and execution. I liked it best when that tree was mine.

I circled the thing again, begging my muse to hit.

"Hello!" Cookie called. She and Caroline strode in my direction, laden with shopping bags and looks of eager anticipation. They split up before reaching me and faced off with the trees on either side of mine. Caroline was on my right and Cookie on my left.

I gave up and sat cross-legged between them as they unpacked and organized their trimmings. "You two look happy."

Caroline beamed. "We just had our first business meeting."

Cookie lined boxes of tinsel and metallic garland on the floor. "She wants to pay me back for the investment, but I don't want her money. If she tries to force it on me, I'm going to have my lawyer make her the sole heir to my estate."

I looked at Caroline.

She puffed air into neat sideswept bangs. "She keeps saying that."

"What do your parents think?" I asked. "They must be glad to see you reaching your goals."

"My parents pretend this isn't happening because it doesn't fit into their plan for my life."

Cookie flung a pinch of tinsel at her tree and shot me a pointed look. "What're you doing to your tree this year, Holly?" An obvious change of subject. "A tribute to American literature? Maine's wildlife? Traditions abroad?"

"No." I huffed. Those were themes I'd already done. "I want to do something new."

"How about mustaches?" she suggested.

Caroline slid a premade sign into the metal stand beside her tree: "Caroline's Christmas Cupcakes." Her fitted Tiffany blue dress was a near-perfect match for her eyes and enhanced the porcelain-doll look she had going on. Her pale-blonde hair hung in ringlets over both shoulders, held back from her face by a wide matching headband. The overall effect was stunning. "Maybe you could do a variation on mustaches," she suggested, "like an American artist in Paris?"

I stuck out my tongue. "Why are people obsessed with Paris?"

Caroline looked as if she'd sucked a lemon. "Because it's Paris."

"I don't get it," I said, turning back to Cookie. "I have a creativity deficit."

Cookie strung white lights around her tree like a professional, hiding the wires among the branches and making the beautiful pine sparkle. "Don't worry. It'll come to you."

I leaned back on my elbows and kicked my feet out in front of me. My jeans were soft and threadbare at the knees from years of wash and wear. My navy-and-brown duck boots were scuffed from the countless cold and wet adventures of a quiet country life.

Caroline's knee-high boots ghosted over the broad wooden floor beams. How she stayed upright in those heels all day, especially in the winter weather, was nothing short of magic. The fact she did it with such grace made me want to clap. She worked methodically from top to bottom, arranging small cupcake ornaments on the higher branches first. The average-sized ornaments went around the center, and giant ones covered the bottom. Every faux cupcake was pale pink or muted white and shimmery as if it had been dusted in sugar before hanging. She strategically attached her business cards to multiple limbs with the help of coordinating clothespins.

"Last but not least," she said, crouching for another reach into her bag, "the perfect finishing touch." She fanned an accordion-pleated tree skirt around the base of her tree. The polka-dotted material was the equivalent of a massive cupcake liner. "What do you think?"

"It's gorgeous," I said.

"I want to eat it," Cookie said.

Caroline uncapped a can of fake snow and shook it. "Why haven't you started yet?" she asked.

"I'm waiting for my muse."

"Well, that'll never happen," she said confidently. "You have to make things happen, not wait around hoping something might happen to you."

I tilted my head back to see all the way to the top of the nine-foot spruce I'd chosen.

Cookie hummed beside me, tossing handfuls of tinsel everywhere. She and Caroline had chosen shorter, fuller trees. Mine looked like an arrow in comparison.

Caroline sashayed closer, stretching a row of wet boot prints in my direction. "Do you need help with the lights?"

"No. I did that much. I just haven't plugged them in. I forgot."

Cookie stopped humming. "She also forgot about the ball until I reminded her last night. She's making me look good."

Caroline squatted next to me. "You've got a lot on your mind. Maybe you just need to get out and clear your head."

She was right. I had plenty of stressful thoughts whirling through my cluttered mind, not the least of which was Sheriff Gray. I whipped my face in Cookie's direction. "Did you plan that sleigh ride for me with Sheriff Gray?"

"What?" Caroline jerked upright and hopped to Cookie's side. Her perfectly sculpted eyebrows were raised halfway to her hairline.

Cookie made wide owl eyes. "Who me?"

"Yeah, you." I pushed onto my feet and braced my hands over my hips. "What did you do that for?"

"I don't know what you're talking about. I only said I'd cover for you if you wanted to go. You're the ones who went scampering off into the night together."

"Oooh," Caroline cooed.

"I didn't scamper," I protested. "I was being polite because you put me on the spot. Then I realized that a sleigh was ready and waiting for us, even though One-Horse Open Sleigh wouldn't officially begin for another hour, and the driver took his sweet time bringing us back."

"That's nice," Cookie said. "I don't know what you're so upset about. It sounds lovely and convenient to me."

"Too convenient." I stared her down. "Don't you think?"

"Nope."

"You sure?"

She scooped her bag off the floor and dug inside. "Nothing can be too convenient. Wait until you're old. You'll see what I mean."

Caroline bounced onto her toes. "You took a romantic evening sleigh ride with Sheriff Gray?" She bit her lip. "Tell me everything. Slowly."

"We. Were. Set. Up." I dragged each word to comply with her request.

She waved her hands. "No. I want details. Tell me about the ride. Did you have to sit close to keep warm?"

"It's a small sleigh."

"Was there a blanket?"

"Yes."

Caroline did some silent clapping. "Did he kiss you?"

"No! Of course not." The dumb mistletoe over Mom's front door flashed through my mind, and my cheeks flared up.

"Liar!" She pointed at my face. "Look at her face," she told Cookie. "Something happened."

Cookie smiled. "You can tell us. We're excellent at keeping secrets."

I refocused on my tree. "There's nothing to tell." A pinch of emotion formed in my chest. Disappointment? Why? I rubbed a hand against the ache. Maybe it was the fruitcake I'd had with my morning coffee.

The fruitcake memory ignited my muse. "Sweets!"

Caroline had the right idea with her tree. The theme should be something I loved. "I'm going to make large versions of my jewelry to decorate with. I'll call it 'Holly's Jolly Jewelry'!" A barrage of images burst into mind. Large mints and candy canes. Gingerbread men and their houses. Gumdrops as jewels in golden rings and lollipops swirled with rhinestones. My tree was going to be the favorite.

"Mom," I called into the air.

She leaned over the railing of her retractable ladder. "Yeah?"

"I'm going to make a run into town for supplies. Do you need anything?"

"No, but Mr. Nettle left his hat when he came for coffee the other day. I put it on top of the refrigerator at home. Will you drop it off to him?"

"Sure." I looked to Caroline and Cookie. "Can I get either of you anything?"

Caroline deflated. "I would've liked at least one juicy detail about that sleigh ride, but I guess a girl can't have everything she wants."

A crazy smile slid over my face. "You want to know what I think of Sheriff Gray? I think he's a nice guy. I think he's a little distrusting and cranky sometimes, but he's very nice and quite handsome. How's that?"

Caroline clutched both hands to her chest. "I'll take it."

Cookie fought a broad grin. "Good. Now get going so you can come back and work. I want to see your finished tree before I have to go home and fix Theodore's dinner." She hung tiny hay bales on the branches of her squatty pine, beside miniature straw hats and figurines that looked a lot like her goat.

I made a trip to Mom's kitchen for Mr. Nettle's hat, then took the first available Reindeer Games truck into town.

The craft store's shelves were as picked over as the toilet paper aisle before a nor'easter. I bought everything I thought might be useful and made plans to locate the remaining items at Reindeer Games somehow. Hopefully a craft closet somewhere on the property had the final few ingredients for a fabulous holiday-jewelry-themed tree.

I paid at the register and loaded bags of ribbon, felt, tacky glue, and foam balls into the truck cab. A powerful electric charge of inspiration ran through my veins. I couldn't wait to get home and get started.

I grabbed Mr. Nettle's fancy gray fedora and locked the truck. I spun the hat on one finger as I moved toward his office building. A little black-and-tan feather fluttered in the wind, anchored in place by the silky hatband. I liked it. It was exactly the sort of hat an olden-time accountant would wear and the polar opposite of anything I'd ever find on Dad's head. Dad wore ball caps from spring until late fall when the weather turned his ears red, then he switched to knitted beanies.

The lights were off at the Historical Society building and Mr. Nettle's office. It was especially dark on the Historical Society's side. I let myself into the foyer and peeped through the windows on the office doors. Security lighting cast an eerie glow on a pile of letters and envelopes inside the door, likely fed through the mail slot in Mrs. Fenwick and Mr. France's absence.

I couldn't help wondering if I'd seen Caleb France moving into Mrs. Fenwick's office the other day or ransacking it. The place had been in substantial disarray. Maybe he'd been looking for something. What? I wished I knew where he was now and why he hadn't called me back. Surely he checked voice mail, wherever he was. Unless I hadn't caught him in the act of changing offices or even ransacking. Maybe he'd been packing his things to leave town after committing murder. Had he fled because I'd confronted him about Mrs. Fenwick? If so, he hadn't gone far because someone continued to harass me in his absence.

Frustrated by more unanswered questions, I turned for the accounting offices across the way, ready to deliver Mr. Nettle's hat and be on my way.

The small waiting room was cheerfully lit but empty. A radio played softly in another room.

I crept to the desk in search of a bell or other means of announcing my arrival. "Hello?" I said aloud. I leaned into the hallway beyond the reception area and rapped my knuckles on the wall. "Mr. Nettle?"

"Coming!" a woman's voice answered.

I took a seat in the waiting area.

Several moments later, a redhead in a wrinkled blouse and skirt arrived. She smoothed a palm over her hair and twisted her clothes until the shirt buttons aligned with her belt buckle. "May I help you?"

I tried not to think of the reason she was a mess but couldn't help myself. I looked away. "I'm just here to drop off Mr. Nettle's hat. He accidentally left it with my parents, and they asked me to return it."

She shuffled in my direction and collected the fedora. "Thank you. I'll see that he gets it."

I chewed my lip. "Thanks. Um . . ." I mentally rearranged the words aching to be free of my mouth. *Do you think Caleb France could be a cold-blooded killer?* I settled for, "Do you know when the Historical Society offices will open again?" *Or where Mr. France may have fled to avoid prosecution?*

"Mr. France should be back before the holiday. Have you met Caleb?" she asked. "He's the one who took over for Margaret after . . . well, you know."

I knew. "Yes. We met once, but I have some follow-up questions about a project I'm working on, and I was hoping to run into him again while I was here. Has he been out of the office long?"

She looked longingly toward the hall where she'd emerged. "I left him a voice mail," I pushed. "I haven't heard back."

"Caleb visits his family in New York this time of year. They rent a cabin in the Catskills and ski, I think." Her words picked up speed. "It's like a big family reunion every winter at Hunter Mountain, then they go back to their lives in progress and celebrate Christmas with their immediate families. You should try back next week."

"Did Caleb have a family in Mistletoe?"

She turned the fedora over in her hands. "I don't think so. He's not married, if that's what you want to know."

"Oh? Do you know him well?" I asked. "Did you know Margaret too?"

Her enthusiasm waned to impatience. I was keeping her from Mr. Nettle, or whomever she'd been canoodling with down the hall. "Sure. You don't work this closely to people and not get to know them. I could probably tell you how they take their coffee."

"Did they get along?"

She hoisted her shoulders. "I think so. They were both highly irritable, if you ask me, but I didn't hear them fight much. I really need to get back to work, if there's nothing else."

"You didn't hear them fight much? But they fought? Did they fight on the day she died?"

"Yeah," she said breathlessly. "I think that's why he took her loss so hard. It messed with him, you know? He even left a little earlier than usual for his ski trip."

Interesting. "Do you know what they were arguing about that day?"

"Money, I suppose. Isn't that why everyone fights?"

Sometimes it was about a yoga instructor.

Sheriff Gray's voice grouched in my head, warning me to knock it off and go home.

"Hello?" Mr. Nettle's voice carried down the hallway. "Sylvia." He dragged the word into several singsong syllables.

The woman's face turned crimson. "I have to go."

I held a finger to my lips, then pointed to the front door with my free hand, indicating I would see myself out. "Thank you," I whispered.

She lifted his hat in her hands. "I'll see that he gets it."

I hurried out the door with no doubt that she would. What I had serious doubts about was whether or not Caleb France was really skiing with his family. I needed to make a few phone calls and confirm he wasn't lurking in Mistletoe to torment me while using his annual family getaway as a cover.

Chapter Twenty

I dropped, half-asleep, onto my bed at crazy o'clock and dragged a pillow over my head. I'd called every lodge in the Catskills looking for Caleb France or his family and come up empty. After that, I'd thrown myself into crafting ornaments and decorating my tree. For hours, I'd thought of nothing but fashioning enormous candy-themed jewelry. It was a welcomed mental break that resulted in dreams of literal sugarplums.

Eventually, my alarm clock forced me out of bed. I dressed in navy leggings and a teal tunic, poured a caffeine breakfast into my travel mug, then went to admire my work. The barn was fully decorated for the ball when I got there. Mom had apparently been up with the sun, finalizing the details. Icicle lights hung from the rafters and lined the displays and tables. Victorian-era Santa statues and vintage-looking village pieces set the stage where a local musician would entertain tonight.

Scarlet carpet ran along the skirts of soon-to-be-raffled trees. The sponsors had come and gone through the evening, adorning their trees before rushing home for dinner or bed. Some had done a great job in a short time; others had repeated their usual boring spiel, creating bland results no wanted to win. But someone would take home the award anyway in the spirit of good sportsmanship.

I approached my finished product with a smile. The previously empty metal sign holder now announced my tree in delightful curlicue script. "Holly's Jolly Jewelry." What had begun as a simple idea at dinnertime had morphed into something fit for a storybook by midnight. I couldn't stop working. Painted Styrofoam balls had become the jewel toppers to enormous rings. Plastic nuggets on fishing line formed royal necklaces fit for a giant princess. Everything I touched seemed to become something more than I'd imagined. I'd ridden the creative high until nearly dawn, and the result was straight out of my childhood dreams, an enchantment belonging somewhere between the North Pole and Candy Land.

Mom approached in my periphery. "It's lovely."

I pressed a palm to my collarbone. "Thank you."

She arched her back and shifted from one socked foot to the other. "I swear this gets harder instead of easier every year. I abandoned my shoes two hours ago."

"Yet you continue to outdo yourself." I dragged my gaze around the gorgeous room. "Everything looks amazing. It feels like we've traveled back in time or maybe into another land. I'm not sure which, but it's breathtaking."

She curtsied. "Exactly the feel I was going for. Your tree is fantastic. I knew you were up late working, but I had no idea you'd manage all this. I should've known you'd come up with something that was over-the-top fun. Your art always made me smile." She approached the spruce with one outstretched arm and ran her fingers over my work. "Beautiful."

Where others had sprayed faux snow, I'd applied glue and a dusting of glitter for an added bit of magic when the twinkle lights went on.

"Your imagination is a true gift," she said. "I always thought you should write children's books."

"That'd be perfect if I could write." I locked my elbow with hers. "Illustrate, maybe, but I could never write."

"Why do you say that?" She craned her neck for a look at me. "You're great with words."

"Well, you've obviously never heard me try to speak, because I'm definitely *not* great with words."

She wiggled free from my arm and fingered my still-damp hair. "I'm so proud of you."

The emotion in her voice raised goose bumps on my arms. "Thanks."

"I would want to be just like you when I grow up," she said, "if it wasn't already too late for me."

I searched her glossy brown eyes. "What's that supposed to mean? Where's this coming from?"

She shrugged. "Nowhere new. I think those things all the time. I just get too busy to say them like I should. You've grown up to be the most marvelous woman I know. You're a great daughter, a wonderful friend, and someone this community can believe in."

A sneaky tear slipped into the corner of my eye. "Jeez. Talk about an ambush," I joked. Mom wasn't the sort to get emotional, and neither was I. Maybe the lack of sleep and abundance of death threats were wearing on us. "I hope you realize that the parts of me you like so much are only that way because of you. It took a strong, patient, happy woman to show me those traits are important."

She hugged me. "I love you."

"I love you too." I batted tear-blurred eyes. I had a few confessions of my own to make. "I'm sorry I never moved home after college and that I didn't visit enough while I was away. It's as if I chose Ben over you, which I never meant to do."

Mom pushed me back by my shoulders and did her best to look stern. "Your father and I have never begrudged you those life experiences. Not for one minute. Children are supposed to grow up and strike out on their own. We wanted that for you. Of course, we'd also hoped that life would lead you back to us one day too, but that's what it's like being a parent. Complicated. Mostly, we just wanted you to be happy." She released me and clutched her hands over her heart. "And it makes me so sad that you aren't."

"Whoa." I pulled her hands apart. "I'm happy."

She wiped tears from her cheeks and laughed. "I meant I'm sorry about Ben."

"I know what you meant, and I'm sorry you spent a ton of money on a wedding that won't happen. Your deposits are gone because I should've been smarter."

"You were in love. *First love.*" She sighed and shook her head. "First love is the worst. Blinding. All encompassing. The sort of thing people fight for long after it's dead."

I laughed. "I guess that's why everyone's online trying to hunt down their high school sweetheart."

"Exactly."

"Not mine," I said. Mine only called when he needed something.

"Well, yours was an idiot." She slapped a hand over her mouth, and her eyes went wide. "I'm so sorry," she mumbled against her palm. "I shouldn't say that out loud."

"It's okay." I laughed. "He kind of was."

Slowly she moved her hands to her sides. "We don't want you to leave after Christmas. Will you stay awhile? Your father and I aren't ready to let you go again just yet."

"Maybe." I looked away. "I don't know. I don't have a job or any savings worth mentioning." I didn't want to be a financial burden on them. They'd already done so much. "I have a lot of things to figure out, but maybe." It was the most I could promise for now.

She dried her eyes and blew out a long breath. "I'll take what I can get, and 'maybe' isn't 'no.'"

She smiled. "Well, I suppose we should get started on the rest of our day. Have you thought about what you're going to wear to the ball?"

I hung my head. "No. I was supposed to figure that out and get in touch with Cookie. She said she'd embellish one of my old costumes for me."

Mom slid an arm across my back and directed me toward the house. "Then let's see what we've got in the attic. Maybe we won't need Cookie. I'm not terrible with a needle."

Unless something drastic had changed, she also wasn't great with one. I'd been teased all through Girl Scouts for the loose threads hanging from my patches. I'd tried to convince the troop that hanging threads were in fashion and that they were the ones who looked silly with their boring perfect stitches. No one believed me. It just gave them something else to tease me about.

"I know you're thinking of the Girl Scouts," Mom said. "I've gotten better since then."

"Oh, yeah?"

"Yeah." She squeezed me against her side as we walked. "I cut the extra threads off now."

"Great."

We slowed at the sight of Dad's work truck speeding up the drive. The vehicle rocked to a stop outside their home, and he jumped out still moving full speed ahead.

"Bud?" Mom called.

He changed direction, rushing toward us instead. "Come on. Hurry up." He grabbed Mom by the hand and towed her up the walk and into the house while I scurried behind.

"Lock the door," he instructed.

"What's wrong?" Mom and I asked in near unison.

He rubbed his forehead and swore.

"Bud?" Mom stroked his coat sleeve. "You're scaring me."

He patted his torso and checked his pockets. "I left my phone in the truck."

I handed him mine. "Here."

He stared at the screen, apparently confounded. My smartphone was a far cry from the ten-year-old flip phone he bought minutes for by the month.

I took the device back carefully. "Who do you want to call?"

Dad raised his panicked eyes to mine. He slid his hands beneath the back of his coat and extracted a large plastic bag from his rear pocket. He handed the bag to Mom. "I need to call the sheriff."

A thousand matches in every length were stuffed into the wrinkled sack.

Mom gasped. "Where did you find these?"

He gripped the back of his neck until his face turned purple.

My hands shook. The little cell phone jiggled in my grip. "Dad?"

"They're everywhere. Scattered through the trees. Around the stables and outbuildings. On the porch at the Hearth. On benches outside Holiday Mouse." His voice was low and gravelly. He turned his gaze to Mom. "It might be time we consider closing up for the season."

I dialed Sheriff Gray, deeply regretting my choice to ask so many questions about Caleb France yesterday.

"Holly?" The sheriff answered on the first ring. "Everything okay?"

"No," I said. "No. Can you come over?"

A door slammed on the other end of the line. "I'm just leaving the pie shop. Where are you?"

"At my parents' house."

"Where are they?"

"Here."

My mind raced with possible suspects and alternate meanings for the possibly spilled matches. Maybe a shopper had a box of matches with a hole in it and left a Hansel and Gretel trail everywhere they went. Maybe this had nothing to do with setting fire to my family's farm.

Dad peeled the phone from my hand, which had gone limp and fallen to my side. He took the call in the kitchen.

Mom and I stared at the bag of matches.

"I'm so sorry," I whispered, but the quavering voice didn't seem like my own. "I did this," I admitted. "I put you in danger."

"No." She dropped the bag on the coffee table and gave me her business face. "The person who did this is desperate to keep their secret. What they've done has nothing to do with you." She pressed cold palms to my flaming cheeks. "Now sit. It sounds like the sheriff is on his way, and he'll get this figured out."

I flopped onto the couch and kept an eye on the front window for signs of a torch-wielding lunatic.

Mom went into hostess mode, and Dad loaded his shotgun.

The sheriff arrived shortly after I'd finished my first cup of tea. Mom was kind enough to use Cookie's special ingredient liberally. As it turned out, peppermint schnapps was just as yummy in Christmas tea as a candy cane, but it made my face tingle.

"Refill?" Mom asked.

"No. Thank you," I said, concentrating on the front window as Sheriff Gray loped up the front steps to our door. I rubbed sweaty palms over my leggings. The schnapps had also successfully loosened the pile of knots in my tummy and unclenched my aching jaw. "He's here."

Mom followed my gaze and opened the door before he could knock.

Sheriff Gray walked inside with a cell phone pressed to one ear. He grunted and nodded before disconnecting. He shook

Mom's hand and stowed the phone in his pocket. "I got here as fast as I could, Mrs. White. Your husband filled me in on the details. I've got deputies on the way. Can I see the matches?"

Mom handed the bag to him.

He slid it into the black shoulder bag I recognized from my last emergency call. "How are you?"

"Shaken," Mom said. "Can I get you something to drink?"

"No, thank you."

She kneaded her hands, growing steadily more anxious with no one to serve. "Do you think this is a real threat? Is it credible? Could it be another empty scare tactic? Should we sleep elsewhere tonight?"

"The deputies and I will assess the situation together and let you know." His cool gaze slid to me. "Sleeping elsewhere would be my suggestion. Though ultimately that's up to you."

Dad marched into view with two steaming mugs and extended one to the sheriff. "Coffee?"

He accepted the offering.

Mom frowned.

The sheriff lowered himself onto the edge of the couch beside me. "Mr. White, I need you to write down everything you told me on the phone."

Dad nodded.

"Have you given anymore thought to closing the farm until this is settled?"

Dad dragged a heavy hand through his hair. "I did, and I can't. Call it pride or stupidity, but I can't bring myself to do it. Reindeer Games has been open through Christmas Eve since my grandpa hung the sign. I'm going to stay here and keep an eye on things. Maybe rent a couple night patrolmen.

But I can't close." He turned an apologetic face toward Mom. "You and Holly should probably get a hotel room in town for a few nights."

She moved to his side. "Don't you dare think for one second I'd leave you at a time like this. My wedding vows said 'for better or worse,' not 'until things get tough.'"

I chewed my shredded thumbnail. "There won't be any available rooms in Mistletoe until after New Year's Day."

The sheriff seemed to mull that over. Thanks to the tour bus business, all inns were full, and he knew it. "You're welcome to stay at my place, if you'd like."

My jaw went slack. I slid my gaze to Dad's darkening face.

Sheriff Gray set his coffee on the side table and clasped his hands in front of him. "I only have one bed, but it's big enough for two ladies." He looked from my face to my dad's. "I could stay here. They could stay there. I can take up one of those night shifts you're hiring out."

Dad's face slowly returned to a normal color.

I would've found the mistake funny if I wasn't in the middle of a stroke. "I think we're all going to stay here." I pinned Dad with my sincerest stare. "No one thinks you're stupid or prideful. This place is family, and families protect one another. I'll take a night shift too."

Mom smiled. "It's settled. I'll put on a fresh pot of coffee."

"Tea." I lifted a finger over my head. "Cookie's recipe."

She winked. "I think I'll make that two. I could use some tea myself."

Dad watched her disappear into the kitchen. "I'll call down to the Moose Lodge and see if anyone wants to earn a little extra holiday cash in exchange for security duty."

"Good." Sheriff Gray moved to the front window and looked out. "You've got a lot of ground, and the plan's not perfect, but it's something. I'll focus my deputies on the buildings and homes. It'd take some effort and a small miracle to get a good tree fire going with all the ice and snow. Plus, another storm's coming tonight."

He moved back to my side and picked up his coffee. He lingered in my personal space, apparently waiting for me to look up. He smiled when I finally did. "You made it one whole day without an emergency. Yesterday was quiet. Peaceful. I got a lot done. You?"

"Yep. Have you had a chance to talk to Mr. Fleece or Paula?" Of all the people I'd spoken with this week, Fleece and Paula were the only two still angry with a dead woman. The fact they used one another as their alibi only made me wonder further about both of them.

He dropped into a squat and caught me in his keen gaze. "I have. Like I told you before, the case is progressing well—solidly and in good time. You need to let me take it from here."

"Sure thing. Think you can finish up before the lunatic burns down my parents' farm?"

His eyes crinkled at the corner for a moment. "Want to fill me in on what you were up to while I was enjoying the quiet yesterday?"

I bit my lip. "I might have peeked in Caleb France's office window and told the secretary next door I had some questions for him."

Sheriff Gray sucked his teeth and glared. "Start from the beginning."

I cast a look over my shoulder, willing Mom to move a little faster. If I was going to unload everything I'd learned from my trip to return Mr. Nettle's fedora and the follow-up phone calls I'd made—after promising to let him handle this—I was going to need her to supersize that special tea.

Chapter Twenty-One

Despite the terrifying threats and my thoroughly shaken family, Reindeer Games' Christmas Tree Ball went on as planned. Mom called her usual crew of girlfriends to assist with crowd control and execution of the event. They divided the night into shifts and assigned themselves to the refreshment booths and raffle ticket sales. Dad rallied members of the local Moose Lodge and every spare farmhand to keep trash cans empty and the floor clear of snow. They were also prepared to load raffled trees into the winner's vehicles or use a company truck for immediate delivery if needed. Sheriff Gray had his deputies on patrol outside the barn and throughout the property. I just had to show up looking less paranoid than I felt. So far, I was the only one failing at her duty.

It didn't help that I'd spent half the night drafting suspect lists in an old notebook found in my high school backpack. I'd drawn hasty columns over the faded blue lines and scribbled the names of our neighbors and friends until three pages were full. I'd started with people who were on the property when the tree markers had arrived at the guesthouse. Then I listed anyone who could've navigated a storm strong enough to close the farm in an effort to freeze me to death. I ruled out the elderly and weak. The killer was capable of transporting a pile of three-foot wooden stakes quickly enough to go unnoticed. I counted out the short.

In the end, I didn't have a suspect list as much as a general profile. Whoever threatened me was local and knew the farm well. He or she had probably visited on many occasions and was likely a man. Someone hearty and tall enough to maneuver those stakes without leaving drag marks on the ground. Once again, Paula and Mr. Fleece came to mind. If they'd worked together, they would have all the advantages, including alibis, access, and knowledge. Hopefully, whoever had planted the matchsticks wouldn't make good on the threat tonight. With two hundred guests at the ball, setting fire to the barn would put innocent lives in danger, and even if no one was harmed, the soot left on Reindeer Games' reputation would reach far into our business future.

My growing paranoia was powered by three hours of sleep and an astronomic amount of fear-fueled emotions. Inconceivably, no one seemed to notice.

The community had taken this year's ball seriously and come dressed to impress. The costume contest was sure to be a hoot. There were angels and snowmen, elves and Sugar Plum Fairies. My parents were Santa and Mrs. Clause for the thirty-second year in a row, but there were plenty of doppelgängers afoot.

I ladled punch into plastic cups while I tallied the worst possible things that could happen.

A line of silver-haired women in matching jingle bell cardigans stopped at my table. The shortest of the four peered into one of my lidded Crock-Pots. "Is that cocoa?"

"It is," I said. "It's peppermint bliss, and there's at least a metric ton of melted chocolate in there." I lifted the lid to let the sweet sting of mint into the air. "This one"—I opened the second crock—"is called salted caramel Christmas."

Their lips parted, and their eyelids fluttered.

"Would you like to try one?" I asked.

The four women pointed in two different directions. Half for salted caramel and half for peppermint mocha. I filled disposable cups and passed them to the women. "Have you had a chance to look at the sponsored trees yet?" I pointed to the red-carpet lineup along the far wall. "You can purchase raffle tickets for a chance to win."

"Oh, yes," they responded with unexpected enthusiasm.

The group's spokeswoman snapped a lid onto her cup and inhaled the steam rising through the air hole. "I want the one with the pickle in it. It reminds me of home."

I scrunched my nose. "A pickle?" Hadn't Dad vetted the trees before setting them into the stands to be decorated?

One of the ladies wiped a chocolate mustache from her upper lip. "We all have favorites."

"Which is your favorite?" I asked.

"Holly's Jolly Jewelry is pretty good," the woman said.

The short lady stretched her hand in the opposite direction of my tree. "I still like the one on the end. I've never been to Boston, but the trip is on my bucket list."

I squinted in the direction she'd pointed. *Did she say Boston?* "Excuse me," I said with a sugary smile. "I don't mean to run off, but I'd love to get a look at that tree. I don't believe I've had the pleasure." I marched painfully forward on the tiny kitten heels of eighty-year-old black lace-up dress boots. The bustle on my backside shimmied with each purposeful stride.

Mom and I had hit the jackpot when we'd opened an old steamer crate in the attic. One of my female ancestors had kept fashionable pieces from a dozen different eras, and I'd chosen a Victorian gown to match Mom's ball decor. I felt enchant-ing in the ensemble as long as I was standing still and ridicu-lous anytime I had to move. The pale-green dress was fitted in the sleeves, bust, and waist, then it puffed out behind me and bing-bonged along as I tried to stay upright on the most uncomfortable boots ever made. It was no wonder Victorian woman carried parasols. They probably used them for balance.

I stopped in front of a busted pine that only a cartoon boy could love. The sign beside it had the large outline of a police shield with the words "Boston Blue, Through and Through" typed on it. I couldn't imagine Sheriff Gray decorating a raffle tree, but who else would have chosen this theme? Tiny rep-lica handcuffs hung from the limbs while blue-and-white lights performed a peppy chase through the sparse and ragged branches. I poked a plastic police badge with my fingertip and smiled. Felt police hats dangled beside little nightsticks to fin-ish off the manly display.

"What do you think?" a man's voice asked.

I jumped back as Mr. Nettle moved into view. "It's one of a kind," I said, trying to catch my breath. "The tree skirt even has an American flag on it. I've never seen that before."

"These all look pretty good to me," he said. "My tree is only about yay big." He mimed a couple feet of space with his hands. "It comes out of the box fully decorated and goes back in one piece when I'm done with it."

"Clever." And a little sad, I thought. Bachelorhood at Christmas must be odd, or at least like nothing I could relate to. The concept brought Sheriff Gray back to mind. Who would he spend the day with on Christmas? His family and friends were in Boston, and he couldn't leave here until the potential pyromaniac was found.

"How are you holding up?" Mr. Nettle asked. "Tomorrow was supposed to be the big day, yeah?"

"Yeah." *The day I was supposed to be married.*

The barn door opened, and a group of people in fancy duds lined up to exchange tickets for passage into the formally dressed barn. Thick white tufts of snow floated gently to the ground behind them. Mr. Fleece led his reindeer through the snow toward their stables. Time for dinner, brushing, and bed, I supposed. Mr. Fleece turned his face toward the barn's interior, and his eyes caught mine. He kept me in his line of sight until the barn door was pulled shut between us.

Ice slid into my pointy black boots.

"Are you feeling okay?" Mr. Nettle asked. "You look peaked."

I forced a tight smile. How could I be feeling okay when I was surrounded by murder suspects? "I'm fine. I was wondering, though—do you know if Mr. France has returned to work? I stopped at the Historical Society while I was in the building to return your hat, but the lights were out. I'd hoped to talk to him soon."

"I don't recall seeing him in the office today, but I was in and out all afternoon, so we may have missed one another. This week is always chaos for me, running errands and gearing up for the extended closing. We won't be open from Christmas until New Year's." He suddenly looked alarmed. "Not that I'm unreachable during that time. I'm always available by phone or e-mail. I just close the office because we never have any appointments at that time and it saves on overhead."

"Of course," I said.

He wiggled his mustache. "I thought you didn't care for Mr. France. You said he was grouchy when you met before."

I forced my mouth shut. This wasn't the time or place for another inquisition, and Sheriff Gray was bound to hear about it and kill me himself. "He was. You know what? It's nothing. Forget I asked."

"I don't mind passing along word that you're looking for him. I'm sure he's just busy. There's so much going on this time of year."

"No. Really. Don't worry about it." I averted my eyes and bopped my head to the tune of a lively string band.

Mr. Nettle turned his body until we were shoulder to shoulder. "Your event has drawn a good crowd tonight. It's a testimony. The farm has done very well considering the blow it took last week. This place loves to persevere."

I inched away from him, haunted by my list of possible killers. "It's a dash of luck and a truckload of determination from the family, I think. The Whites are hardheaded that way."

"Don't I know it." He clapped me on the shoulder and walked away.

I watched with rapt curiosity as he moseyed into the crowd. Was it paranoia, or was there a dual meaning behind his words?

Mr. Nettle stopped several yards away, near the woman from his office. She smiled, and he hugged her.

This round goes to paranoia.

I went back to my drink station.

Ray Griggs stood behind my table looking like a *GQ* ad in tan dress slacks and a white formal shirt. He was ladling punch for a little ballerina. "There you are," he said to me. "I thought I missed you."

"Here I am," I said, making goofy jazz hands.

He handed the cup to the little girl. "Merry Christmas, young one."

I eased into the space beside him. "Thanks for stepping in. You didn't have to, but it's nice."

"It's no problem." He rearranged the array of waiting cups. "Your mom told me you were here, so when you weren't, I figured you'd be back. Where'd you go?"

"I was checking out the tree competition."

Ray gave the line of decorated trees a weird look. "I thought it was a raffle."

"Sure, for the people buying raffle tickets, but the people who decorated the trees probably want theirs to be the favorite."

He smiled. "Did you decorate a tree?"

I waved to a baby in a passing stroller. "Merry Christmas."

Ray chuckled. "You did. And you want to be the favorite."

240

I shot him a goofy smile. "It's so stupid, right?"

"No way. Which one is yours?"

"There." I pointed. "It's covered in giant candy rings and necklaces."

"Cute."

I turned narrowed eyes on him. "You think it's *cute*?"

"Sexy?" he guessed.

"No!" I laughed. "Whimsical. Fantastical. A sheer delight."

"Wow." He whistled the sound of a falling missile. "You're humbler than I remembered from high school. I don't think *fantastical* is a word."

I pushed his arm. "It is a word, Mr. Reporter. You're going to have to expand your vocabulary."

"Words are hard."

I laughed again. "I just told my mom the same thing." I reached under the table and grabbed my thermos.

"Liquor?" he guessed.

"No. It's coffee. I love the hot chocolate, but if I keep drinking it, I'm going to start looking like the Pillsbury Doughboy. How's your article coming along? Find an angle that will get you a byline?"

"Not yet, but I've got a new strategy."

"Yeah? What's that?"

He dipped his head and moved in closer to keep whatever he was about to say between us. "I'm going to follow the sheriff. He's chasing leads. Pulling reports. Talking to everyone. I'll stay close to him, and when he makes the arrest on Fenwick's killer, I'll be on the scene. The first reporter with the scoop. The paper will have to run my story."

I suspected Sheriff Gray would spot him and threaten him with obstruction long before his plan unfolded, but at least he had a plan. I unscrewed the lid and poured a cup.

Ray tapped my bustle. "What is this thing?" He hit it again like a bongo drum.

"Hey!" I spun around, swinging it out of his reach. "Stop that."

He circled me, reaching for it. "My word. What do you keep in there?"

I swung away. "Stop." I swatted his hand and tried not to choke on my coffee. "It's a bustle, and it's none of your business what's in there."

He craned his neck. "It's fascinating. Can you sit on it?"

"No, you don't sit on it."

"Is it like one of those cushions that sports fans take to football games so their bottoms won't get cold or fall asleep on the bleachers?"

"No!" I laughed. "Bustles were a fashion trend during the eighteen hundreds. I wanted to coordinate my costume with all these Victorian decorations."

Ray examined me from head to toe, lingering his gaze in a few key places and making me mildly uncomfortable. "It looks new." He swept a finger across the snow-white fur outlining my cuffs. Cookie had sewn the accents along my neckline and hem as well.

"The trim is new. The dress is old. I'm not sure how old. I think it was a costume for someone else. There's no way it lasted over a hundred years in our attic without falling apart."

"What I'm taking away from this is that you want to win the costume contest and have the favorite tree."

"I never said either of those things." Though who wouldn't want them?

"Greedy." He pinched the end of his Rudolph-themed tie, and a little red light blinked on the reindeer's nose. "Does this count as a costume?"

"No." I finished my coffee and refilled the cup. "Are your mom and aunts here tonight?"

"Yeah. They're talking with your mom."

I scanned the crowded wonderland with a fresh dose of nerves. She'd specifically mentioned thinking I looked happy at bingo with Ray. "I should go say hello."

"Sure. I'll handle the hot and cold libation operation," he said, filling and setting another cup among the selection already waiting to be chosen.

"You don't have to," I said. "You can come with me."

He pulled his phone from his pocket and looked at the screen. "Hang on."

I hadn't heard the device make a sound. Not even the little buzz created by a cell phone set to vibrate. Was the incoming call strangely coincidental? Was there really a call at all? Did he have a reason to avoid chatting with me and his mom again?

He pressed the phone to his chest. "Looks like I might get that byline after all, White." He hastened toward the exit at a jog, one thumb raised overhead.

He was the second man to leave me without a good-bye tonight. I was tempted to check my antiperspirant.

I set a fresh pile of disposal cups between the Crock-Pots and erected my handmade "Be Back Soon. Please Help Yourself" sign. I needed to catch Mom before she said something that might be misconstrued by Ray's mother as encouragement for her son's flirting and passed on to Ray. I didn't have time for that. My head was boggled enough without a mother-driven romance.

I crossed the room at a clip, bustle bobbing at my back.

Mom lit up when she noticed me. "Holly! We were just talking about you." Her bright-red dress and rosy cheeks made her look more like Mrs. Clause than any drawing or photograph I'd ever seen in a book. Her sweet, selfless disposition made it hard to believe she wasn't something more than a mother to one grown child. In a way, I supposed the whole town was in her care. She cooked for everyone who was sick or injured, was newly married, or had just had a baby. She led a book club, ran the Hearth, and stayed at the ready in case anyone she knew needed help.

I waved to the trio of Ray's family members. "Nice to see you all again." I flinched as a strange sensation crawled over my skin. Someone was watching me. I turned in every direction but found no one. The wave of paranoia was strong enough to knock me off my aching feet. Mr. Nettle had left me abruptly. Ray had jogged off. Mr. Fleece had stared me down from thirty yards away. Was I imagining it, or were all the men I knew behaving squirrely tonight?

"Hon?" Mom set her fingers on my wrist. "You look flushed. Maybe you should sit down for a while."

I pressed my hands to my ribs. The corset, which hadn't given me much trouble up to that point, suddenly seemed to squeeze the air from my lungs. "I could probably use something cold to drink. Ice water. Maybe punch." I ran the back of one hand over my forehead. "Have you spoken to anyone working outside?" I asked Mom, using a perkier voice than I'd thought I could muster. "No one found wandering, I hope?"

She glanced at Ray's family. "Nope."

Ray's mom made a strained smiled. "Your dress is lovely, Holly."

"Thank you." I fanned my face as another blast of anxiety and heat blew over me. "Maybe I should sit down."

Mom led me to an open bench near a stone planter of plastic poinsettias. "Do you want me to get you anything or walk you home?" she asked.

I pulled in deep lungfuls of air, concentrating on the sounds of my breath and trying desperately to block the barrage of scary thoughts swarming my mind. "I'm okay," I told Mom. *The barn will not explode into flames. I won't be the reason for two hundred deaths. Mr. Nettle, Mr. Fleece, and Ray are the same people they were a week ago. They are not out to kill me.* I rolled my shoulders back and pulled myself together. There was plenty of time for a proper breakdown later. For now, I had a cocoa stand to manage.

Mom lingered, clearly unsure if she should leave me.

I was safe inside the barn. Whoever wanted to kill me was probably planning a sneak attack when I was alone and at my most vulnerable.

I wiggled my phone from the pouch attached to my gown and dialed. "I'm going to check in with Sheriff Gray," I said. "I'll feel better once I get an update that things are quiet out there."

Mom squeezed my hand. "If you're sure." She headed back into the mix of guests.

"Holly?" The sheriff's voice boomed in my ear.

I started. I'd almost forgotten I'd sent the call. "Hi. I'm just checking in."

His breath rattled the speaker. "Thank goodness. I thought something might've happened."

"No." I pushed onto my feet and pointed myself toward the drink station. "Things are good in here. Everything okay out there?"

"Quiet as a mouse," he said. "I've got a deputy circling the barn every few minutes and two others keeping watch on your house and the stores. I'm making rounds to check on them. We've got it covered, so you can relax."

"Good." I slowed at the drink table and sucked down a glass of punch. "I was feeling a little panicky. I think I just needed to hear that things are okay."

"Feeling better now?"

"Yeah. Sorry to bother you." I dropped my empty cup in the trash. "You know, if you get cold or hungry out there, we have an assortment of hot drinks and cookies in here."

"I'll keep that in mind." There was a smile in his voice that spread to my face.

The little ballerina Ray had helped earlier ran back to the table. She lifted the thermos cup.

"Oh." I waved to her. "That's mine. You don't want that."

She looked into the little cup and made a disgusted face. "Ew. Gross." She tossed the drink onto the table and ran away.

I jumped back to avoid the splash. "Whoa!"

"What happened?" Sheriff Gray's voice snapped in my ear.

I lifted a finger to the filthy puddle of coffee racing toward a village of prepoured punch cups. Four coffee-soaked matches rode the ugly brown current in my direction.

Chapter Twenty-Two

Christmas Eve came in, appropriately, with a storm. Wind whistled around the old farmhouse windows all night long, adding to the edge I was already feeling. By dawn we had another four inches of precipitation, but the weatherman predicted a high of twenty. The late-night blizzard and early morning rush to clear roads would have been a nightmare for my wedding, but it was perfect for the final Reindeer Game of the season. The annual Christmas Eve Snowball Roll.

I peeled my eyes open, unsure I could muster an emotion anywhere near enthusiasm, but I was determined to give it the old White try. I swung my legs off the couch, careful not to wake Mom. We'd slept in her living room, fully dressed and curled against the armrests in either direction. Dad had kept watch in the recliner until his eyelids gave up their duty. Sheriff Gray stayed in the kitchen, serving coffee to deputies as they arrived, checked in, or completed their shifts. I rubbed my surely puffy face and shuffled in the general direction of my morning brew, eyes squinted, mind scrambled. I huffed against one palm to test my breath. *Not good.*

The sheriff poured a mug of liquid pep and extended it in my direction. His hat was on the counter and his hair was mussed. He'd removed his heavy sheriff jacket and button-down uniform shirt since I'd seen him last and hung both over the back of a kitchen chair. "How'd you sleep?"

I dragged my gaze away from the dark-gray T-shirt stretched over his broad chest and accepted the coffee. "Good." I tried not to think about my own ensemble. I'd had the sweat pants since college, and the cat on my long-sleeve T-shirt wore a Santa hat and chased a ball of twinkle lights. The caption beneath him was "Meow-y Christmas!"

Sheriff Gray pulled out a chair and motioned for me to have a seat before sitting across from me. "It was quiet through the night. Nothing to report beyond the matches in your coffee."

I gave my cup a long look. "If everything's quiet, then what's wrong?" I asked. "Please don't say 'nothing'; just tell me the truth."

"Truth is I've been sitting here all night thinking about this case. I haven't had to give many things this much thought since I came to your town." He tapped his finger against the worn wooden tabletop. "I almost miss it."

"And?" I prompted. Surely that wasn't the end of his answer.

He kicked back in his chair and hooked one elbow over the rungs of the backrest. "We didn't see or hear anything unusual during the ball, not even when someone was dropping those matches into your coffee. The whole thing was very stealthy.

Very undercover. Contrived. I can't help thinking this is sheer psychological terrorism and not a valid threat." He lifted a palm off his lap. "We're still treating it as a threat. I just can't stop thinking that we've seen a lot of warnings and no action. Seems like the culprit is attempting to keep you quiet without getting his hands dirty again. That could be a good thing."

I let the words simmer a minute. "You think whoever is behind the threats would rather I just shut up. In other words, the killer's unlikely to act unless I force his hand." I liked that idea more than the one tumbling around my head. In my version, I was being stalked by a sadistic lunatic who delighted in my continued state of terror.

"I'm not saying this is someone to play with, only that whoever it is has been slow to act and quick to threaten. You should never underestimate the capacity of a killer. This person has a lot to lose."

"And people generally prefer to get away with murder," I said.

Sheriff Gray fought a small smile. "Yes. The good news is that I don't think we're dealing with a seasoned villain. Mrs. Fenwick's death was most likely a crime of passion and opportunity. Now someone's trying to put that night in their past, but you're making it very difficult to reach their goal."

"What about you?" I asked. "The town sheriff must be making the same trouble I am. More, probably. Any death threats coming your way?"

"No." His smile spread, and he rubbed a hand over his mouth. "Seems all your shenanigans have kept the criminal's attention. Aside from running to your newest crime scene every few days, I've had ample opportunity to pursue my leads."

I finished my coffee and checked the bottom of my mug for matchsticks. Safe, I went back to waiting impatiently for him to expound, which he didn't. "And?" I fussed. "Don't people have conversations in Boston? Is the concept new to you, or do you intentionally leave me hanging at the worst possible moments?"

He slid away from the table and stretched to his full height with a yawn. "Usually the second one. Can I get you a refill?"

"No. I've got to get ready for the Snowball Roll." And apparently, he had no intentions of expounding on all those leads he was allegedly chasing. "I saw you questioning Ray last night, but he didn't do this."

"He was alone at the booth with your thermos immediately before the incident. Plus, he's been acting fishy. Lurking around everywhere I go."

I made a show of rolling my eyes. "It wasn't him. I saw Mr. Fleece outside the barn not too long before I found the matches. He stared at me. It was weird."

"He was with the other farmhands. I spoke with all of them. Before you ask, Paula was at home."

"Can she prove that?" I asked.

"Maybe. She says she was on the phone. I'm working to verify that, but it will take a couple days." He refilled his mug with a quizzical expression. "I saw the Snowball Roll advertised on the flyers. I assume it's what it sounds like? A race to see who can roll a snowball the fastest?"

"Wrong." I rested my elbows on the table and dropped my chin into waiting palms. "You've been in Mistletoe six months and you haven't heard about the Snowball Roll? Do you ever talk to anyone besides the pie shop waitress?"

He didn't answer.

"Well, you're in for a treat. This is my event." I cracked my knuckles and made a semidramatic exit from the kitchen, then slunk upstairs feeling the weight of a night on a couch shared with my mother. I stood under a hot shower until my knotted-up muscles stopped aching and my fingertips were wrinkled unrecognizably. Then I slowly turned the water temperature down until the shock woke my brain.

I slid into a warm, comfy sweater and pants fit for chasing a snowball. If I couldn't feel human on too little sleep and too much stress, I could at least play the role. I curled my hair into something feminine and drove a gloss stick around my lips. For good measure, I even swiped mascara on my stumpy lashes. The reflection in my mirror looked nothing like I felt. Voilà. The miracle of makeup.

I flipped my ringing phone over and spun it around for a look at the caller ID. I didn't recognize the number. "Merry Christmas," I answered. "This is Holly."

"Ms. White, this is Caleb France returning your call."

I pushed back on my little cushioned seat at the vanity. "Mr. France! Thank you so much for getting back to me."

"I wouldn't have called on Christmas Eve, but your message seemed urgent, and I can make this short. I can't help you. Your questions were all based on bad information."

"What do you mean?"

"For starters, we didn't get the mill grant. We didn't start any work there because we weren't awarded the money, and we didn't submit a grant proposal for the covered bridge before the mill because the mill was in greater need."

"But . . ." I squinted at my reflection in the little oval mirror. "I saw photos of the mill on the HPS website."

"Photos were part of the application process."

"Why would they post pictures of a project they weren't backing?" To make it look like they'd completed all those projects? If so, how many of the pictures in their digital gallery had actually gotten funds?

"I can't say. I wasn't in contact with HPS."

I had been, and they'd given me another story completely. "An HPS representative told me the grant was awarded. Why would she lie?"

There was a long pause before he answered. "I don't know, and that's a really interesting question. Maybe there's something in it for them? I'll see if I can get more information on this next week."

"Thank you." This was the kind of cooperation I'd been hoping for. "Will you let me know what you find out?"

"I suppose. Give me at least a week. I don't expect a company that's up to something to have the answers I'm looking for right away."

"Okay. Thank you." I smiled against the receiver. "Merry Christmas, Mr. France."

"Ms. White?" he said before I could disconnect the call.

"Yes?"

"I want you to know you were right about something."

"I was?"

"I shouldn't have piled Fenwick's things up like trash. You'd probably like to know that a member of her extended family stopped by yesterday and caught me checking the messages. I told him he was welcome to anything of hers he wanted. All he took were the photos, but he seemed glad for them."

"That was very nice of you." I tapped one finger against my knee, still hung up on why the HPS granted money to the mill but Caleb France didn't know about it. What happened if the HPS board granted the money but the check was sniped? Who was accountable? How would anyone know?

A slow tremor played over my hands. Poor Mrs. Fenwick might've had these same questions. Could that be the reason she was dead? Did someone on the other end of the equation keep the funds? Had Mrs. Fenwick discovered the crime? Had a member of the HPS team made an early trip to Mistletoe to shut her up? No. I backpedaled. HPS accounting would know if the grant check was cashed. That could be traced.

"Like I said"—Mr. France's voice registered through my racing thoughts—"stop into the office at the end of next week, and I'll let you know what I hear. If I hear anything."

"Thank you."

We ended the call, and I stuffed the phone into my back pocket. I liked an HPS affiliate for the crime, but why would they still be in Mistletoe haunting me? It seemed like a visiting murderer would've taken the next ride out of town, especially at Christmas. Also, how did I know Caleb France was telling me the truth?

I tugged my favorite boots on and let the smell of bacon pull me down the steps. I parked my backside in a kitchen chair and stole a slice of bacon from the pile on the table.

Mom was alone and happy as could be.

"Good morning," I said when she came bebopping past.

"Morning, hon." She hummed her way through the kitchen flipping pancakes and pulling crispy bacon from a bubbling pan. "Merry Christmas." She tossed a wink in my direction. "I know someone tried to cast another shadow over our holiday last night, but I can't help myself. It's Christmas Eve, and I swear I can feel the joy in my bones. There's so much to be thankful for. Our baby girl has come home. We're together again, all happy and healthy and well. It's going to take a lot to bring me down today."

"I think you cooked happiness right into the bacon," I said, biting into another slice.

"I added maple syrup to the pan."

I stifled a satisfied moan.

She set a short stack of pancakes in front of me. "Don't forget the pancakes." She pushed a decorative basket in my direction. "I've got three kinds of syrup if you aren't in the mood for maple."

The basket held a shaker of chocolate chips and two small bowls, one with fresh diced apples and another with brown sugar and a spoon. "Can you think of anything else?"

I ladled the brown sugar over my short stack. "Not unless you can tell me why I ever left home."

"Hormones. A search for yourself. Rite of passage. That sort of thing." Mom snapped her fingers. "Whipped cream." She tugged the refrigerator door open and shook a can with gusto. "There." She made a fluffy white funnel on top of my breakfast. "Now that looks good."

"Truth." I pressed the tines of my fork into the soft, buttery layers and lifted them in her direction. "Have some."

Mom rubbed her hands in the fabric of her apron, then cranked the burners on the stove off. She joined me at the table with another plate of bacon. "Don't mind if I do."

"Where are Dad and Sheriff Gray?" I asked. The house was strangely empty without them.

"Gone to set up at the Snowball Roll. Don't worry, they left a deputy on the porch, and I fed them all while you were in the shower." She eyeballed my boat-neck sweater. "Cute top."

"Thanks." I stuffed another bite between my lips and smiled as I chewed. "Either your happiness is contagious or you really did fry it into this bacon."

"Nonsense. You're a White. This is Christmas. Of course you feel the thrill of it. How could you not?"

I hadn't for years. I set my bacon aside and rested one hand on Mom's arm. "Thank you for always taking care of me no matter what."

Mom tipped her head and pursed her lips. "Aw, sweetie." She stroked a stray hair off my cheek with soft dimpled hands. "That's what mothers do."

We cleaned up after breakfast and walked to Spruce Knob together. The tree-barren hillside was used for many things over the years, but the Snowball Roll was my favorite.

I used to race my friends down the hill on plastic sleds as a kid. We'd even had a few community sled challenges over the years, but nothing got Mistletoe excited like the Snowball Roll. I think the tradition behind it was the biggest draw. People in historic towns loved to be part of history, and locals had been chasing their balls down our hill since the early twentieth century.

My great-grandfather held the first event nearly seven decades back when Reindeer Games was still a small and floundering tree farm. The enthusiasm it drew today was a direct result of his dedication to local outreach all those years ago. Grandpa White grew the business to a thriving success when it was bequeathed to him years later, but it was his father who'd made Reindeer Games a real part of our community.

I smiled brightly as we walked, refusing to give my secret tormentor the satisfaction of knowing how much he was getting to me. I also didn't want anyone oblivious to my recent threats to think I was upset about my canceled wedding, so I put my chin up and my shoulders back.

Unfortunately, my best efforts were under attack by the elements. Cold December winds stung my cheeks and knocked curls into my face. I peeled freshly styled locks from my lips with woolen mittens that seemed to deliver more hair than they removed. My semifashionable outfit was hidden beneath a puffy, knee-length down coat. A thick knitted scarf buried half my face, and a matching hat pressed bouncy brown locks to my ears. Hard to feel cute when I looked like the kid from *A Christmas Story*.

A few more steps and the low roar of a crowd arrived on the heels of extraloud Christmas tunes piped through massive outdoor speakers. Mom and I exited the narrow treelined path from her house to the site a moment later.

"Holy hotcakes," I gasped as the scene took shape. People in brightly colored snow gear lined the broad hill on both sides. Food vendors and crowded tables filled the space at the bottom. Two winding lines extended from the area marked as registration. "It looks like the winter Olympics."

Mom smiled sweetly at the controlled chaos before us. "This has become a town favorite the last few years. More popular than all our other games combined."

"Do the people know they're freezing their bottoms off on Christmas Eve to see a bunch of silly tradition-loving yo-yos roll a snowball two hundred yards?"

"Yep."

I moseyed along at her side in awe of the spectacle my favorite event had become.

We found Dad in the thick of the food congestion, where he'd nestled a circle of logoed camping chairs between the funnel cake trailer and a steak on a stick vendor. It was a brilliant strategy, really. The trucks were excellent food choices and doubled as barriers against the frigid wind. As an added bonus, we were engulfed in the mouth-watering scents being expelled from both as they cooked.

I only lasted a few minutes in my assigned seat beside Dad. The crowd had me too pumped up to sit around and watch. "I'm going to register." I kissed his cheek and got in line behind a man dressed like an Olympic bobsledder. I hadn't been part of the Snowball Roll in years, but it was high time I changed that.

"Next!" The middle-aged woman seated at the registration table gave me a waiver of liability. Her black-and-white coat and hat were sparkly. Her personality was not. "Read it carefully and sign at the *X*," she directed in a monotone. I complied, and she drew a check mark in the corner. "You're in lane one. Stay in lane one." She peeled the back off a three-by-five-inch sticker with a large number one on it. "Lane one," she repeated, rubbing the sticker securely onto my sleeve.

My upper body shook with her efforts. "I'm sorry. Which lane?"

She shot me a droll expression and let go of my arm. "Go around the crowd to the top. Don't climb through the race area to get to the starting line. We don't want the snow being tromped through before the event begins. It ruins the pictures."

"Gotcha. Any last advice?" I ventured. She clearly had no idea that I'd won this event six times.

"Yeah. Don't fall." She blinked stoic eyes. "You'll start a pileup, and then we'll have to call the volunteer EMTs again. It's Christmas Eve. They deserve the day off, don't you think?"

I laughed.

She didn't.

"Sorry. Right. No falling." I tucked that in my hat for later. Mom hadn't told me anything about people pileups. I stepped aside to let the next contestant register.

"Sheriff Gray." I perked. "What are you doing in this line?"

He frowned at the lady briskly sealing a nametag to his coat sleeve. "You made this sound like a big deal, and I'm trying to fit in here. I figured I'd go roll a snowball and make it happen."

I snorted.

"Any advice?"

I glanced at the stone-faced lady checking his waiver. "Yeah. Don't fall." I hooked my arm in his and directed us toward the crowded hillside. We climbed the space behind the spectators slowly, careful not to bump into anyone or accidentally roll their stuff down the incline. Holiday music blared obnoxiously as we drew nearer to the top.

Sheriff Gray chuckled. "This is like a rock concert with really bad seating and music, or maybe the X Games intermission show."

"It's definitely something," I agreed.

He'd swapped his sheriff gear for a black all-weather coat and dark-gray knitted cap. "What?" he asked.

"Nothing," I mumbled, caught staring once again. "It's just that you look surprisingly at home in the snow. I had you pegged for a city boy."

"We get plenty of snow in Boston."

"Yeah, but that's not what I mean."

He looked away, dragging his focus over the crowd and the horizon. "So what do we do now?"

I tugged the material of his sleeve for a better look at the number on his sticker. "You're in lane two. That's good. I'm in lane one."

"Yeah? You were hoping to watch me pass you from close range, then?"

"Ha ha." I edged around the final cluster of onlookers and mounted the crest of the hill where a mass of contestants rolled snowballs behind a red line. Lanes and numbers were spray-painted on the snow but disappeared a few feet away from the starting line. We made our way to the back of the pack and surveyed the competition. People of every age, shape, and size chatted on the hilltop, ready to race to the bottom.

"You go over there," I told Sheriff Gray. "There are twelve lanes, and the lines will get you started on the right path, but all that goes out the window when everyone's snowball goes the wrong way fifty yards down the hill."

He scooped up a wad of snow and pressed it into a hard ball. "How big of a ball do we start with?"

"Doesn't matter," I said. "As long as you can hold it in your hands until the whistle."

He gave me an odd look. "Are you telling me I can start out with any size ball I can carry?"

"Go for it."

He made a deep throaty noise of superiority, then rolled the little nugget around his feet and watched it grow. "All I've got to do is be the first one to the bottom of the hill, right?"

I gathered snow in my mittens. "You have to have your snowball with you when you get there."

He stopped to stare at the drop-off. "Don't fall," he repeated in a whisper. "This is where all the EMTs went last year, isn't it?"

A bubble of laughter rose in my chest. "Yes. How'd you know?"

He hung his head. "I hear the guys talk about it some-times, but I've never asked. I'm always on the outside looking in around here."

I grinned. "Not anymore."

He dropped his snowball onto the ground. "Only in Mistletoe are all the volunteer EMTs called out for a people pileup on Christmas Eve."

"Any questions?" I asked.

"What happens if more than one person gets down there with their snowballs at the same time? There are a lot of people up here, and I don't see any timers or judges to make the call." He squinted in the direction of the food trucks and registration table, all tiny as toys in the distance.

"The crowd will know, but if there's any doubt as to who got there first, they'll measure the snowballs."

He nudged his with his toe. It was already the size of a basketball.

I molded my snow into a smooth sphere, then packed it tighter and bigger until the music cut out and Cookie's faux British accent echoed through the network of outdoor speakers.

"Merry Christmas Eve!" she said. "The White family and I would like to welcome you to the seventy-fifth annual Snowball Roll! For those of you who've been here before, cheerio and welcome back!"

The crowd erupted in applause.

"For those who are new, welcome!" She opened her arms dramatically. "Now I'd like to ask the contestants to lift their snowballs overhead and prepare for the whistle. First one to get their ball to the bottom in one piece is the winner. Everyone else is a loser!" She dragged the last word into two syllables.

A round of feedback and white noise erupted as Mom wrangled the mic away from her. "On your marks," Mom said.

The whistle blew, and the horde of contestants started down the hill.

"What about 'get set' and 'go'?" Sheriff Gray asked.

"Go!" I yelled. I launched forward with my ball at my feet, passing a number of slow starters and leaving the sheriff firmly in my dust. Players came and went in my periphery, catching up and falling back in intervals as they struggled with their snowball amid unexpected drifts and speedy competition.

The crowd chanted and hooted until I felt the cadence of their voices in my chest. *Go! Go! Go! Go!*

I leapt over challengers' balls and rejoiced inwardly when mine missed racing-human obstacles, pulling me ahead of the pack in no time. The process was exhilarating, freeing, an incredible high. Until Sheriff Gray appeared at my side, guiding a ball the size of a boulder with his instep like a soccer pro instead of a small-town sheriff chasing half a snowman.

My squatty ball hadn't grown that much. Every kick I gave the sucker seemed to send half of it scattering back into flakes. How was he doing it? More important, how was he passing me? We were approaching the second dip in the gently rolling hill, a naturally formed halfway mark, and the hill only got steeper moving forward. If he didn't slow down, then I couldn't slow down, and the odds of losing control would grow. Snowball Roll wasn't a game of speed like everyone thought. It was a game of strategy. When everyone else lost their snowball, footing, or both, I'd jog past and claim the victory with calm control.

A trio of contestants up ahead tangled their legs together and collapsed. I dashed right with my ball, deftly avoiding the mess, but Sheriff Gray's megamonstrosity collided and burst against one fallen player's head.

"Sorry!" he yelled, steering the remains of his lopsided chunk back down the hill. "Move it, White," he called, coming up fast behind me. "Unless you want to be run down on your own hill."

I stopped short to startle him.

He hollered and lost his footing. The hunk of snow he called a ball clunked to a stop, and Sheriff Gray sprawled belly first onto the ground, skidding slowly toward the finish line.

I laughed, unsure if I should help him up when I was so close to the end.

"Watch out!" a woman wailed behind me. I turned to judge the situation, and she plowed into me, sending me tail over teakettles down the hill. My ball was gone. The ear-splitting scream that streaked out of me was enough to drown out the obnoxious holiday music overhead.

A hush seemed to roll over the frozen crowd as I jetted past them, face down, arms wide, and flailing. My ball was gone. The woman who'd leveled me had collided with a local cameraman and thudded to a stop. Meanwhile, the more I wiggled and protested my predicament, the faster I went. There was no way to avoid the handful of players still upright and ahead of me. Snow sprayed my face as I clipped their feet and ankles with my outstretched arms. They landed on their backsides as I propelled ahead.

Cookie stood frozen in my path.

"Move!" I called, choking on ice and snow. There was less than a few seconds left until certain impact, and I was twice her size and moving at a ridiculous speed. My legs caught on a stalled or lost snowball, which spun me sideways. I covered my eyes and dug my toes into the ground, praying for purchase and hoping I didn't kill her. The effort forced me into a clunky log roll. I immediately regretted all the breakfast bacon.

Chants from the crowd morphed into hysteric laughter as my world began to spin out of control.

Dad's voice boomed.

My eyes opened in time to see him swing Cookie out of the way.

Hallelujah! A burst of nausea and relief exploded in me. It was a Christmas miracle!

My body flipped once more and jerked to a stop as I wedged beneath the belly of the Patsy's Popovers truck.

Mom's boots hustled into view. "Holly!"

I army-crawled out from under Patsy's and flipped onto my back for a cleansing breath. "I'm okay," I lied.

Everything I had hurt, and I had no idea where my snowball had gone, but at least I'd beaten Sheriff Gray to the bottom.

Chapter Twenty-Three

I propped my probably sprained ankle on a throw pillow at the end of my parents' couch and tugged a quilt around my shoulders.

Mom set a tray on the coffee table and poured me a cup of tea. "Just the way you like it. Are you sure there isn't anything else I can get you? A snack or a book? A doctor, perhaps?"

I laughed and regretted it. "Ow."

"Be still." Mom fussed. "That was the most terrifying thing I've ever seen." She tucked the blanket around my legs and adjusted my foot pillow. "You're a mess. I can only imagine the bruises under those flannel jammies. What were you thinking flying down the hill like that? You know you have to pace yourself to make it to the end."

I'd been thinking I wanted to beat the sheriff, but I wasn't about to admit that. As for the bruising, I'd taken my time in a hot shower, making sure all my parts were accounted for. Everything was still intact, though some pieces were a bit touchier than others. "I'm going to be fine. Besides, you should've seen the other guy," I teased.

"Oh." Mom made a terrible face. "We did. The poor woman toppled into you after she tripped on that wonky barrel-shaped thing Sheriff Gray was kicking. She could barely get up when she stopped rolling. The cameraman she plowed over next will surely put his footage on the nightly news."

I swallowed the urge to scream. "I hope they're both okay."

Mom tipped her head back and forth over her shoulders. "Embarrassed more than anything, I think."

Understandable. At least I'd had a rescue team.

Mom and Dad had loaded me into a work truck and whisked me into hiding after my one-hundred-yard skid and roll down Spruce Knob in front of five hundred cheering fans.

"Well," Mom said, threading her arms into the sleeves of her coat, "I'd better get back. I put your clothes in the dryer and hung your coat in the mudroom." She layered more toasty blankets over me. "There's a deputy on the porch if you need anything, and I've got my cell on me. Enjoy your tea. I'll be home in time for dinner. Don't forget the memorial for Mrs. Fenwick is tonight at seven. A short candlelight vigil before the tree lighting in the square. Rest up so you don't have to miss it." She kissed my forehead and smoothed my hair.

"Okay."

She slipped out, and I sipped my tea, desperate to doze off, but the way my week was going, the house would most likely burst into flames if I got any sleep. Cindy curled on my legs and let me pet her fluffy calico fur until I felt a little better. "Do you want to watch a movie?" I asked her. "We're on our own for another couple of hours."

She rubbed her face against my belly, then flopped onto her side and bit my fingers.

"Stop." I flipped channels on the remote until the Grinch's green face lit up the screen. "Oh, look!" I set my cup aside and dragged her higher on my lap for a proper snuggle. "This is where you got your name, Cindy Lou Who." I nuzzled my cheek against her head. She struggled to paw my mouth and chew my nose. "If I'd have known then what I know now, I might've named you after a different character."

She jumped off the couch and gave me a backward glance before slinking away.

"I interpret your rejection as love," I called after her.

I wiggled deeper beneath the blankets, warmed inside from the tea and outside from the thick pile of covers.

"Knock knock." Sheriff Gray poked his head through the newly opened front door.

"What's wrong?" I asked, straightening myself begrudgingly on the cushions. "Why didn't my mom lock the door?" What if he'd been the killer, or if I'd been indecent? What if I'd been binge-eating maple-covered bacon and not in the mood to share?

"Sorry," he said shyly, pushing the door shut behind him and extracting the key. He lifted it near his cheek. "She gave this to me in case of emergency. I'll give it back when this is all over."

My muscles went rigid. "Is there an emergency?"

"Well, no, but I could see you resting from the window and didn't want you to have to get up, but . . ." His expression puckered. "I probably shouldn't have assumed you'd let me in."

"I would have let you in," I sighed. "I just don't think I'll be much company."

"I won't stay. I was just checking in with my deputy." He posed awkwardly beside the window, apparently unsure what to do with my house key or his hands in general. "I thought while I was here, I'd see how you're feeling after that nasty spill."

I groaned as memories of my out-of-control penguin imitation flooded back to mind. "I don't want to talk about it."

"You say that a lot."

"I mean it a lot." I moved the end of my blanket pile off my sore legs. "You can sit with me if you hold my feet. Normally, I'd hop up and get you something from the kitchen, but my ankle's tender, and I'm being a baby. You could sit in the recliner, but then you'll miss the best holiday movie ever made." On-screen, the Whoville townsfolk held hands and sang.

"Well, that looks familiar."

"Seen it before, have you?"

He hung his coat on the rack and made his way to the couch with a soft chuckle. His clothes were dry despite his earlier tumble. Apparently, I wasn't the only one to go home and clean up. Though I was probably the only one vowing to take a few practice runs before the big event next time. "Yeah, every morning at the town square."

I laughed. "Mistletoe isn't quite that jolly."

"Oh, no?" he asked with a grin.

"Sorry I can't get you something to eat or drink. You can share my tea." I hooked a thumb in the direction of my cup. "There's more in the kettle, but I only have one mug."

"I don't need anything. I visited one or two food trucks before I came over." He lowered himself into the space I'd made for him and placed my legs across his lap with careful hands.

I flipped the pile of covers back over us. "*The Grinch* is my favorite."

He spread his arms along the back of the couch, looking suddenly uncomfortable. He crossed his arms instead and gripped his elbows.

I smiled. "Are you trying not to touch me?"

"What? No." His gaze darted to the door.

My smile grew. "You're afraid my dad's going to come in here and freak out, aren't you?"

He didn't answer.

"You know, there are at least seven layers of clothes and blankets between us, I think my dad would let you live if he walked in, plus I'm getting the impression you're a gentleman. He appreciates those."

The sheriff moved cautious green eyes to mine. "You think I'm a gentleman?"

"You're polite and compassionate, you never take advantage of your authority, you always thank my mom for the things she does, and you're the first to pitch in when someone needs help, even a lonely, hungry cat. Plus, you don't yell at me, even when I deserve it and think you are."

"So you admit I don't yell," he said. "Good. But if you get me mad enough, I might arrest you."

"Doubtful," I said. "I've been kind of a pain, and I'm still free."

His cheek ticked up on one side. "I've got to admit, I didn't know what to think of you at first, always turning up with a side dish of trouble. Now I think you're just being you. Curious and stubborn, sure, but I don't think you irritate me intentionally."

I let my mouth fall open. "I irritate you?"

"Not intentionally."

My cheeks hurt, and I realized I was smiling. "So what are you really doing here?" I asked, desperate to turn his attention away from me as my cheeks grew warmer.

"Checking in," he said. "You worried me back there. Everyone else crossed the finish line on their feet."

"I crossed first, though."

"Yeah, face first and without your snowball."

"Now you're just being picky," I told him.

He laughed. "My snowball was smashed to smithereens. I finished without it, and I think I bruised my spleen. You guys should think about adding rules to that game—or an age limit."

"Rude." I laughed. "Who are we to say when someone's too old to chase a snowball?"

"It's all fun and games until you're stuck under a food truck. That's all I'm saying."

I raised my eyebrows. "I wasn't stuck, and it's not up to us—or you—to decide who plays."

His expression fell, and he finally rested his hands on my lower legs, looking utterly defeated. "I know."

I tried to imagine the frustration he had when people made poor choices. "It must be hard to be the hero all the time."

He rubbed the back of his head. "I can't protect everyone from everything, right?"

"Right, but I'm confused," I said. "Are we still talking about the Snowball Roll?"

He turned sharp green eyes on me. "I went to the Historical Society today."

"Oh." I fiddled with the hem of my top blanket. "When?"

"After I stopped at home to change clothes following the snowball race. I ran into Mr. France."

"Hmm." I pressed my lips tighter to keep from getting into more trouble. Suddenly his impromptu visit to "check" on me seemed more like an ambush to tell me I was busted. "He called while I was getting ready for the Snowball Roll. I planned to tell you about it, but I got sidetracked when I saw you were going to race."

He folded his hands on the pile of blankets over my legs. "Go on."

"He got my message and returned my call."

"Do you think he was really out of town all those days?"

"I'm not sure. He sounded sincere when we spoke, but I don't know what's real anymore or who's lying. Maybe the call was a ruse."

"What did he say?"

"He says the HPS didn't award the grant for the mill, but someone at HPS told me they did." I swung my legs off the sheriff's lap and winced. "Maybe we can go talk to him together and find out what made him think the grant was denied. He says he didn't talk to HPS directly, but surely there are files on the matter among Mrs. Fenwick's things." If Mr. France hadn't dumped them in the trash yet.

Sheriff Gray extended an arm to stop me from jumping off the couch. "I've got this. You stay here and rest. It'll mean a lot to a whole bunch of people if you make it to the square."

"But I can help," I said. "We can revisit her home office. She had a ton of information on HPS there."

He gave me a sad smile. "You can't even sit up without hurting yourself. You need to stay right where you are and let me handle this. It's what I do."

I wanted to argue, but he was right about the pain. My body felt like a piñata after the party. I relaxed against the armrest, somewhat thankful he was as stubborn as me. "Fine."

He cocked a disbelieving eyebrow.

"What if I promise to stay out of trouble until after Santa comes? That should give me time to heal up and make a new plan."

"No new plans. I'll handle the plans."

"You aren't the sheriff of plans," I said. "If I'm going to be stuck on the couch, you know I'm going to be thinking about what to do next."

Sheriff Gray leaned forward and pulled my legs back onto his lap. "On second thought, as much as folks would like to see you tonight, I think everyone will understand if you want to get some sleep instead. The whole town saw you collide with Patsy's Popovers."

"I went under it."

"Uh-huh." He turned his attention to the movie as a cartoon dog's sled went out of control. He kept watch on me from the corner of his eye, as if I wouldn't notice.

"Mr. France said someone from Mrs. Fenwick's family is in town. Will you have to give Whiskers back?"

He smiled. "I met they guy at her place to turn over the house key. He's staying at a hotel outside of town. Cat allergies."

"Well, that's too bad." I smiled at the television. "I guess Whiskers gets to stay."

At the next commercial break, I muted the television. "Who are you spending Christmas Day with?"

"I'm working."

"What? Why?"

He shrugged. "The deputies are on call, but they've all got families. They should be with them. I can hold down the fort."

I didn't like the idea of him being alone on Christmas. "What did you ask Santa for this year?"

"World peace?"

"No."

He squeezed my calf gently through the blankets and chuckled. "I don't know. I guess I'd like to have this case wrapped up. The sooner the better." He turned sincere eyes on me. A look of determination lined his brow. "And I want to keep you safe."

My mouth opened, then silently shut. A familiar heat crawled over my cheeks, and I simultaneously loved and hated the effect he had on me. "Me too."

He rubbed his suddenly ruddy cheeks with one hand and grinned. "What about you? What does a woman like Holly White want for Christmas?"

"I'm not sure." For the first time in far too long, I felt 100 percent like myself. I didn't feel as out of place as I'd suspected I might on my drive from Portland. Instead, it was as if I was the last piece of a puzzle that had been waiting for me. Despite the twisted ankle and recent scares, I was happy, wrapped in cozy blankets at my childhood home, sitting with a handsome new friend who kept me safe and made me smile. What else could I ask for?

"There must be something," he pressed.

I looked him in the eye and smiled. "No. I've already got everything I've ever wanted."

His bright smile lifted my heart. "Well, if you're sure."

I forced the front door mistletoe from my thoughts. "Pretty much."

Chapter Twenty-Four

The sheriff only stayed until the movie was over, and I couldn't seem to get warm again without him. The house was too big. The wind was too strong. I didn't even know the deputy who was keeping watch on the house, supposedly guarding me. I should've asked for an introduction before the sheriff left, but I didn't think of that until I was alone with a stranger as my personal "protection." For all I knew, the deputy was the killer, a suspect I hadn't considered because he'd covered his tracks so well. I flipped myself around on the couch to keep both eyes on the front window, but neither eye was open when Mom and Dad arrived on a cloud of icy wind that nearly scared the tea out of me.

"We're home," Mom chirped, in case the blast of frigid air hadn't woken me. "The Twelve Days of Reindeer Games are officially over until next year." She kicked off her boots and hung her snowy things on the rack beside the door. "How was your tea?" She lifted onto her toes to kiss Dad under the mistletoe before locking up.

He bent at the knees to receive her little peck.

I worked to right my hazy thoughts, which had been yanked sharply from the Land of Nod.

Mom approached me with a frown and pressed a frigid palm to my head. "You look like you've seen a ghost. Look at her, Bud. She's pale, isn't she?"

"Peckish?" he guessed.

Heavens, no. If I ate anything else, I'd pop the button on my pants.

Mom moved her hand to my cheek. "Are you fevered or is my hand cold?"

"Your hand is a block of ice," I told her. "You startled me, that's all. I must've fallen asleep for a minute."

"That's good." Dad collected my tray and carried it to the kitchen. "I think we could all use a little rest after the week we've had," he called to us.

"It was a good day," Mom said. "Injuries aside." She lifted my achy legs and put them on her lap, snuggling in next to me. "How's your ankle?"

"Sore but not sprained," I said. "I can put some pressure on it. It's probably just bruised, but I'm going to keep it up until morning." I waited for her to hear the other message in my statement.

"Morning? You aren't coming to the square tonight?"

I made my best puppy dog eyes. "I don't think so," I admitted. "I'm emotionally and physically spent, and I don't want to go into a crowd on an achy ankle. I thought I could stay here and rest up for tomorrow." Unless things had changed since the last Christmas I'd spent at home, half the people in the square tonight would show up here tomorrow with food and Christmas wishes for my folks. "I can set a nice table for when you get back. Cookies. Cakes. Drinks. Maybe some old-fashioned wassail."

Dad reemerged from the kitchen with a bag of frozen peas. He lifted all but one blanket from my ankle and arranged the peas over tender muscles.

Mom stroked his arm. "We haven't had wassail in years, have we, Bud?"

He eyeballed the peas. "Maybe I should stay with Holly."

"Nonsense," Mom disagreed sweetly. "She's a big girl. There's a deputy out front if she needs anything, and we always watch the tree lighting together. Plus, this year we have the vigil for Margaret. I hear some extended family will be in town."

Dad gave me a peculiar look. "She's right."

"I know. It's okay," I said. "I'll be fine on my own, and you won't be gone long. Plus, I have a security detail these days." I motioned to the front porch. "Do you guys know him?"

Dad walked slowly to the window with a deep look of concern. "Not well. He's new to Mistletoe. Probably only been in town five or six years."

I smiled. Only in a historic town was someone still considered new after five years.

Dad spread the curtains with his fingertips. "Sheriff put him on a circuit. He circles the house and checks the garage, then back to the porch every few minutes. I don't like it."

"Why?" Mom and I asked in unison.

I couldn't help wondering about her objection. Mine was that I didn't know the guy from Adam, and apparently neither did my folks.

Dad turned back to us, abandoning his post at the window. "Every time he's out back, someone could walk right through the front door, and when he's here, someone could walk in the back."

"The doors are both locked," I reminded him. "Even if someone tried to break the door down, I could leave through the opposite one."

Dad dug a mass of keys from his pocket and worked one off the ring. "Keep this on you. It's for the new pickup. You can drive it until you find something else or just don't want it anymore. I won't have to worry about you getting stranded anywhere or stuck in the snow as long as she's your ride. I filled the gas tank last night and parked her out front beside your mom's truck."

I accepted the key with a full heart. "Thanks, Dad."

"Anything goes haywire while we're gone, you get to that truck," he said. "I keep a shotgun in the rack."

I looked at Mom.

She patted my shoulder.

The truck was a great gift. I wasn't sure how I felt about needing a gun to protect myself from a lunatic who might chase me out of the house.

Dad headed for the staircase. "If I'm going out, I'd better get cleaned up."

I waited for him to disappear around the corner before turning back to Mom. "I love when he says that, then comes back looking just like he did when he left." Dad was like the guy on those paper towel ads, perpetually in plaid flannel and jeans.

Mom sighed. "When you marry a lumberjack, you get a lumberjack. You know what I mean?"

"We are who we are."

"All day." She squirmed free of my legs, no longer able to sit still. "I'll fix you some soup. That'll make you feel better."

"And grilled cheese," Dad called down the steps.

Mom smiled at the ceiling. "Nothing wrong with his hearing."

"I can hear a squirrel sneaking past at twenty yards," he said.

"Take your shower!" Mom called. She rolled her eyes at me and mouthed the word *men*.

I hobbled into the kitchen to help with the soup and grilled cheeses, mindful of my slightly swollen ankle. I couldn't eat another bite, but I could be useful. I collected cheese and butter from her fridge and set them on the counter near the breadbox. "We had a great turnout today."

Mom lit the burner under her favorite soup pot and cracked the tops on a couple jars of her tomato soup. She loved canning her produce almost as much as growing it, and Dad loved eating it, which made her infinitely proud. One more reason they were the perfect couple. "You and Evan seemed to be having a nice time. It's good to see the sheriff finally making friends."

I slid my knife across the butter and worked to balance on my good foot. "He's a really nice guy. A little uptight, but that probably comes with the job."

"I'd imagine so." She dried her hands on a dish towel and came to my side. "Let me help you butter the bread. All I did was dump the contents of a few jars into a pot." She'd made the soup and the bread, but she probably wouldn't see that as contributing to the immediate efforts, so I moved over.

"If you see him at the square tonight, you should invite him over tomorrow. I think he plans to work and then spend Christmas alone."

"Ha!" she said, obviously shocked. "Not on my watch."

I smiled, utterly pleased, and grabbed a pan from the rack overhead. I set it on the stove beside her soup pot. "How about you fix 'em, and I'll fry 'em."

"And I'll eat 'em," Dad's voice boomed overhead.

Mom pointed her buttery knife at the ceiling fan. "See what I mean?"

*   *   *

The house was extra toasty from the help of a heated oven when my parents finally left for the square. Mom had refused to leave me without dessert, so she shoved a pan of fudgy brownies in to bake after they finished off the soup and sandwiches. Ignoring the rich chocolate scents wafting from the stove was almost as difficult as pretending my cat wasn't provoking me for entertainment.

Cindy peered from the recesses of our Christmas tree, shaking the limbs and rattling the glass bulbs as she climbed. I would've chastised her if I thought it would make a difference, but I knew better, and the prowling and rebellion was partially my fault for strapping a Velcro elf hat onto her furry head when she came looking for her dinner.

I texted Sheriff Gray a picture of her in the tree, dragging garland on the tip of her pointy felt chapeau. He responded with a picture of Whiskers curled lovingly on his lap.

I turned my phone to face the tree. "Do you see that?" I asked her. "That's how nice kitties behave."

Cindy growled and knocked another line of ornaments onto the tree skirt.

I flicked the television off and rubbed my belly. "If we're going to stay here," I told her, "I'm going to need to take up jogging or cross-country skiing." There was no chance of my willpower withstanding mom's constant cooking, and my metabolism wasn't what it had been in high school. "I need a high-intensity outlet or a new wardrobe." The second option cost money I didn't have, so for now I'd have to do jumping jacks. As soon as I healed from my last attempt at physical activity.

The deputy paced across the front porch and back down the steps before disappearing around the side of our house for his umpteenth trip of the day.

I opened an old copy of *Mistletoe Magazine* from Mom's coffee table and thumbed through the pages until I couldn't stand the silence. The air seemed weighted, and the hairs on the back of my neck stood at attention. I looked to the tree, wishing Cindy was more of a cuddle cat when I was being a baby.

A quick rap on the front window set me on my feet with a squeak. I jerked my sore foot off the floor and peered into the darkness beyond the glass. Twilight had bled into night faster than I'd realized.

"Hello?" a muffled voice called. "Holly?"

I slid into my fuzzy slippers and hobbled to the switch plate, flicking the light on outside.

"Oh!" The man on my porch rocked away from the window waving his hands over his face.

"Mr. Nettle?"

"Yes!" He blinked and rubbed his eyes. "Goodness."

I checked in both directions for the deputy but didn't see him.

"My parents have already left for the square," I said through the window.

"I know." He popped the collar higher on his coat. "I saw them there, and your mother said you were looking to talk with me. I spoke with Mr. France today."

"You did?" Caleb France must've been making his rounds.

"Yes. We had a lovely talk. You know, your parents seemed a little disappointed you weren't with them tonight. I slipped away, thinking I'd fix two problems with one move."

"I'm not following."

He opened his palms and grinned. "I'll bring you to the square, and they'll be thrilled. Meanwhile, we can talk about Mr. France on the way. Though I'm still not clear what's so interesting about him."

A strong gust of wind rattled the windowpanes and popped the fedora off Mr. Nettle's head. He pulled his shoulders up to his ears and hunkered down in his tweed coat as he chased the hat across our porch. Wisps of gray hair fluttered over his bald spot, seeming to join him in the cap's pursuit.

Mr. Nettle's car was parked beside the deputy's cruiser, so when he made it back around, he'd know I wasn't alone, and there'd be no mistaking who was with me.

I cranked the dead bolt and pulled the door open. A blast of snow hit me in the chest. "You're welcome to come inside for a minute," I called against the brewing storm, "but I'm not leaving. I hurt my foot earlier in the Snowball Roll."

Mr. Nettle pinned his hat against the porch railing. "Gotcha!" He shook it back into shape with a look of victory. "I heard about your tumble." He cast a remorseful look at my feet. "You'll be okay?"

"Yeah. It's just tender. I guess I'm a little older than I realized."

He laughed humorlessly. "Aren't we all?" He dashed his toes against the welcome mat and accepted my offer to step inside. "You should sit. I didn't mean to keep you standing in the cold on a bad foot."

I waved him off. "Let me get you something warm to drink. You can even take it with you. We keep disposable everything at the ready." Or we used to. "Let me see what I can find."

"Don't go to any trouble on my account." He turned his face toward the kitchen. "Are you baking?"

I smiled. "Mom couldn't resist. Her brownies are just about ready to come out of the oven. At least stay until they cool so I can send one with you, and maybe a cup of hot tea or cider too."

He looked around, uncertain.

"It'll only take me a minute."

Mr. Nettle took a seat and rested his hat on his legs. "I suppose there's always time for tea."

"Good." I smiled. "Make yourself at home. I'll be right there."

I grabbed my phone off the coffee table and headed for the kitchen.

"What was it that you wanted to ask me?" he called.

"Um, give me just a second," I called back to him. I hopped to the stove and tapped the sides of a barely warm kettle. I'd have to reheat it. I slid oven mitts over my hands and set the piping hot brownies out to cool, then switched the oven off.

I bumbled back to the living room and leaned against the doorjamb. "It's nothing now. I'd planned to ask you about Mr. France, but he called this morning, and I was able to talk with him for a bit."

"Is that so?"

"Yes. He's not as bad as I'd originally thought. I must've caught him at a bad time before."

"Everything's fine, then? Got all your questions answered?"

"Not really," I admitted.

Mr. Nettle rested one foot on the opposite knee and stretched his arms over the back of our couch. "Maybe I can still help."

I rolled my head against the doorframe. "Only if you've got any experience with grants or the HPS in California. Did you say you wanted tea or cider? I've already forgotten."

Something strangely uncongenial flashed in Mr. Nettle's eyes. "Are you looking for a grant?"

"No. It's a long story," I said, levering myself off the wall. "Never mind."

The air had changed inside my home, sending gooseflesh over my arms and standing the little hairs on the back of my neck at attention.

"I just remembered you said tea." I smiled. "I'll go heat the kettle."

I hopped through the kitchen toward the stove, fighting a rush of inexplicable fear.

An ugly possibility needled my mind. If Caleb France hadn't been in direct contact with HPS, who had? Was it Mrs. Fenwick, or someone else?

If the Historical Society had used a third party, like an accountant, to handle grant applications and receipts, the accountant could have lied. He could have kept the monies for himself. He'd have good reason to keep his crimes hidden. Would anyone check up on an alleged grant denial? Maybe not, and if Mrs. Fenwick hadn't applied for a second grant this year, maybe no one would've known at all. I wetted my suddenly dry lips. What if Mrs. Fenwick had caught someone stealing the grant money, but the thief wasn't in California. What if he was in my living room?

I checked my pockets for my cell phone and new truck key, then cracked open the back door silently. An arctic blast of snow whipped through my pajamas. My coat and boots were in the living room. I said a silent prayer.

"Where are you going?" Mr. Nettle's voice sounded behind me at close range.

I didn't look back or bother to answer. I jumped into the snow with a wince and fell immediately over something on the ground. Panic jutted through my limbs as the object came into focus.

The deputy in charge of my safety was sprawled beside a striped tree marker and a growing puddle of crimson blood.

Chapter Twenty-Five

Mr. Nettle looked down at me from his perch inside my warm house. "Come back inside. There's no reason to go out like that. You're hurt. Your feet will freeze in those slippers, and you've got no coat."

Sharp winter wind sliced through my thin pajamas, reinforcing his point and chilling me to the core. My body heat had melted the snow on my fleece pants, and the temperatures were attempting to freeze the cloth to my skin. Even so, going inside seemed like a decidedly worse option.

"No, thank you," I said politely while taking inventory of my capacities. The cold was doing a marvelous job of reducing my ankle's sting, and adrenaline was working overtime to convince me it was warm enough to run and I was a track star. Unfortunately, neither of those things was true.

I scrambled backward on the ground where I'd fallen over the deputy, avoiding his blood and a high drift of snow along the stone patio. I took stock of my fallen protector's equipment as I put some distance between myself and Mr. Nettle. "You should get your coat from the living room," I said. I didn't want the deputy's gun, but there was a radio on his shoulder. The spiral chord disappeared beneath him, attached to something I couldn't see. "I'd hate for you to leave it behind as evidence when the sheriff gets here and finds us missing." More so, I'd love for him to give me a head start running to the pickup out front.

Mr. Nettle's expression dimmed. "I'm not leaving you alone out here so you can skitter off and hide, and I don't leave evidence. You should know that by now. I'll be long gone— coat, hat, car, and all—before the business at the town square is done. Now come inside so we can talk this over."

I swung my chin left to right, trying not to fixate on the deputy. He was young and strong. His chest continued to rise and fall in shallow pulls. Movements so small, it seemed Mr. Nettle hadn't noticed. The deputy could survive what Mrs. Fenwick hadn't. I just needed to lure Mr. Nettle away before he finished the job. I also needed to call for help before he gave my head a whack with that tree marker.

I rearranged my arms and legs, forcing myself onto my feet. I swayed gently with the wind. "If I come inside, what will happen?" I stalled, slipping my hand inside one pocket to work the buttons of my cell phone. The power button was easy enough, but there was no way to blindly discern anything else about the smooth screen's surface. How could I make a call when I couldn't see the numbers? I could have been updating my Facebook status with gibberish for all I knew.

"You said you wanted to talk," Mr. Nettle said. "Come back inside and we'll talk."

I stepped forward, and he opened the glass storm door wider, extending his free hand to beckon me in.

A knot of determination sank low in my gut as I resolved to make the only move I could. Mr. Nettle didn't have a banged-up body and busted ankle like me. I had to slow him down any way I could.

"Hurry up," he grouched. "There's no reason to drag this out."

I hung my head and lowered my eyes in a show of inferiority, then lunged at the open glass door and slammed it against his reaching arm with all my might, smashing the limb against the doorframe and shattering the glass in the metal frame.

A shower of swears and spittle spurted from his mouth as he stumbled back, clutching his likely broken arm. Shards of glass tumbled into the snow-covered ground.

I dove onto the fallen deputy before Mr. Nettle could get the door open again and wrenched the nightstick and sidearm from the deputy's belt.

Mr. Nettle fumbled onto the patio opposite me, still gripping his arm. "Get back here you nosy, no-good troublemaker, and I'll at least give you the dignity of a final good-bye. I'll stage a suicide and let you write the note." He tented his eyebrows, as if to ask if that was a deal.

I ran for the trees.

The back door slammed shut behind me, sending a wave of echoes into the night. He must've gone back inside for his coat, but I was already headed in the wrong direction, into the shadows, away from the house and truck. I had nowhere to go. No coat. Sopping-wet slippers. What had I done?

I couldn't keep going. I needed to hide. Every step I took sent blades of pain through my aching foot and cast a sheen of sweat over my freezing forehead, not to mention the path through the snow that led straight to me.

I cut between the rows of trees, where reaching branches had restricted the amount of precipitation on the ground. I pressed my back to a tree trunk for support and dialed the sheriff.

A cheerful whistle raised into the air. "Holly," Mr. Nettle sang. "Come out, come out, wherever you are."

The call at my ear connected with a loud click. "This is Sheriff Gray."

I pressed a shaking hand to my mouth, suppressing the sudden torrent of emotion. Help was just on the other end of my phone, but I couldn't speak, could barely breath. I didn't know where Mr. Nettle was or if he'd hear my voice if I answered Sheriff Gray.

"Holly?" The sheriff's voice came again, louder and firmer this time.

I sucked in a rattling breath and scurried deeper into the trees, catching the limbs with numb fingertips in an effort to support my awkward stride. I slipped from row to row in the densest part of the forest. "Help," I whispered into the phone, cupping one hand around my mouth to direct the sound into the receiver. "Help me." I crouched to bury the gun in a pile of snow. I wasn't going to shoot anyone, but I also didn't want to be shot.

Twigs snapped in the distance. The familiar stride of a brisk walk drew nearer by the second.

Darkness loomed over me like a suffocating blanket, and my throat burned with each new inhalation. The light from the house and garage was long gone, swallowed up by the night, buried beneath the horizon of a rolling hill. Even the plastic light-up Santa at the chimney was vanquished from existence. There was only Mr. Nettle, myself, and the trees.

I ducked under the wooden perimeter fence and into the trees at Reindeer Games. My heartbeat pounded in my ears.

"Where are you?" the sheriff demanded. "I've dispatched another deputy to your parents' home. Are you there?"

"No."

"Then where the hell are you?" The words were pointed and lethal.

"Hiding." The word lifted from my lips in a cloud of white steam that I was certain Mr. Nettle could see.

"Where's Phillip?" he asked next.

"Who?"

"My deputy. The one protecting you," he demanded.

A tiny sob escaped my trembling lips. What now? Speak? Don't speak? Have a conversation while Mr. Nettle sneaked up and bashed my head with a wooden stake? "I'm in the trees at the farm," I said as softly as possible. "Phillip is down."

"Ah-ah-ah," Mr. Nettle taunted. His hot breath blew over my burning neck.

I tensed. A fiery battle of fight or flight warred inside me. I couldn't outrun him. Not tonight.

A heavy hand landed on my shoulder, and I spun on instinct. Even before the decision was fully formed, I swung the stolen nightstick at the man behind me. My weapon connected with a sickening thud, and Mr. Nettle cursed. I dropped my phone in favor of a two-handed grip on the club and lashed out a second and third time until he released his grip on me with a shout.

My feet were in motion, carrying me over the snow, leaving a trail anyone could follow. I ignored my body's protests—the pain in my ankle and the burn of the air.

I jetted through the field, guided only by the moon and an array of distant twinkle lights on rows of Reindeer Games' trees. A renewed sense of hope rushed through me. I could do this. A killer had had his hand on me, and I'd earned my freedom. All I needed now was somewhere to hide until the sheriff or his deputy arrived.

A lump formed in my throat. My phone was gone. My already sprinting heart beat unfathomably faster. I'd lost my lifeline, but the sheriff knew I was in the trees at the farm.

I moved again, vanishing between rows of towering evergreens, begging the sting in my hands and feet not to mean what it could—frostbite. I slowed to rest my foot as the trees grew more and more sparse. "Why'd you do it?" I listened for signs of Mr. Nettle's location in the dark.

"Do what?" his voice echoed through the trees, carried on the groaning wind.

I pressed my back against a mature fir and struggled for another painful breath. The adrenaline had run its course, and my body temperature was plummeting. My swollen ankle had become stiff and uncooperative. My fingers and toes had gone from burning to numb.

"Why'd you kill Mrs. Fenwick?" I pushed. "Was it because she caught you stealing the town's grant money?"

I needed a better plan than waiting for help to arrive. Hypothermia was a frighteningly real possibility, and I didn't have long before the effects took hold. The wet and freezing material of my pajamas seared my skin. It was too dark to see my fingertips, but they were undoubtedly the color of the snow. By now, blood had likely stopped trying to save my extremities in favor of keeping my organs pumping.

I swallowed a brick of ice and tried again to make Mr. Nettle talk. "When she sent the grant application to the Historical Preservation Society for the covered bridge, she learned that they'd already given money to Mistletoe this year, didn't she? Did she come to you and ask why the HPS said they'd sent a check but you'd told her the grant had been denied? How many other grants have you stolen? How much do you owe this town?"

Projecting my voice stole the last of my energy, and soon my shaking knees gave out. I dropped into a squat against the tree and prayed to live.

There was movement in the row of evergreens opposite me. A shadow stretched and morphed under power of the moon and stars until there was no doubt—it was my hunter.

I mashed my chattering teeth together and scanned the greater picture. A squirt of adrenaline pushed me back into motion. I needed a new place to hide.

A familiar tree caught my eye as I slipped away, moving toward it as quickly as possible. The tree in my sights was separate from the others and possibly too good to be true. I strained to acclimate myself for confirmation. Had I really come so far on adrenaline and fear? All the way to the property's edge in pajamas and slippered feet? I struggled to blink frozen eyelids, hoping it wasn't a mirage.

Salvation was less than one hundred feet away. The sinkhole I'd leapt over for fun as a youth would save my life tonight. All I had to do was summon the energy to make it that far, through drifting snow, past the man who wanted to kill me, and jump.

My eyes warmed and blurred as I hobbled toward the pit. What if I couldn't make the jump? What if I fell in and Mr. Nettle followed me down? He'd surely kill me like he had Mrs. Fenwick. What if I fell and he didn't? He'd walk away, collect his car, and leave. I'd be long dead before anyone found me, frozen among the discarded limbs, and Mr. Nettle would get away with murder. Again.

He stepped through the trees, as if on cue, a crazed look on his haggard face.

I didn't wait for him to speak.

I flew in the direction of the pit, yipping with every step. My twisted ankle felt suspiciously broken, but that wouldn't matter if I failed.

"Stop running!" Mr. Nettle screamed. His fingertips brushed my elbow as I stayed just beyond his reach.

I raced toward the finish line. I ran for justice. For my town. For my folks. I couldn't die on the land that had provided and sheltered us all these years. I wouldn't.

The pit came closer with each new stride. I counted silently and with unmatched determination. *Three . . . two . . . one . . .*

I pushed off the ground with everything I had, leaping into the air, deftly clearing the pit, now camouflaged in darkness and snowfall. My victory was stunted as I bounced on my chest against the frozen earth. Wind expelled from my lungs with a deep whoosh.

Behind me, Mr. Nettle's footfalls were replaced by a terrifying scream and a thunderous crack. He'd run directly into the pit.

My lids fell shut as the weight of my predator disappeared, and I dreamed immediately of my name on Sheriff Gray's lips.

"I dropped the phone," I whispered to the sky. What I heard wasn't him. It was delirium. It was my body giving up and the cold sleep of death come to give me rest.

My hazy thoughts drifted to a brighter day, when Mom and Dad waved to me from their front porch rocking chairs and the sun warmed my cheeks. I relaxed into the memory until the light began to blind me.

I grimaced and shook my head as the beam seared my eyelids. Sounds of machinery and engines pulled me away from my family and back into the frozen night.

"BP sixty-two over forty," an unfamiliar voice informed no one in particular. "Low but stable. Pulse is weak, but she's got one. I count that as a win."

My limbs sprawled and dangled a moment before being tucked against my sides. Something hugged my head and neck.

"You have the right to remain silent," Sheriff Gray's voice thundered like the Great and Mighty Oz. Whoever had crossed him in that disposition was unlucky to be sure.

I attempted to turn my head toward the sound but couldn't.

"You're going to be just fine," the same unfamiliar voice promised.

Multiple flashes of light burst beyond my frozen lids. Was someone taking pictures?

"Griggs"—Sheriff Gray's voice was sharp and deep—"get the hell away from here. What are you doing? Following me?"

A woman with round cheeks and a knitted cap smiled down at me. The little green-and-red yarn ball on top of her head bobbed along with each of her steps.

"Where are we going?" My gummy tongue stuck to the roof of mouth, distorting my speech.

"You're on a gurney, and we're taking you to Mistletoe General for a few tests and a nice warm bed."

"She going to be okay?" Sheriff Gray's voice arrived nearby.

I wiggled on my little bed, straining to see his face.

"We'll know soon," the smiling woman said.

I had so many questions, but when I opened my mouth, a sob came out. Reality exploded in my heart and head like a hand grenade. I wasn't with my parents on a warm summer day. I was cold and wet; I was nearly murdered by a middle-aged accountant.

"I've got her." The sheriff's face swam into view as I peeled my frozen eyes open. He bumped the lady out of his way and took control of my gurney. "How you doing, White?"

My vision blurred, and a hot streak swiveled over my cheek then landed in my ear. "I was hoping to run into you."

Sheriff Gray produced a handkerchief and wiped the wetness away. "You scared me," he said. His honest green eyes burned with emotion. "When I promised I'd keep you safe, I had no idea you were going to make it so hard."

"Phillip," I croaked, suddenly recalling the name of his deputy.

"He's okay. He called from your parents' landline thirty seconds after you hung up on me."

"I lost my phone."

The rosy-cheeked woman popped back into view. "That's what she was saying when I got here. Mean anything to you?"

"Yeah," he said. "She needs another phone." Red light passed over his face as we stopped behind the ambulance, and he released the silver bedrail. "I'm sorry I wasn't there for you when you needed me most."

Together, he and the woman hoisted my gurney into a well-lit ambulance, where a waiting EMT snapped an oxygen mask over my face and a glowing clip onto the end on my finger. I lifted it slowly like a doped-up E.T.

Sheriff Gray climbed inside and took a seat beside the woman preparing an IV. He leaned his face to mine and bound my hands in his. "You're going to be feeling lots better as soon as that medicine kicks in."

I fought heavy eyelids as the needle punctured my skin. "Don't go," I mumbled.

"I won't."

The vehicle rocked to life, and we began a slow roll away from my worst nightmare.

Sheriff Gray lowered his lips to my forehead and left a kiss behind. "You did good tonight."

Chapter Twenty-Six

I woke in my old bed the next morning, rested but not. The hospital had discharged me after several hours of observation, and whatever they'd put in my IV had helped me sleep, but the night was filled with horrid dreams. I levered my stiff body off the bed and used the steam and massage of a hot shower to loosen my kinks. Recalling the looks on my parents' faces when they'd arrived at the hospital was almost as dreadful as the reason I was there. I'd fallen asleep vowing not to worry them when I woke.

I took my time getting ready, sorting through my muddled thoughts and list of lingering questions while choosing something appropriate but comfortable to wear. A soft white cashmere sweater and my favorite black leggings seemed to fit the bill. It was Christmas after all, and people tended to stop by throughout the day for a taste of Mom's custom cocoas and snickerdoodles. I was thankful in advance for the inevitable distractions. It hurt to bat my eyes and put on lip gloss. Fooling my mother into thinking I was less than miserable would take intense theater training that I didn't have.

What I did have was another Christmas in my favorite place with the two people I loved most in the world, three if Cookie came to visit. I worked at my vanity for a long while, until even I couldn't tell how shaken I still was by last night's adventure.

Emotion clogged my throat, but I cleared it away. Mr. Nettle was a criminal. He'd badgered me, chased me, and threatened me, but in the end, he'd lost. Justice had prevailed. Karma had broken both his legs, and he'd spend his holiday in the infirmary ward at the county jail. I suspected his trial wouldn't be much more fun. Good luck finding a sympathetic jury of his peers in this town. Those were my happy thoughts. They helped me deal with the other ones. The ones where I hated him for what he'd done to Mrs. Fenwick and for what he'd tried to do to me. I rolled my shoulders back and forced the anger away before I ruined my makeup. There'd be time to wallow later. Besides, letting him haunt me would be like letting him win. And I'd won.

Once there was nothing more to be done about my appearance, it was time I showed my parents that I was okay. I set my good foot on the top step and puzzled. The murmur of voices had risen into a low, happy roar. I took the stairs carefully, ever mindful of my fractured ankle and now booted foot. The crowd came into view as scents of cinnamon and coffee lifted up the staircase to my nose. Every face I'd ever met in Mistletoe seemed to be gathered in our living room, standing around the tree and in front of the fire, along narrow tables that had been erected at the front window and loaded with food in the mismatched dishes of a dozen homes.

I reached the landing before the crowd of faces turned to me.

Mom beetled into view. "There you are." She waved me down while jogging up to meet me. "Merry Christmas, sweetie." She offered her arm for balance and pressed warm lips to my cheek, surely leaving a print of puckered red lips behind.

Slow applause began at the center of the room and rolled outward in waves as Mom helped me into the midst of our neighbors and friends.

I sat on the couch, and Mom brought me a plate. Dad delivered the coffee, and Cookie fielded the trickle of questions about my recent ordeal for more than an hour. It was the closest thing Mistletoe had ever had to a press conference. Fortunately for me, the press seemed to be elsewhere.

I gave all the details I had freely, baring myself in an attempt to put worried minds at ease and dissuade gossip from springing up later. Better to issue the facts now than sort a thousand lies in the future. I didn't want Mr. Nettle to become an urban legend. He didn't deserve the honor of being remembered. It was bad enough he'd made history as Mistletoe's first killer in forty years. I wouldn't allow him to become infamous.

Mom sat beside me and stroked hair off my shoulders. "I still can't believe Mr. Nettle did something like this. I should've seen him for what he truly was."

A thief and a killer.

"Why would you have known?" I asked. "He was your accountant." The obvious fell onto my head like a sack of bricks. "I'll bet he's the reason you and Dad never had anything extra. He probably took as much as he could without drawing your suspicions."

"We think so," she said. "Your father's hiring someone to review the Reindeer Games financial records and an attorney to insist on restitution if we find Mr. Nettle was stealing from us too. That will all take time. Right now, I'm just glad you're okay."

I tipped my head against her shoulder.

The doorbell rang just after lunchtime, and the nearest guest answered it for us, as had been the custom all morning.

Caroline darted inside, carrying stacks of bakery boxes and knocking snow from her boots. "Merry Christmas!"

Cookie went to help with the boxes.

"There's more on the porch," Caroline said, nodding over her shoulder. "You could grab those."

Cookie opened the door and stared out. "That's enough cupcakes to feed an army."

"Four hundred dollars' worth." Caroline passed her boxes into Mom's waiting arms, then came to hug my neck. "I couldn't stand the thought of you losing that big deposit because of some idiot's decision to break off your engagement five minutes before the wedding."

I glanced around the room, wondering who had heard her and who had already known.

Dozens of disgusted faces nodded in agreement.

Caroline peeled her coat and gloves off with a smile. "I used your deposit and the supplies we'd already purchased for the cake and made cupcakes instead. There are some sugar cookies and cutouts in there too, but those aren't as good as your mom's."

"Thank you." I hugged her back. "You're a good friend."

She rolled her eyes. "If that were true, you'd think I'd have more friends."

"Me and you, then." I smiled. "A team of two."

Her face lit and her eyes twinkled. "I like that."

Mom crammed the hot dishes together on the buffet tables, making room for Caroline's bakery boxes, which were pushed into the free space and pried open immediately.

Glistening white cupcakes traveled through the room, passed hand to hand.

Caroline brought a little pink one to me. "I'm glad you're home," she said with a bright smile.

"Me too."

"Me three," Cookie added, rubbing frosting from the tip of her nose. Her eyes crossed as she worked. "Hopefully you've had such an exciting time this week, you'll think of staying awhile."

I scanned the room for my parents and found them laughing together near the fire. "I'm not staying for the excitement," I said, "but maybe I could see how the jewelry-making business goes."

Caroline settled beside me on the couch with a second cupcake. "To revived friendships and young female entrepreneurs." She tapped her treat against mine and curved an arm around my shoulders.

"Hear, hear!" I smiled, then ate my cupcake with shameless enthusiasm.

It was late in the afternoon when Sheriff Gray arrived. I'd secretly hoped he'd make an appearance, and the sight of him stole my breath. A bad habit that seemed to be getting worse instead of better.

He made his way to me, hat in hand, and lowered into the place where Caroline had spent an hour regaling me with the funniest moments from her all-nighter of cupcake baking.

"Holly," he said slowly.

"Sheriff Gray."

His cheek kicked up in the boyish way I loved.

"Why do you call me that?"

I flicked my gaze to the place where his nametag hung on his uniform. "It's your name."

"My name is Evan."

I smiled, feeling suddenly awkward. "I know."

"How'd you sleep?"

The smile fell from my face, pulled away at the mention of my night. "There were nightmares," I whispered. I glanced around the room, unsure why I'd admit such a thing and hoping no one else had heard.

Evan leaned closer. "They'll pass," he whispered in response. "I promise. Nightmares, anxiety, all sorts of reactions are perfectly normal in the aftermath of an experience like yours."

I bobbed my chin, willing his words to be true. "Okay."

"You're very brave," he said. "The odds were against you, and you persevered. No light. No coat or boots. No phone. No plan." The final word was clipped.

"Why did he do it?" I asked, altering the subject slightly. "Why did Mr. Nettle kill Mrs. Fenwick? Did she find about the stolen grant money and confront him? Why would he steal from her to begin with?"

A number of listening ears turned our way.

Evan gave the room a passing glance before answering. "According to his confession," he said, "Nettle was financially overextended and thought borrowing some of the grant funds was the answer to his problems. His intentions weren't sinister, though they were certainly illegal. He was desperate and thought he had a good plan. He told the Mistletoe Historical Society that the mill grant was denied so he could use the money to get himself out of debt. He assumed he'd have plenty of time to put the money back before spring, which was the soonest the work on the mill could begin anyway. Once he'd repaid the money, he planned to surprise Mrs. Fenwick with news of a reconsideration. He'd hoped she'd be too thrilled to question the reason."

"That's sad," I said. "None of this should've happened."

"You're right."

I hated the troubled expression on Evan's face and the fact I could sympathize with Mr. Nettle. One bad decision had led him to a commit a whole slew of crimes. I knew firsthand how things could get out of control when you started down a questionable path. I'd begun asking questions about Mrs. Fenwick's murder in an attempt to make Evan look beyond our farm for a suspect, and when I couldn't stop, I'd nearly gotten myself killed. "I'm sorry I pushed this so far."

"I should've gotten here sooner."

"It's not your fault," I said.

His jaw clenched and pulsed. "I was building a case against France when I realized what had likely happened and turned my interest to Nettle. I'd been to his home and office looking for him last night. When I saw your parents at the square without you, I got worried. When they said Nettle had just spoken to them, I knew it wasn't a coincidence. I tried contacting Phillip while I beat a path through the square to my cruiser, but he didn't respond. I was terrified by the thought of what might be happening to you because I'd been too slow to put the clues together, but then you called." He released a slow breath.

"And I confirmed your fears."

One stiff dip of his chin said what he couldn't: he'd thought I was going to die.

"Why couldn't I have just let you finish building your case?" Frustration built in my chest. I'd asked myself the same question a thousand times.

A tiny smile budded on Evan's lips.

"Why are you smiling?" I sniffled.

"I was sitting around building a case. You trapped him in a hole. Your way was faster."

A low rumble of laughter drew my attention away from Evan. I hadn't noticed the room grow still around us with interest in his story.

The bottom line to all of it was that if Evan hadn't been en route when I called, it wouldn't have mattered that Mr. Nettle fell in a hole; I would've frozen to death. Evan had saved me. I turned back to him, full to the top with gratitude, and wrapped my arms around his shoulders. I buried my face into the curve of his neck and squeezed him tight. "Thank you for coming for me."

He ran broad hands over my back and tightened his fingers against me. "Always," he promised in a fervent whisper.

Someone cleared his throat obnoxiously, and we sprang apart.

I expected to find Dad glaring at us but instead found Ray Griggs with a pile of daily newspapers. "Hello," he said. "Holly. Sheriff Gray. Merry Christmas."

Evan released me. He stood to shake Ray's hand. "Sorry for the trouble I gave you last night. You did all right." He clapped Ray on the back, then saw himself out without a good-bye.

I did my best to hide the sting of disappointment plucking at my skin. "What was that about?" I asked.

"He caught me following him around, and he was pretty mad, but I got a picture of Nettle stuck in that pit." A wide smile split his face.

"Did you get your story in the paper?" I asked, pointing to the stack of *Mistletoe Gazette*s tucked under his arm.

"Yeah." He turned the papers around, giving me a clear view of the headline.

"'The True Meaning of Christmas,' by Ray Griggs," I read. "This isn't about Nettle."

"Nope." He slid the top paper onto my lap, then passed the rest of the papers through the room.

A tear fell onto the paper as I finished the article on the guaranteed revitalization of Pine Creek Bridge. "Really?" I raised my eyes to his.

"When these people heard about what happened last night and why"—he opened his arms to indicate the crowd filling my parents' home—"they started forming a mob outside the Historical Society."

Bright smiles and blushes spread over the faces of our town. "I don't understand," I admitted.

Ray rocked back on his heels with a goofy grin. "When I finished the article at dawn, donations of time, supplies, and cash totaled over seventy-five thousand dollars," he said. "More than enough to restore the bridge and dedicate it to Margaret Fenwick and her family."

My mouth fell open with a gasp. I covered my mouth to stifle a sudden sob.

"In the true spirit of Mistletoe," Ray continued, "there will be a formal ceremony in her honor next Christmas when the restoration is completed."

A hearty round of hoots and applause broke the silence. The folks before me patted one another's backs and exchanged handshakes and hugs.

Ray's headline was right—this was the true meaning of Christmas.

"Thank you," I said, first to Ray for the article, then more loudly to the room of celebrators. My gaze slid to the front door, wishing Evan had stayed a moment longer to see this with me. This was Mistletoe.

A number of guests abandoned their snacks and donned their coats, forming a sudden exodus through our front door.

"Don't go," I said, struggling onto my good foot.

Ray moved back into view. "I have one more thing to show you." He offered me a hand and steered me to the end of the exit line.

I checked the crowd behind me to see if I was in anyone's way.

The lingering bunch smiled and waved.

"I don't understand," I told Ray.

"The article was from me, but this is the work of your people." He propped me against the doorjamb and moved away, allowing me an unobstructed view of the world outside.

A crowd of carolers began to sing "We Wish You a Merry Christmas." They filled the porch, front steps, and lawn. Behind me, guests in our home joined along with the chorus.

I blinked to make sense of the sheer numbers. I'd thought everyone who knew me had been in the living room, but there were many new faces singing in the snow.

Mom unhooked my coat from the rack and handed it to me. "Come on," she said. "You'd better get out there and invite them in."

I slid my arms into the coat sleeves and hobbled through the open door. A thrill pinched my chest as I took in the beautiful sight.

Slowly, a handsome tenor emerged from the pack. Sheriff Evan Gray climbed the porch steps with a gentle smile. "Holly?" he asked, casting a pointed look at the mistletoe over my head.

"Yeah," I answered, catching two handfuls of his coat in my hands.

"Merry Christmas," he whispered, and he lowered his lips to mine.

Acknowledgments

Huge, heartfelt appreciation to my agent, Jill Marsal, for believing me in. My world is changing because of you. To Crooked Lane Books and their kind, dedicated team. Matt Martz, Anne Brewer, Jenny Chen, Sarah Poppe, thank you. Also, to my personal cheer and support squad, Keri Ford, Jennifer Anderson, and Janie Browning. You make my stories better. Finally, to my mother-in-law, Darlene Lindsey, who deserves a gold medal in love, support, and encouragement, and of course my sweet family. I'd be lost without you. And if you are reading this, I thank you too. They say it takes a village. You are my village.